A Pretty Picture

Two blondes and a redhead, all about thirty, had stepped into view at the point where the draw joined the canyon. All three acted in concert to raise their hands out from the bulky fabric of their bouffant skirts—to aim six revolvers of various makes at Edge. In common was the fact that all were cocked.

"Well ain't that pretty as a goddamn picture?" Nick Price drawled.

"You gonna trust my word about the deal still standin' Edge?" Harlan Price asked. "Or you gonna believe we Prices are as black as we're painted?"

"Appears I don't have much of a choice, feller," the half-breed answered as he showed a cold grin to the three smiling women. "Since these ladies have so artfully made me the only target in a shooting gallery . . ."

Other titles in the **EDGE** series from Pinnacle Books

EDGE 1: THE LONER
EDGE 2: TEN THOUSAND DOLLAR AMERICAN
EDGE 3: APACHE DEATH
EDGE 4: KILLER BREED
EDGE 5: BLOOD ON SILVER
EDGE 6: THE BLUE, THE GREY AND THE RED
EDGE 7: CALIFORNIA KILLING
EDGE 8: SEVEN OUT OF HELL
EDGE 9: BLOODY SUMMER
EDGE 10: VENGEANCE IS BLACK
EDGE 11: SIOUX UPRISING
EDGE 12: THE BIGGEST BOUNTY
EDGE 13: A TOWN CALLED HATE
EDGE 14: THE BIG GOLD
EDGE 15: BLOOD RUN
EDGE 16: THE FINAL SHOT
EDGE 17: VENGEANCE VALLEY
EDGE 18: TEN TOMBSTONES TO TEXAS
EDGE 19: ASHES AND DUST
EDGE 20: SULLIVAN'S LAW
EDGE 21: RHAPSODY IN RED
EDGE 22: SLAUGHTER ROAD
EDGE 23: ECHOES OF WAR
EDGE 24: THE DAY DEMOCRACY DIED
EDGE 25: VIOLENCE TRAIL

EDGE 26: SAVAGE DAWN
EDGE 27: DEATH DRIVE
EDGE 28: EVE OF EVIL
EDGE 29: THE LIVING, THE DYING AND THE DEAD
EDGE 30: WAITING FOR A TRAIN
EDGE 31: THE GUILTY ONES
EDGE 32: THE FRIGHTENED GUN
EDGE 33: THE HATED
EDGE 34: A RIDE IN THE SUN
EDGE 35: DEATH DEAL
EDGE 36: TOWN ON TRIAL
EDGE 37: VENGEANCE AT VENTURA
EDGE 38: MASSACRE MISSION
EDGE 39: THE PRISONERS
EDGE 40: MONTANA MELODRAMA
EDGE 41: THE KILLING CLAIM
EDGE 42: BLOODY SUNRISE
EDGE 43: ARAPAHO REVENGE
EDGE 44: THE BLIND SIDE
EDGE 45: HOUSE ON THE RANGE
EDGE 46: THE GODFORSAKEN
EDGE MEETS ADAM STEEL: TWO OF A KIND
EDGE MEETS ADAM STEEL: MATCHING PAIR

Best-Selling Series!
#47

EDGE

THE MOVING CAGE

BY

George G. Gilman

PINNACLE BOOKS NEW YORK

This is a work of fiction. All the characters and events portrayed in this book are fictional, and any resemblance to real people or incidents is purely coincidental.

Edge #47: The Moving Cage

A Pinnacle Books edition, first published in Great Britain by New English Library.

Pinnacle edition / November 1984

ISBN: 0-523-42266-0

Cover art by Bruce Minney

Printed in the United States of America

PINNACLE BOOKS, INC.
1430 Broadway
New York, New York 10018

9 8 7 6 5 4 3 2 1

for:
A.S.
a new hand on
the new spread

Author's Note

MORE than four years ago, the thirty-fourth book in the Edge series was published. Entitled *A Ride in the Sun*, it told a contemporary story interrupted at the end of each chapter by a flashback to an incident in the past of the man called Edge.

The creation of that book was triggered by certain readers who wrote to me requesting background information about Edge (and some secondary characters in the series) which I had failed to present in the full-length books. Since these incidents had no connecting thread, except for Edge himself, and were scattered widely in time and place, it seemed appropriate to comply with the readers' requests by using the short-story form.

In my introduction to *A Ride in the Sun* I wondered, with some trepidation, how the mass of readers who had not asked for such flashbacks might feel about such a book—and the technique of its presentation. Apparently, I need not have worried. There was no adverse comment and, of course, this new book is concrete evidence that a sufficient number of readers were impressed enough to request more of the same.

Naturally, I am always pleased to have reader reaction to my work, be it favorable or otherwise (and occasionally it is the latter!). But I was particularly happy to discover that a second book of this nature would be welcomed, thereby enabling another group of Edge fans to have their curiosity satisfied.

These are the readers who have learned that Edge short

stories were published by magazines of which they were unaware at the time. A trio of these stories are to be found in this book, slightly rewritten where appropriate. They are:

"Getting the Message," which was first published in *Club International,* December 1973, as "Raw Edge."

"The Quiet Gun," published in *Western Magazine,* October 1980, under the same title.

"The Vengeance Guns," which appeared with this same title in *Short Stories Magazine,* February 1981.

It is perhaps of interest, too, to point out that the story which appears in this book as "Gundown at Twin Oaks" is loosely based upon a tale called "Guns at the Silver Horseshoe," which appeared in the January 14, 1955, issue of *Reveille*—and was the first Western fiction I ever wrote.

I hope that those readers who are not already familiar with these stories will enjoy them, and that those who read them in their original form will not feel cheated to have them served up again in their amended versions.

As for the book as a whole . . . ?

It is my earnest hope that the entire readership will enjoy it—particularly you.

THE MOVING CAGE

Chapter One

THE fat man driving the prison wagon spat at the rump of the gray gelding on the left and growled wearily, "You know what I think, Ray?"

From inside the wagon an equally tired-sounding voice countered: "Crap, Cody. If you got anythin' to think with, it's in your ass. So whatever comes out has to be—"

"You're a condemned man, Price!" the rider to the left of the wagon snarled, and made a token gesture of draping a hand over the jutting butt of his holstered revolver. "But it's me makin' a last request to you! Keep your friggin' mouth shut!"

"Last request because Ray ain't gonna tell you no more times!" the rider on the other side of the wagon sneered. And emphasized the threat by jerking his repeater rifle partway out of the forward-slung boot, then thrust it angrily back in again.

There was a low murmuring of resentful talk among the bunch of prisoners in the cage wagon, and all their eyes burned with contempt for the guard who had spoken last.

"Which of them three Prices made with the mouth, Ray?" the driver asked dully.

"Hell, Art, I don't know."

"Harlan, Art! It's always Harlan Price makes the worst trouble! He's the leader of the whole lousy family! The others, they just fall in with what he—"

1

"Okay, Mel," the driver cut in on the sneering man who was relishing the almost palpable hatred being directed at him through the safety of the bars of the moving cage. "Nothin' more for us to do except deliver the freight. Just needed to know the name. So I can get paid back for the favor I done Charlie McMullen."

"Charlie's the hangman that's goin' to set you bastards swingin'!" Mel Snyder crowed.

"Wouldn't want you other two Prices to suffer overmuch on account of what the other one done," Art Cody droned. "But Harlan, it's gonna take you longer than most men to get strangled while you're kickin' and twitchin' on the end of Charlie's rope. Can promise you that."

"And Art wouldn't lie to a dyin' man, Price," Ray Nixon added.

Then nobody said anything for a long time: the men behind the bars perhaps giving brooding consideration to the image conjured up by the driver's words; their guards watching the same scene in imaginations untroubled by doubt. Then, tiring of this, Ray asked, "What was it you were thinkin', Art?"

"Thinkin'? Oh, yeah. I forget now. Shit, ain't that a bastard?"

There was another low swell of mumbling among the prisoners, and even a harsh half-laugh of derision. But whatever the association of ideas that had triggered the exchange, it was not strong enough to be sustained. And the men in the cage became morosely silent again, before any of the guards felt sufficiently moved out of their lethargy to snarl an order. For many minutes, the clop of hooves, creak of timber and leather, and crunch of turning wheelrims were left to provide the only sounds to disturb the natural peace of the scrub desert through which the condemned men were being transported.

They were moving, at a slow pace dictated by the glaring heat of the afternoon sun, in a north-eastward direction through that area of New Mexico Territory known as the San Agustin Plains. At their backs and to their left, temporarily shrouded by the shimmering heat haze, were

2

the high peaks of the Continental Divide. Not so many miles ahead, and barely visible in blurred outline through that haze, were the ridges of the Gallinas Mountains. They had not yet come close enough for the San Mateo Mountains to be seen on the right of the little-used trail they were following. The desert plain encircled by the heat-misted high ground was not flat: its floor constantly rose and fell and was featured with countless outcrops, mesas, and bluffs. Infrequently, where primeval natural violence had created an easier way, the trail made by generations of men cut through ravines or curved along the bottoms of minor canyons. When this happened, the shade thrown by high walls of rock provided only an illusion of coolness, as transitory as the tantalizing images that came and went in the rim of distant shimmer that kept the dusty yellow land from touching the clean blue sky. Vegetation was mostly scrub grass and scattered cacti: spindly ocotillos and phallic saguaros, spreading prickly pear and bulky barrels. Brush grew in widely scattered clumps, and even more scarce were stands of timber—live oak, juniper, mesquite, and cottonwood.

To those with an eye for natural beauty and an inclination to indulge his perception of God as an artist, the scenes on every side of the wagon and escorts would have been a constant source of pleasure: while their aesthetic senses would have been abused by the sight of the wagon, its occupants, and the outriders that comprised such an ugly blot moving across the ruggedly beautiful landscape.

The wagon was an old army ambulance that had been converted for its present occupation—the transport of prisoners. It now had a solid timber roof and partition separating the back from the driver's seat, while the sides and rear were formed of steel bars. These bars, which were an inch and a half in diameter and spaced four inches apart, stretched from bed to roof and were strengthened by a flat horizontal bar at a midway point. The only door to the wagon was at the rear, fastened with two padlocked chains. The rig's timbers were bleached and cracked and warped, and the bars were rusted, with just a few patches of black paint clinging to the metal. But the solid bars were still firmly secured in sound wood at top and bottom.

There were seven captives confined behind the grille of bars, trapped in a space of some fifteen by twelve feet. Six white men and one Indian, ranging in age from twenty to fifty. None of them was fat; but some were heavily built, others lean. The Comanche was the shortest man, and the tallest was an inch above six feet without boots. None of the prisoners wore boots, or hose. All wore shapeless gray pants and tunics and forage caps. Six of them had heavily bristled faces—only custom made the Indian appear clean-shaven. Everyone had sweated a great deal, and the salt moisture stained clothing and caused dust to adhere to exposed flesh. The denim penal uniforms and the prisoners' skin were ingrained with old dirt. A pungent stench of stale sweat and other human waste emanated from the wagon and attracted the unremitting attention of desert flies. Such flies were not always brushed aside by the weary men whose filthy flesh they settled on.

Some prisoners sat or squatted on their haunches while others stood, leaning against or gripping the bars. Nobody made any effort to move about in the restricted space.

The fat driver was the oldest of the three Territorial Prison Service guards. Fifty-some and soft-looking in terms of flesh, but with a moderate degree of intelligence visible in the alertness that showed in his bright blue eyes even when the rest of his face appeared slack. The guard named Ray Nixon was at least half Cody's age: tall and lean and strong with a naturally mournful countenance. On the other side of the cage wagon, the thirty-five-year-old Mel was beanpole thin with a gaunt face that looked wrong unless his features were twisted into a scowl or a cruel grin.

All the guards wore military-style uniforms that had been pale blue in color when new. But the tunics and pants had been new a long time ago, and now the captors looked as disheveled as the captives: the uniforms were soiled and torn and shapeless with the original brass buttons some-times replaced with mismatches. The leather of their boots, gunbelts, and holsters was dulled and cracked by neglect. The faces of the driver and two horseback riders were as bristled and dirt-grimed as six of the prisoners'. The geldings in the wagon traces and the two with riders on their backs were as ill cared for as the men and their equipment. And looked as gloomily dissatisfied with their circumstances as did the men inside and outside the moving cage.

"What I was thinkin', Ray," Cody announced unexpectedly, capturing the lethargic interest of everyone, "is that a week from tomorrow it'll be my birthday."

"That a fact, Art," Mel growled sourly.

"We gonna sink a few glasses, Art?" Ray asked, genuinely interested in an answer.

"Be fifty-three a week from tomorrow," the fleshy driver continued, in a tone of voice that suggested he was thinking aloud rather than talking to Ray or anyone else.

"Proves what they say, Cody," one of the prisoners muttered. "It's just the good that die young."

"When they hang you, Delany, it'll give the lie to that crap!" Mel taunted the youngest man in the cage. "And when they hang the whole bunch of you, me and Art and Ray'll get in some drinkin' practice for Art's birthday party! And if they knew about the hangin's, a whole lot of other folks'd be raisin' glasses, too!"

Some of the prisoners met the guard's challenging stare with scowls of hatred, but most elected to ignore him. One of those who did not give the blustering rider the satisfaction of rising even tacitly to his bait was Harlan Price, whose surreptitious attention was focused outward, on a single aspect of the arid terrain beyond the confines of his cage. While his fellow captives either dwelt miserably on various facets of their circumstances or openly directed their ill-feeling toward the guard they hated most, the eldest of the Price brothers stood tight against the rear door of the cage: urinating out between the bars as he peered at the strip of slick-looking heat shimmer in the southwest, hoping for another glimpse of the lone rider he was certain he'd seen twice already. But he temporarily lost the opportunity to confirm it was not a mirage he had seen when the wagon started on a downslope into a ravine and red rock reared up to block his view.

The ravine was just three times as wide as the wagon at the start, and the sound of slow-moving hooves and sluggishly turning wheelrims echoed off the flanking cliffs and drowned out all other noises. The riders, uncomfortable being so close to the prisoners, dropped back to ride behind the wagon. Once out of range of the longest arm that might be thrust through the bars, both Ray and Mel rode in relaxed attitudes again: the younger guard maintaining what he thought of as a steel-eyed watch over the wagon while the other man gazed in the same direction with undisguised scorn. The wagon did not roll fast enough to stir up more than a few small puffs of dust, and the stink that trailed behind the closely confined prisoners was no worse than that which had been spreading to either side throughout this day and the two that had gone before.

"You should have held off takin' the leak until now, Harlan," one of the younger Price brothers snorted. "Really shown that bastard Snyder what we think of him."

"I ain't seen you relieve yourself lately, Nick!" Mel Snyder countered scornfully. "You wanna go now, go ahead. But I give you fair warnin': you wave your pecker at me, boy, I'll shoot it off."

"Your mouth is all you can shoot off, Snyder!" a prisoner snarled.

"And he's so full of shit, I don't reckon he ever relieves himself," another added.

Hidden from sight by the solid wood partition that segregated him from the prisoners, Art Cody felt his temper rising as he listened to the ill-humored voices and maintained a nerve-taxing watch on the widening ravine in front of him. Cody was afraid, but was unable to provide himself with a logical explanation for his fear—beyond the fact that the ravine was a good place in which to stage an ambush. But during the past two and a half days there had been a dozen or more places along the trail where an attempt to jump the wagon and free the captives could have been made with an even greater chance of success. Although he was equal in lowly rank to Ray Nixon and Mel Snyder, Cody was by dint of age and experience acknowledged by the other two as in command. He knew, though, that his token authority would be lost the minute he started issuing orders rather than making requests. And he had alerted the men to the possibility of lurking danger too often already. Progressively, the fear of ambush he had communicated to Nixon and Snyder had lessened in degree as earlier anxieties had proved groundless. And, as the younger men's fears abated, their confidence in his leadership waned and their sharpness in keeping watch was dulled.

If it was going to happen anywhere, this was the place where a prisoner's friends were going to try to set the captives free: Art Cody knew this for certain, but in a hundred years could not have explained why he was so sure. And he had a lot less time than this to convince Nixon and Snyder that they'd better take note and shape up this time. Otherwise, Ray would pay highly for his laziness and Mel would wish he'd spent less time baiting the trapped men and more time keeping watch for those free to direct more than harsh looks and words at him.

But then the wagon rolled clear of the ravine, out of the shade and into glaringly bright sunlight again. The downgrade ended and the trail snaked across a level area, twisting and turning around the thickly scattered boulders that prevented a straightaway. It was dangerous terrain, still, but Art Cody was already feeling better. He had visualized men moving into view on the flanking rims of the narrow ravine and pouring vicious gunfire down on himself and the two guards on horseback: an attack against which there would have been no effective defense. Especially if the ambushers also had men at ground level—in front of the wagon or behind it, or even both.

This was not so dangerous, Art Cody allowed to himself as he swallowed hard and used the back of a filthy hand to wipe stinging sweat from his eyes. Eyes that still did not see so clearly as they recovered from gazing fixedly up at the dazzlingly bright strip of sky which had been caught between the tops of the ravine sides. Strained eyes that

7

nonetheless were able to cooperate with the line of his mouth in showing a smile. It was an expression of relieved tension and self-satisfaction: the latter with a twofold reason—that as a man renowned for his even temper he had once again managed to control threatened rage, and that he had not further undermined his insecure authority over Snyder and Nixon by once more appearing to fear that which turned out to be nothing.

Then, just before his vision returned to normal and his features resumed their neutral set, the smile became self-mocking: the man acknowledging a feeling of foolishness he was glad had not been made public.

This did not last for long, and when the final trace of the smile was gone he became as composed in his mind and his attitude on the seat as he was in countenance. Until he heard the gunshot. Snapped his head around to peer off to the right of the trail. Felt something hit him hard in the chest as a small puff of smoke appeared against the dark figure of a man beside a light-colored boulder.

"Holy Mary, Mother of God," he rasped through gritted teeth. As he reined the two-horse team to a grateful halt and moved a trembling hand to explore the source of the slight pain in his chest.

Two other gunshots exploded, a space of no more than a second between them. They sounded against a barrage of raised voices from the other side of the partition against which Art Cody pressed his back as his probing fingers touched wetness on his uniform tunic. The frenetic thudding of fists on timber began to accompany the raucous shouting, and he felt the partition vibrate against his back. He raised his hand rather than lowered the direction of his gaze so that he could peer at the crimson stain on his fingertips. And it was shock, rather than any physical effect of the bullet in his chest, that caused a nervous spasm to lance through him from head to toe. And he involuntarily half rose and leaned forward, lost consciousness on his feet, and tipped off the front of the wagon: thudded hard to the ground between the twitching hind legs of the pair of geldings. He was bitterly aware of releasing his hold on the reins with the hand not stained by his own blood and of dragging the Colt revolver from its holster. All this as he saw the man who had shot him turn away and disappear behind the boulder. And heard the taunting voice of Harlan Price from in back of the partition:

"Fifty-two is as old as you friggin' get, Cody!" Then all was silent and black, the driver protected by unconsciousness from the pain of his jarring impact with the ground, as the prisoner added, "Weren't nobody left to go to your birthday party, anyway!"

The way the two guards at the rear of the wagon had been shot vindicated Art Cody's strong hunch about the ravine. For a man was crouched up on the south rim just short of where the ravine ended: and in rising to his feet after the wagon and escort had gone by below him he'd signaled his partner in the boulder-strewn area to shoot the driver. And, an instant after the bullet had driven into Cody's chest, the man on the rim had triggered his own rifle. Back-shot Ray Nixon in the heart. And while the dead man was still twisting stiffly out of his saddle, a second bullet was levered into the breech of the repeater and exploded toward the turning form of Mel Snyder. The younger guard died instantly and easily, knowing nothing beyond the fact that he had heard a single shot and seen the men in the cage wagon become ecstatic with pleasure. Snyder, however, had heard the shots that hit both Cody and Nixon, had a second longer to see the reactions of the prisoners, to realize what it all meant, and even to hear one of the Price brothers start yelling, "Don't kill that bastard! We want him alive to—"

The wagon came to an abrupt halt and Snyder turned to find out where the shot that hit Nixon had come from. In his mind was a vague, panic-inspired idea to spur his mount into flight. But then a curse shaped his lips as terror widened his eyes. And this expression became his death mask, for the fatal bullet belched from the rifle muzzle just as Snyder spotted the man standing on the wall of rock. Because he was turned from the waist, the shot entered his heart from the front: and its impact caused him to twist even further, so that he fell backwards off the side of his saddle. And came to rest in an untidy heap close to the equally inert form of Nixon.

The mounts of both men backed off a few paces as another small billow of dust rose a short way up from the trail. Then, as the excited shouting of the men in the cage faltered and faded, the horses halted and calmed.

"Goddamnit, Harlan, you knew this was gonna happen!" one of his brothers yelled accusingly.

"Did I hell, Ethan? I didn't know a damn thing! I just had trust in friendship!"

"We all get to be free, Price?" the prisoner named Delany asked a little nervously.

"What the frig?" the eldest Price growled. "What kinda guy you think I am? Damn right everyone gets turned loose! Even the Injun, and I ain't overly keen on Injuns! But we're all of us in the same boat, and now we been rescued, I ain't about to toss anyone overboard!"

"Thank you, Mr. Price," the Comanche said, softly but tautly.

"Hey, Rod!" Nick Price yelled from the barred door in the rear of the cage wagon. "It's gotta be Johnnie that give the driver what he had comin', right?"

"Right on, Nick!" the man who had been on the ravine rim shouted in reply. He was leading his horse among the scattered boulders after coming down off the high ground.

"Yeah, I see Johnnie!" Ethan Price called, laughter in his voice, from where he was pressed to the bars at the front right corner of the wagon. "How you doin', Johnnie?"

"Shootin' good as ever!" came the reply.

"Two best rifle shots I ever rode with," Harlan Price announced to the prisoners who were not his brothers. "Why, I bet both of them guys could have got in a lot closer if they'd wanted. Wasn't no need, though, the way they shoot."

He could have sounded no prouder if he'd been boasting about his own prowess as a marksman.

"I'm real grateful to get turned loose this way," the youthful Delany said in a relieved tone. "But I reckon I'm just as pleased your buddies give the friggin' flies somethin' else besides us to keep them occupied.''

All of the men in the wagon looked out to where swarms of desert flies were noisily feeding on the fresh blood that had blossomed on the tunics of Snyder and Nixon.

It was the low but harsh humming sound of flies scavanging his own blood that roused Art Cody to the first stage of a return to consciousness. Then the shouted greeting issued by Ethan Price to Johnnie. Before the man who had shot Cody had completed his response, the driver was fully conscious again. His eyes were open, he could feel a dull ache in his chest, taste blood in his mouth, and recall all that had happened up until the moment he lapsed into a shock-induced faint.

Without moving his head, Cody was able to orient himself. He was lying on his left side between the hind legs of the docile wagon team, knees folded up toward his pained chest. His left arm was trapped under his body; but his right was draped free, his hand still fisted around the butt of the uncocked Colt. Above the excited talk of the prisoners, he heard the clop of hooves. A horse approaching the wagon from the rear and another from the side. It took what seemed to Cody an inordinate length of time for his eyes to alter focus from the Colt, some two feet away, to where Johnnie was leading his horse by the bridle a hundred feet away.

Fearing that pain, hatred, or simply his determination to do his duty might glint in his eyes and show Johnnie that his victim was not dead, Cody closed his lids. Which helped him to concentrate on the not easy task of playing down his breathing: this made harder by the fact that the ache in his chest was no longer dull and constant. Every now and then he felt a sharp pain, as if someone were probing him with a long needle in a relentless attempt to find his heart and finish his life.

But the injured man need not have worried: he had only to keep from crying aloud in reaction to the mounting pain. For the arrogantly confident man who had shot him

11

did not even glance at the motionless form he was sure
was a corpse as he came to a halt beside the wagon. Close
to where Rod had stopped a few moments before.

"My you boys do smell high," Rod said with a grimace.

"And our tempers are gonna be about as sweet as we
smell if you don't let us outta this cage right now!" the no
longer good-humored Ethan Price growled.

"Sooner the better, Johnnie," Harlan Price urged in a
brittle tone. "Before we rolled down that draw I spotted a
rider way off to the southwest. Maybe he ain't the kind to
mind his own business. And maybe if the shots bring him
gallopin' here, he won't be so welcome as you two guys?"

"Sure thing, Harlan. Blast the locks, Rod."

"No!" Harlan Price snarled as Rod moved toward the
rear of the wagon, a hand going to the Colt in his tied-
down holster. Then lightened his tone to add: "I'd trust
you guys, either of you, to blast a friggin' cherry pit off
my nose at a hundred paces. But I don't trust no ricochets
through these friggin' bars. Art Cody's got the key that fits
both locks."

"Cody's the fat guy that was drivin'," Delany supplied
in response to a quizzical look.

"Hell, you know I don't like messin' with dead people,"
Rod muttered uneasily.

"Shit, one of you get the friggin' key and let us outta
this cage!" Harlan Price roared.

The sudden loudness of his voice and the rap of hooves
on hard-packed dirt as the horses were disturbed served as
adequate cover for the sounds made by Art Cody as he
thumbed back the hammer of the Colt.

"You're crazy!" Johnnie accused as he swung around
and moved to calm the team. "Dead men can't give you
no trouble. It's the ones that are alive you gotta watch out
for."

He was still directing a mocking smile toward the squea-
mish Rod when he sank smoothly down onto his haunches.
But he snapped his head around to show Cody the incredulous expression on his face when the wounded man said:

"Ain't that the truth, bastard."

It was Cody, however, who vented a shrill cry of pain, when the act of raising his hand off the ground sent a powerful bolt of agony through his heart. But the strangely cool satisfaction of seeing a torrent of blood gush from the other man's face in the wake of the first gunshot defused the fresh hurt. The blood came out through the hole where Johnnie's disbelieving right eye had been. Was seen for just part of a second before the instantly dead man was sent backwards off his haunches to end up inert and spread-eagled.

Blasphemy, profanity, and shouted questions filled the air, totally masking the suddenly angrier buzzing of flies disturbed at their feeding. The voices and the gunshot that had signaled them also unsettled the horses again. Dust was kicked up in Art Cody's face and the coughing fit thus induced caused an almost unbearable assault of pain to knife through him, and it was not just confined to his chest now. But that determination to do his duty which he had been fearful of communicating too early was as firm as ever. And even as he gave vent to an even shriller scream, he had the presence of mind to thumb back the hammer a second time. A moment later, as he curtailed the cry and snapped open his eyes, Cody saw clearly that his time of pain was a moment removed from its end.

The spooked team of horses had staggered forward, raising dust as they hauled the cage wagon that had been Cody's cover away from him. Leaving the wounded man, as the dust settled on and around him, totally exposed in the brilliant sunlight of the spring afternoon. The four saddle horses, infected by the nervousness of the team, backed away. Three corpses were slumped in stillness kept from perfection by the activity of the flies foraging on the wounds that had killed them. One man stood tall and strong and full of life, his every fiber directed to the act of killing Art Cody as he extended his arm to full stretch and sighted down the length of it: thumbed back the hammer with a motion that was not transmitted to the unwavering barrel of the revolver in his fist. But he held off from squeezing the trigger to complain to the man on the ground in a tone of disapprobation:

"Johnnie never didn't kill a man that way before."

Then he shot at Cody, who had abruptly unfrozen from his fetal posture on the center of the trail. Once more Cody was unable to control a vocal release of agony as he shoved himself up into a partial sitting attitude, swung the hand holding his gun. On this occasion, the pain that engulfed his entire being was too powerful to allow his punished consciousness consideration of anything else. And so he cared nothing that the Colt in the other man's hand exploded a bullet toward him: he could not taste the fresh blood that rose into his throat, and was unaware that it gushed out from his screaming mouth like liquid vomit. He could hear nothing, see nothing. He felt only pain that built to a greater intensity by clearly discernible stages, each of which seemed impossible to surpass in terms of conscious endurance.

To Art Cody it seemed that the torment would continue for all time: and perhaps it did, if that was what comprised his private hell. But to the watchers crowded tightly against the bars at the rear of the again stalled cage wagon, the man with a bullet in his brain was already dead an instant after Rod's shot drilled through the center of his brow. So it was a spontaneous nervous spasm of a dying hand that caused Cody's finger to twitch against the trigger of the unaimed Colt and explode a bullet into Rod's flat belly.

The twice-shot Cody collapsed back into his former attitude in the middle of the trail, but now he was utterly inert and the gun slipped from his unfeeling grasp. The one with a bullet in his belly stood for several seconds in a splay-legged stance, his gun hand hanging limply down at his side while his other hand seemed to be trying to keep the blood from leaking out of him and staining his shirt. If he heard the majority of the imprisoned men screaming at him to get the key and release them, he gave no sign of it. He just peered down through sightless eyes at the dark crimson oozing between his fingers, while he rasped through clenched teeth the words of a part remorseful–part profane

14

plea for deliverance. Then, head still bowed, he let go of his Colt and lowered himself slowly onto his haunches, sat on his rump, legs splayed again, and clutched at the wound with both hands. And only now did he raise his head to show his tear-run face to the men still shrieking at him through the bars.

"Hey, Rod, snap outta it, old buddy!" Harlan Price said entreatingly after snarling at his fellow prisoners to keep quiet. "Quicker you get the key off that old buzzard and let us outta here, sooner we can fix up that little scratch you got."

"Scratch, my ass," Rod muttered, and returned his gaze to the blood on his fingers. "Damnit, I gotta have a crap!"

"Kick his ass is what I'd like to do!" Nick Price snarled.

Some others spoke in harsh agreement with this, as they balefully watched the wounded man's cautious act of leaning backwards—Rod unable to arrange himself completely flat on his back, since his head was resting, slightly crookedly, against the base of a boulder at the side of the trail. His hands dropped away from the wound and the inevitable flies hummed in to settle on the crimson patch.

"He can no longer hear you," the Comanche said into a brief pause in the chorus of acrimonious pleas hurled at Rod.

"The Injun's right," Ethan Price rasped as everyone became silent and stared with growing despair at the unmoving form and blank-eyed face of an obviously dead man.

"Sonofabitch, and he said we smelled bad!" Delany growled, pulling a face.

"Man emptied his—" the Comanche began to explain.

"Shuddup!" Harlan Price snapped, and swung an arm in a chopping gesture. Then cocked his head in a listening pose as he peered expectantly back over the five sprawled corpses and between the four no longer concerned horses into the ravine.

Everyone else aped his attitude, and on the faces of the intently listening men, hope replaced despondency.

"A horse, Harlan," Nick said huskily.

"The guy you seen before?" Ethan wondered.

"How the frig would I know?" the eldest brother countered caustically. "He was friggin' miles away."

Now a man astride a chestnut gelding rode into clear view just a few hundred feet away. He did not pause, nor show any subtler reaction to the scene of carnage when he saw it for the first time, but continued up the gentle grade of the ravine and out onto the level trail among the boulders at the same unhurried pace.

A man over six feet in height and two hundred pounds in weight, the silent prisoners in the wagon saw. His build was lean yet powerful-looking. He was dressed predominantly in black—spurless riding boots, pants, shirt, kerchief, and Stetson. His gunbelt with a bullet in every loop was also black. The saddle in which he rode easily and the accoutrements that hung from it were also dull hued and lacking in ornamentation. The Winchester jutting from the forward-hung boot and the Frontier Colt in the tied-down holster looked to be standard models, a great deal older than the man's attire and the rest of his gear—except, perhaps, for a once colorful necklet of strung wooden beads that had been subdued by the passage of time.

The man's build and the way he rode so loose limbed in the saddle suggested at a distance that he was younger than he was seen to be as he closed the gap on the wagon beyond the scattering of sprawled dead. Forty-some, with at least one line for every day of his life etched into his darkly burnished face. It was a long and lean face with high cheekbones, a hawkish nose, narrowed eyes that glinted ice blue, and a mouthline that warned of a cruel streak just beneath the impassive surface. A face of contrasts that told of mixed bloodlines: framed by no longer jet-black hair that reached to his shoulders in unruly waves. Strands of gray showed in the black, and there was grayness too among the dark bristles that grew on his lower face, left to flourish a little more thickly along his top lip and to either side of his mouth in an underplayed Mexican-style moustache.

"Another Injun!" Delany blurted sourly as the newcomer pulled his mount to a halt some twenty feet short of the cage wagon. And draped the reins over the saddlehorn as he dug the makings from a pocket of his shirt.

"Nah, he's a Mexican, right *hombre*?" Nick Price corrected and questioned.

"You're half right," the man rolling the cigarette answered with a negligent wave toward the youngest Price brother. "But it seems to me it doesn't matter what I am . . . so long as I'm not the law? Far as you fellers are concerned."

"That's friggin' right, Mr. . . . ?" Harlan Price began, a broad grin of happiness spreading across his filthy face.

"Edge." The stranger angled the freshly made cigarette from a side of his mouth and heeled his gelding forward, one hand on the reins while the other delved inside the shirt pocket for a match.

"Damn right, Edge!" Price hurried on, and swept a warning glower over the eager faces of his fellow prisoners, as if afraid that one of them might speak out of turn and spoil his play. "And since you ain't the law, I figure you'll be interested in makin' a deal? A cash money deal? Big money? We ain't in no shape to even try to screw you, like you can see plain enough."

Harlan grasped two bars so tightly that the knuckles of his fists showed white despite the dirt ingrained in the flesh. The expression of earnest sincerity on his face was no less intent. And this look of solemn probity was only momentarily marred by a flicker of latent rage when Edge leaned to the side and struck a match on the bar just a few inches away from the man's nose.

Then Edge sat square again in the saddle, and moved into a slightly more comfortable position. Invited, on a stream of tobacco smoke: "Okay, feller. On freedom of speech, no sweat."

"Easy, Harlan," Ethan murmured, recognizing the signs that his brother was close to losing his temper.

"That's right," Edge agreed, running his glinting gaze over the cage wagon and its embittered, filthy, foul-smelling human cargo. "I never was a sucker for a hard cell."

17

Raiders in the Rain

Until now the earliest episode in the life of Josiah C. Hedges to be related in full rather than as a recollection in a contemporary account was told in "The Drummer," the first short story in A Ride in the Sun. The story which now follows pre-dates that by fifteen years.

AN IOWA storm was brewing. Although the sky was still clear blue immediately above and to the south, east, and west of the small farmstead, there was a thickening belt of grayness above the northern horizon.

The medium-tall, stocky Mexican with the unlikely name of Jose Hedges came to the open door of the single-story frame house and grimaced when he saw the ominous buildup of clouds. Then vented a sigh of resignation and used the nail of a forefinger to pick a piece of his just finished lunch from between two teeth. Called back over his shoulder:

"Ingrid, *querida Hijo*. There is bad weather coming, I think!"

"I'll go help Pa, okay Mom?" the eight-year-old Josiah

18

Hedges shouted loudly, and his father grinned. Knowing the boy was eager for an excuse to get out of helping with the dishes—shouted so loudly to invite backing if his mother should object.

"One day I will have another child to enlarge this family," the woman said, and her voice carried to the doorway easily without need to raise it, hardly accented at all with her native Swedish. "And I intend to give birth to a sister for you. So that I may stand a chance of—"

"I'm real obliged, Mom!" her son cut in excitedly. "And if I get to have a sister, it'll be fine! I won't have to do no women's chores then, right?"

"Wrong, young man!" Ingrid Hedges called after him. And might have been inclined to start on a lecture about a family sharing in all things, those pleasant and those not so pleasant. But from where she was starting to clear the dirty dishes off the table she could see the boy halt beside his father who briefly draped a paternally protective arm around his thin shoulders. And she knew from experience of the man-to-man glance they were exchanging—a shared look that held them bound together even after it was finished, bound in a world from which she was not exactly excluded but was admitted only as a guest.

"Hey, you take care of the stock, huh?" the father suggested. "While I finish on the roof. What d'you say, Joey?"

"I say no sweat, Pa. And I also say please stop calling me Joey."

"That's right," Ingrid Hedges agreed with her son, moving on to the threshold of the house to look out and see for herself the kind of threat posed by the gathering storm. "Josiah is how we had our firstborn baptized, and it is how he should be called."

She winked secretly at the youngster and he responded with a conspiratorial look—which his father saw and grinned at. For, as always, he welcomed the way in which their son knowingly took part in the good-humored rivalry of his parents who, through their child more than anything else, had learned to compromise on the many differences

19

that existed between the ingrained tempestuousness of the Hispanic man and the heritage of stoic reason that was such a strong characteristic of the Scandinavian woman.

Taking time to watch as Josiah started gathering the chickens from the yard to drive them into the barn, while Jose climbed up the ladder to reach the house roof, Ingrid marveled yet again at the attractive manner in which the boy had been endowed with such a fine mix from each side of his parental ancestry. The light blue eyes, basic facial bone structure, tall and slender frame, and composed temperament she knew without false modesty had been inherited from her. While from his father he had derived the texture and coloration of his hair, the skin hue that owed little to being out of doors so much, and a brand of self-reliance that sometimes shifted over the line from independence to almost insulting arrogance.

Then, far to the north, where the gray clouds were visibly encroaching across the clear sky, a brilliant fork of lightning streaked. Before the thunder rolled far enough to reach the farmstead as an anticlimatic sound effect to the spectacular flash, the tall, blonde, statuesque woman had swung off the threshold to return to the house. Where she hurried to complete the after-meal chores in case she should be needed to lend a hand outside when the storm broke over the Hedges farm.

Sitting astride the ridge of the roof, Jose could hear his wife start to sing a familiar cheerful song from her native land, and he could see his son as the boy made short work of rounding up the chickens before running into the corral to bring the milk cow and the four horses into shelter. The boy was obviously as happy as his mother, Jose reassured himself yet again. And he was *feliz*, too, he acknowledged with a broad grin as he recommenced the chore of fixing the hole in the roof caused by the decay of neglect. That word of his native language said exactly what he was—happy because he was lucky and because there was nothing of any consequence that could cause him to be anything else.

He had not always been so lucky—especially in those

days when he was a gambling man known to his friends as Bet-Hedging Aviles. But then he had met Ingrid Ohlson and, a decade ago this year of 1843, he'd had the good sense to marry her and move away from his old haunts to start this little place on the edge of the prairie. Out of good sense had come good fortune. Not in a monetary sense, for whatever cash they came by was put right back into the farm. A place that on this day was comprised of the four-room frame house and a larger storage barn with the yard between and a picket fence surrounding the buildings. To the south of the east-facing house and barn was the corral. Further south and to the west and north were fields of crops—corn, wheat, and hay grass. To the east, beyond the shade oak and the front fence, was the wagon trail that reached to the small and as yet unnamed community that would one day be a town.

It was the hope of Jose and his wife that it would be a town, anyway. A place where, when they got to be really prosperous, they could go to buy a few luxuries. For themselves and for their home, which would be much bigger by then. And for Josiah and his young sister. Ingrid was wanting their next—and last, she insisted—to be a girl. Jose did not mind . . .

A breeze suddenly rustled the summer foliage of the oak tree, the moving air as humid as the still air had been for several days now. Then a large warm spot of rain hit Jose on the sweat-tacky forehead. And he was jolted out of the reverie that had kept him langorously idle on the ridge of the roof for several minutes while his wife and son conscientiously attended to their own chores. The sun was suddenly obscured by the rapidly advancing clouds and then a whole flurry of raindrops sprayed over the Mexican, freshly soaking his shirt which was partially dampened by sweat. Then, with one final glance of quiet pride and satisfaction across the full extent of his domain visible from his vantage point, he set to work with a will. Aware, with a sense of guilt, that since he had abandoned gambling for money, his most serious fault was a penchant for daydreaming. Which, in itself, was not a cause of friction with Ingrid—

but daydreaming did go hand-in-hand with idleness. And now he worked frenetically at patching the roof, as much to impress his wife and son with his industry after wool-gathering as to get the chore completed before the full force of the storm hit.

When he had cast that contented glance over the farmstead, Jose Hedges had paid little attention to the vista beyond the boundaries of his property. Perhaps noted that the sky was now almost totally domed by low, dark gray clouds so that the sun shone just in the far south—and there for just a few seconds more. And that the rain harbingered by the strengthening wind was so heavy in the north that it created a belt of thick mist formed by the driving force of its angling fall and the vapor it triggered from the warm land it assaulted.

It was a rapidly moving belt, powered southward by the unusually warm north wind. And by the time the man saw it, on the periphery of his vision, it had advanced close enough to the farmstead so that it cloaked the band of six Sioux Indians moving inexorably toward the place.

Then sheet lightning lit the entire countryside, and its clap of thunder sounded with no measurable time lapse. The wind roared and the rain lashed. Jose had to release the hammer and bag of nails, fling himself forward along the new boarding of the ridge, and cling to the roof with his hands, elbows, knees, and feet to keep from being snatched off his perch and hurled to the dirt out back of the house. Dirt that only moments ago had been hard packed but was now on its way to becoming a morass of puddled mud as the torrential downpour exploded out of the storm that had transformed day into near night.

In the instant of the lightning flash, Jose could have glimpsed the Indian band had he happened to be looking in their direction. Would have seen them clearly enough in the brilliant, short-lived luminescence to count five braves and one squaw, two of the braves leading a pony each by rope reins, the animals lightly laden with the group's meager possessions. There would not have been time, and the more than a mile of distance intervening was too great, for the Mexican to see the band in any greater detail than this. To note that their emaciated bodies were clothed in rags and their faces were scarred by disease. That they were old before their time, but determined to survive as best they could. Ill armed with tomahawks, knives, one Mississippi rifle, and two single-shot handguns. All these weapons hung from belts or carried in the packs on the backs of the ponies until the lightning flash revealed to the Indians how close to the farmstead they had trudged. When, startled by the alarmingly loud crack of the thunder, the braves drew their weapons. And those leading the ponies delegated that duty to the squaw.

But Jose Hedges saw not a sign of any of this. Instead, as he abandoned his tools so that he could concentrate entirely on not being plucked off the roof, he saw one of his horses rear and kick in panic as Josiah was about to steer him into the barn. Saw it was the black gelding that was the strongest and most high-spirited horse on the place.

He knew he could do nothing except yell at the top of his lungs for his son to let go of the animal and get inside the barn himself. But Jose shrieked only a few words of advice, half in Spanish and half in English, before he realized there was no way his son could hear him above the roaring of the wind and the thrashing of the rain into and around the buildings and the fences and the live oak.

At the moment of this realization, he was forced to squeeze his eyes closed against the assault of wind and water. Perhaps a full two seconds later, as the power of the wind died down, he felt able to shield his eyes with a hand and peer once more at the front of the barn. He saw that the doors were firmly closed. The gelding was in a bolt, terror of the flash and the crash of lightning and thunder urging him into a flat-out gallop across the yard and out through the gate that had been wrenched off of its catch and opened by the wind. Josiah was nowhere to be seen in the front yard that was now a rain-pocked quagmire. And there was suddenly another instant of blue brightness and a deafening clap of electric noise, which caused the panicked horse to strive for greater speed and enabled Jose to see that Josiah was definitely gone from sight.

"Bueno, Josiah," Jose yelled, pronouncing the boy's name the Mexican way. And the venting of the exclamation was almost indistinguishable from the laugh of joy that followed it. "It is better to lose *estupido caballa* than the best son a *padre* ever had!"

He did not know if the eight-year-old had ducked into the barn or scurried across the gap to seek the more comfortable shelter of the house. What he also did not know—because he had been too intent upon looking for his son to glance elsewhere when the lightning lit the Iowa prairie—was that the five Sioux braves had apparently disappeared off the face of the earth while the squaw continued to lead the two ponies openly toward the farmstead.

"Jose, Jose! Are you still up there, Jose?"

Once again the noise of the wind and the rain had subdued, and the man on the roof heard the urgently anxious voice of his wife: looked toward its source and saw the top of the ladder, which had been knocked down by the first major assault of the storm, jut above the eaves of the roof.

"Si, mi amada," he yelled above a fresh barrage of storm sounds. "You hold it still, huh?"

"Hurry, Jose! *Pronto* Josiah, he has gone with the horse!"

The man's joy at considering his son safe and his happiness over Ingrid's concern for him was abruptly replaced by fear. And fear led to recklessness. Jose released his previously tenacious hold on the ridge of the roof and slithered rather than climbed down the angle of the pitch. Had to struggle to turn himself so that he did not come clear of the eaves headfirst. Succeeded in getting his feet to the front of the slide, but missed the ladder and crashed heavily to the ground some six feet to the side of where Ingrid stood staring at him. Water and mud splashed up in all directions. Jose Hedges quickly rose in its wake, saved from injury by the sodden softness of the ground.

Lightning, sheet and forked, ignited the sky and the land for perhaps two seconds. And in its harsh illumination, both Jose and Ingrid Hedges wrenched their fear-widened eyes away from each other. Sought a panic-stricken glimpse of their son. Saw the squaw with the two ponies on lead lines coming through the storm-lashed wheat planted in the four-acre field to the north of the house and barn. The woman with the animal was just two hundred yards or so away, which was close enough for the Hedges to see she was attired in Indian style. Close enough, too, for them to see she was leading the animals with both sets of reins in one hand. For when she saw the whites looking at her, she raised a free hand in an apparently friendly greeting. While, so startled were they to see the stranger, Jose and Ingrid found themselve for stretched seconds staring at her to the exclusion of all else.

This as young Josiah Hedges saw the squaw with the horses, too. From a different and more distant viewpoint. But saw her and the animals and his parents as just component parts of the whole dangerously developing situation. For, as he felt himself rooted to the spot by the dazzling brilliance of the double flashes of lightning, then twisted from the waist to stare back the way he had dashed in pursuit of the runaway horse, he glimpsed a scene that filled him with greater dread than if it had been the one he had expected to see. Because, so terrifyingly tumultuous was the thunder in the wake of the lightning, that he felt sure the farm buildings had been struck by a bolt from the torrenting, nightlike sky. And his mouth was gaped wide as he prepared to utter a scream of horror.

But nothing yet had been destroyed by act of God—or man. And, even at his tender age, Josiah C. Hedges had the presence of mind to impose self-control over his urge to give vent to his fear of what was actually happening, as the murk and mist of the deluge blanketed the farmstead again.

Indians! At least six of them, the boy forced himself to admit as he dropped to his haunches in the muddy, swirling water of a temporary pond that had formed in a natural depression several yards from the east trail, at the edge of the wheat field. There had been so little time to be sure before the bad light clamped down again, making it seem darker than it perhaps was in contrast to the glaring brilliance of the fleeting flashes. Indians. One of them making no attempt to hide in the wind- and rain-lashed crop. Leading two horses with one hand on the reins while the other was raised in a pretense of friendly greeting. While five others, for certain, stalked through the wheat, crouched down behind the cover of the horses.

Good grief, maybe the whole Sioux nation had risen and was about to slaughter every white man, woman, and child in the country! Burn everything the whites had built! Like some of his Pa's friends said was sure to happen one day if the Indians weren't hit first! Why, even the soldiers who infrequently patrolled the area never failed to make a point of warning folks to be on their guard against a hostile uprising any day. And this could be it.

It sure as hell . . . ! Just thinking the word, not even speaking it aloud, and despite the fear-filled tenseness of the situation, Josiah felt both excited and ashamed at the same time. This sure as *hell* was not the usual kind of run-in his Pa and Ma had had with Indians in the past. Most there'd ever been at one time, far as he could recall, was three. Lots of times there had been two. Every now and then, just one. And the Sioux had never sneaked up under cover of bad weather or night or anything before. Came to the place large as life and twice as ugly, as his Ma often said about lots of things she didn't like too much. Then tried to be sneaky in the way they wanted to trade for food or a horse or liquor or trinkets. Except for the one time when three braves rode up like crazy, firing off their pistols and giving out with war-whoops. And Pa had shot one of them in the hand with the ancient Hall breechloader rifle from over the fireplace. That had sure as hell scared them off! That bunch had been drunk of firewater, Pa had figured.

More lightning flashed, making the day brighter than it had been when the hot sun was glaring out of the high sky.

And more than a second—maybe more than two or three—passed before the crackle of thunder sounded. So the center of the storm was gone on by the area of the farmstead.

"Aw shit!" The skinny, dark-complexioned youngster actually whispered aloud this most forbidden of words. His fall from grace in the sodden privacy of the murk and the deluge triggered by self-anger displacing fear. Anger that he was indulging in relief that the harmless storm was passing while his grasshopper mind was filled with futile memories of other Indians when another bunch of Sioux was getting to be a greater and more real danger by the moment.

In that last instant of illumination, just the squaw and the horses were in sight close to the yard side of the field as his Ma waved back eagerly in response to the Indian's gesture of greeting. And his Pa looked anxiously around—maybe spotted the still galloping runaway horse but failed to see his hidden son. Just as Josiah was unable to see any sign of the braves who must now be on their hands and knees or even their bellies as they neared the picket fence with the two buildings and the white couple on the other side.

With the final sound of the thunder rumbling out of earshot across the vast prairie, Josiah checked an impulse to whiplash up to his full lanky height and jump in the air to emphasize his presence as he yelled a warning at the top of his voice.

Just maybe one or both of his parents would see him appear above the wavering top of the wheat field, but they would certainly not be able to hear his shout against the sounds of rain and wind that lashed the crop. The Indians would not be able to hear him, either. But to see him would be sufficient.

Josiah half rose up out of the deepening pool of water in the basin, and raced in the same half crouch into the wheat—his right hand going to that side of his belt where one day he would carry a pistol in a holster tied down to his right thigh. As an eight-year-old he carried what was made as a toy but was intrinsically a weapon thrust into his belt at hip level. But he did not draw it yet. He did begin to gather

27

ammunition, though, as he darted through the crop: sweat oozing from his pores to mix with the rain that soaked his calico shirt and homespun pants. The times when he had most often heard his father use the forbidden cuss words was when this very field was being ploughed and the share kept snagging on rocks.

Yet more lightning streaked brilliant illumination across the low sky and the vast flatness of the Iowa landscape. Josiah Hedges had no inclination to count off the seconds until the thunder started now. For he was in the first position he had been aiming for, and now rose just high enough to get a clear view of the squaw and the horses from almost directly behind. Over a range of fifty or sixty feet. At such a distance did not need lightning to show up his target clearly. And could see, almost as plainly, his Ma as she hurried across the yard toward the fence which the squaw would reach first, and his Pa, who was still devoting all his attention to a peering search for his missing son.

Just for part of a second, as he drew taut the vee of tough elastic from the top of the Y-shaped wood catapult, the eight-year-old boy considered shifting his aim. But, before the compulsion became too strong to resist, he released the square of buckram to send the chunk of rock zinging through the torrenting rain. Felt his lips pulled into a satisfied grin as the sweat beads of excitement squeezed more rapidly from his wide-open pores. But he did not now waste time with vanity in his skill as he heard the Indian pony on the right snort his pain and saw him start to rear in response to the stone impacting with his rump. While he enjoyed a sense of triumph that briefly excluded all other thoughts from his youthful mind, he automatically reached in his pants pocket to produce another rock and load it into the catapult.

Now there was no temptation to aim at the back of the squaw's head, as the female Sioux screamed and half turned in an attempt to keep control of the spooked and pained horse. For the rearing and hoof-flailing animal gave her temporary cover. Josiah sent the second rock speeding toward the rump of the other horse and the grin on his face had a fixed quality that made him look older than his years when he saw that animal react much like the first when he was hit.

Both horses broke free, wheeled away from the barrier of the fence, and lunged into bolts of pain-induced panic. While the squaw yelled, his Ma yelled, and his Pa yelled. And two of the stalking braves yelled as they were forced to their feet by the necessity of throwing themselves out of the path of the terrified animals.

Jose Hedges had a good idea of what was happening when he saw the sudden rear of the first pony. And connected it with the fact that Josiah was nowhere to be seen. For the only time he had ever raised his hand to his son and come within a moment of striking him was when the boy had fired his catapult at the horse hauling the plough across the four-acre field that spring. Not Josiah, nor Jose, nor even Ingrid was ever likely to forget the harsh words, high tension, and latent violence that had followed that incident.

And now . . . the second pony vented a body-quivering snort and came up on his hind legs, forehooves beating at the rain-lashed air. And as the squaw snarled at them in her native tongue, Jose was certain his son was responsible. Ingrid, recalling the same springtime incident, reached the same conclusion. And did not need to hear the bellowed warning of her husband as she gave vent to her own fear-filled feelings. For she knew, just as he did, that Josiah had a better reason than youthful devilment and a childish urge to experiment with cruelty to reenact such a spiteful performance.

Then, just as Ingrid Hedges was about to acknowledge to her husband that she shared his foreboding, they both saw the two braves rise into sight above the wind- and rain-thrashed wheat. And each of them responded with something close to the brand of composure that had been inherited by their son and would someday be finely honed by him. They were worried for him, as on this storm-filled day he was worried for them, but they—like Josiah—knew they could only help each other by rejecting reckless actions spurred by panic.

Jose Hedges was close to the cover of the house and he ducked into it. While his wife whirled, wrenched open one of the barn's double doors, and plunged inside. This as the whole Indian raiding party abandoned every effort at stealth and launched a frenetic assault on the farmstead buildings— war-whoops venting shrilly from the throats of the braves as they scrambled up and over the picket fence. This while the squaw whirled to give chase to the pair of runaways.

Josiah had moved closer to the fence, unseen by anyone in the fear-filled excitement that followed the two opening catapult shots. But now the boy fired a third rock, and this one struck a human rather than an animal rump—the pain of the impact forcing a cry from the brave it hit. The Indian was in the process of leaping off the fence into the yard as he brandished his pistol over his head. But he hurled the gun away, reaching with both hands for the source of his agony, and tumbled rather than jumped to the yard. Pitched full length into the morass of mud.

Spiteful triumph of the worst kind now gripped the boy as he relished the pain and humiliation he had delivered to an enemy. And he leaped to his feet and let out a war-whoop of his own.

He was seen on the periphery of her vision by the running squaw, rather than heard. And anger displaced any fear she may have been feeling as she gave up pursuit of the ponies to veer toward the mere boy who had spoiled the Sioux plan of a sneak attack.

Abruptly, twenty feet away from where Josiah Hedges turned toward her, the squaw slithered to an apprehensive halt in the sodden field. She was a full-grown adult of more than twenty-eight summers. A head taller than the white boy, but with perhaps not much difference in their weight: since she was sick and hungry and he was in fine shape. Still, he was only a boy. Why was she suddenly so afraid of him? His light-colored eyes fixedly stared at her from between slitted lids while his lips were drawn back in a grin of evil joy.

A gunshot sounded. The boy seemed not to have any desire to turn and see another brave fall from the fence, while the squaw found herself unable to do so. Ingrid Hedges's voice was heard shrieking, but the sense of her words—urging her son to run—was lost in the lessening sounds of the passing storm.

The squaw started to say something to the boy in her native tonge: her tone of voice and the expression on her gaunt, pocked face making it clear that she was pleading with him.

"You oughta be laughing," the boy rasped through his clenched teeth as he took aim with the catapult primed to near breaking point, his target her pulsing throat. "Seeing as how you're going to the Happy Hunting Ground."

At the open doorway of the house, Jose Hedges thrust the once-fired flintlock revolver into the front of his belt and snatched up the newer but still elderly Hall rifle. This as the brave with the Mississippi rifle landed in the muddy yard and exploded its single shot, his excited whoop of triumph becoming a wail of despair as he saw wood splinters kicked out of the door by the .54-caliber bullet. But the Mexican did not aim his rifle at this brave or the two others still on their feet at either side of the two fallen in the mud. Instead, the long barrel was tracked toward a target in the wheat field. Fired at that target.

The squaw took the bullet in the side of her head and died on her feet—to fall with the rigidity of a lightning-struck tree into the sopping-wet crop. Lightning flashed and the boy was able to keep from letting go of the buckram pouched rock as he saw the Indian female topple, a welter of blood spurting in an arc from her head wound.

The rain eased as the wind slackened.

Jose Hedges bellowed: "*Ponerse en marcha.* Get on out of here before—"

The five Sioux braves and Josiah stared at the Mexican as he hurled down the spent rifle and jerked out the revolver to brandish it at the intruders. Then all attention was abruptly switched away from him and he broke off his yelling when the barn doors were flung wide. The statuesque Ingrid Hedges stood on the threshold, her sodden dress pasted to her full body as she held a pitchfork in a double-handed, threatening attitude.

Just one brave still held a firearm—a pistol that he seemed on the point of swinging toward the blonde woman whose weapon was useless in such a situation. But then another of the braves vented an authoritative string of words. And the gun was hurled bitterly into the mud. This same Indian gave further orders with less urgency, and two of the dejected braves moved to aid the one who had been shot in the shoulder. The man hit with a stone was left to painfully regain his feet himself.

"We are hungry and weary and in need of help, white-eyed tiller of the soil," the leader of the band announced in faltering English.

"You stay that way, *indio!*" Jose Hedges snarled, with a dismissive gesture of the gun. "But you do not stay here!"

"You should have asked, redskin," the woman in the barn doorway added as the braves backed off across the yard and began to climb over the fence. "Instead of trying to take."

The Sioux and the whites alike were suddenly aware that the boy was no longer to be seen in the wheat field under the lightening sky. The Indians were angered by his disappearance. Ingrid Hedges was at first anxious for the safety of her son, but placated by the reassuring look with which her husband responded to her worried frown. Josiah was still missing from sight after the braves had carried their dead and injured off the Hedges property and recaptured the runaway ponies.

"Jose," the woman started, "perhaps the boy is afraid to return after—"

"He does not look frightened," her husband interrupted as he draped his free hand around her waist and waved with the pistol along the east trail beyond the dripping live oak and the gate now swinging gently in the wind.

She looked away from where the dispirited and beaten band of Indians was heading back north again, and saw

Josiah at the moment he caught their runaway gelding. Then her relief expanded to the point of joy and found outlet in a burst of uninhibited laughter. Jose made one final check to see that the Sioux had retreated before he dropped his pistol to the muddy ground and, laughing himself, took his wife in a double-arm embrace.

The wind ceased to blow entirely, the rain stopped falling, and there was a quality of finality about the way in which a distant flash of lightning showed above the horizon far to the south. The sky seemed to visibly rise higher above their heads as the couple recovered from their initial bout of uncontrollable excitement.

The woman shuddered.

The man held her more tightly and calmed: "It is all right now."

"Josiah, he was about to shoot that thing at the squaw. He could have killed her."

"I know this, Ingrid."

"Also, you never killed anybody before . . . that I know of?"

"I never have, *mujer*."

She nodded her belief in the truth of what he said. Then asked, frowning: "You will live without regret about this, my husband? It was necessary to protect what is yours."

"What is ours, Ingrid," Jose Hedges corrected. "Josiah is our son. There will be time enough in his life to come for him to endure such a regret. Better that I . . ."

He allowed the sentence to remain unfinished as Josiah rode the now composed horse into the yard. And the boy grinned foolishly at his parents who regarded him with love and pride.

"I do all right?"

"You do very fine, son," his mother assured him.

"Aw shit, I only—"

The forbidden word slipped out, a complete accident, as the still-embarrassed youngster was swinging down from the bare back of the horse. And he curtailed what he was about to say as soon as he realized what he'd already said.

"Josiah!" his mother shrieked.

33

"Gee, I'm sorry!" the boy countered hoarsely.

"Just where did he pick up such bad language, Jose Aviles?" the woman demanded rhetorically. She only used her husband's actual name when she was furious with him.

The man, in comradeship with the boy against his wife again, was as discomfitted as Josiah had been. And at this moment the gelding lifted his tail to heap a pile of horse apples in the mud of the yard. And Jose, with a surreptitious wink at their son, turned to his wife:

"Sometimes, *querida*—"

"Don't you 'darling' me, Jose Aviles!"

"On particular occasions, you will understand? It is easier said than dung."

Chapter Two

HARLAN PRICE spoke earnestly as he struggled against the urge to anger: "We figure close to twenty thousand cash, Edge! Plus a whole mess of jewelry that could maybe make as much as that again if sold in the right place! Or, could be, even more! Me and Ethan and Nick, we ain't no experts on that stuff!"

The impassive-faced half-breed dropped his cigarette to the parched ground and crushed it under a boot heel: this as he straightened up from where he had been leaning against a boulder while he listened to the eldest of the three Price brothers propose the deal.

No more than ten slow minutes had passed since the lone, taciturn rider's arrival at the fly-infested, corpse-littered scene of the abortive ambush on the boulder-strewn area beyond the ravine in eastern New Mexico Territory.

"So the trinkets could be worth a whole lot less than the cash money, feller?" Edge drawled as he moved without haste around to the blind side of the boulder. "Since you and your brothers aren't experts?"

"Hey, where you goin', mister?" the youngest of the seven prisoners in the cage wagon demanded, his voice shrill with anxiety.

"No place without his horse," the stoically composed Comanche Indian pointed out flatly.

The chestnut gelding, still saddled, was hitched to the

35

team in the traces of the wagon, so that the Winchester which jutted from the boot was far beyond the reach of all the wretched-looking, foul-smelling, variously tempered prisoners. The saddle horses of four of the dead men, each with a similar rifle in a boot, had wandered away from the wagon of their own accord to search for shade and grazing and water. They would find relief from the direct glare of the blisteringly hot sun as it inched inexorably down the southwestern dome of the near cloudless sky. But the unmoving air in the shade would still make it feel like there were fires burning fiercely closer to the surface of the parched ground than hell. Forage and water—dumb animals domesticated by man had to be optimists.

Just the half-breed's Stetson-shaded head showed above the top of the boulder as he urinated against the rock and eyed the wagon and its unwilling passengers over a distance of fifty or so feet.

"Takin' a leak is all," one of the men growled.

"The kinda people and places we rob ain't cheap, mister!" Nick Price argued. "So the watches and the rings and the fancy bits and pieces we got off the women . . . they wouldn't be no crap bought at a small-town notions store, would they?"

"Maybe he's one of them strange kind, Harlan," Ethan Price suggested in a sneering tone. "A Holy Joe religious nut that don't want money like normal people? Maybe he's just told us what he thinks of the deal."

"He don't look religious to me," Delany muttered as Edge refastened the front of his pants and emerged from behind the boulder.

The youngest prisoner's full name was Billy-Joe Delany, Harlan Price had told the newly arrived rider after introducing himself and his two brothers. Delany was twenty or so, short and skinny with a hollow-eyed, sunken-cheeked face under blonde hair which, like that of his fellow prisoners, had been cropped to a length of no more than a quarter-inch all over his skull.

The Comanche was a match for Delany's five feet three inches in height, but he had a more powerful build. There was more flesh on his face, too, with its broad forehead, wide mouth, and firm jawline. The Indian was about thirty years old and during those years had gotten used to accepting with sullen equanimity his status as low man in any group of whites. He looked for no better treatment from Edge, to whom he'd been introduced simply as the Comanche.

Austin Gatlin was in his mid-forties, and the prison barber hadn't had much work to do cropping his hair, which was comprised of a horseshoe of gray around the back and sides of his skull. He was of medium build and height and had the kind of face that, when it was not long overdue for a shave, probably was instantly forgettable. His complexion was patchy red, except where his skin was dry and pale and peeling—he looked like the indoor type, not used to the rigors of the trail. Gatlin was the only incarcerated passenger convicted of murder plain and simple, Harlan Price explained in his catalogue of the prisoners' felonies. Gatlin had used a shotgun to blow the head off the man he found in bed with his wife and then wielded the same weapon as a club to beat his wife to death.

The tall and broad and dull-eyed Chester Rankinn was also on the wrong side of forty. Green-eyed and red-haired with an element-processed face that had probably worn a mean look even before he acquired the livid scar angled across his left cheek. Like the Comanche Indian, Rankinn had been sentenced to death for rape and murder.

The trio of Price brothers, in common with Billy-Joe Delany, had been sentenced to death for killing and robbery—the youngster for his lone attempt at raiding a bank, while the brothers were wanted in numerous towns and counties for stage and train holdups.

Harlan was forty-five, Ethan perhaps ten years younger, and Nick another ten short of this. The wide disparity in the ages of the three was very evident, but it was equally plain to see that they were close blood relations. They all had black hair, blue eyes, and good teeth in wide mouths. All were close to an even six feet in height. Harlan's time-worn face was more heavily wrinkled, of course, and

37

he had more excess flesh hanging at his belly and chest and rear than the other two. Ethan's well-built frame advertised muscular strength, while Nick looked lean and quick.

Although Harlan was obviously the undisputed leader of his family, Gatlin and Delany appeared to accept him without reservation as their spokesman too. The mean-faced Rankinn remained in brooding isolation within the close confines of the cage, never saying a word as he gazed like a captured wild animal at Edge—resenting the half-breed's freedom. The Comanche also remained his own man in captivity, and even when he spoke his tone of voice seemed as detached as everything else about his attitude.

"Well?" Harlan asked as Edge approached the stalled wagon again. "You believe we got us a cache of cash money and high-value loot hidden away?"

"You got good reason to lie," the half-breed answered as he rasped the back of a brown-skinned hand across his bristled jaw.

"Shit, mister—" Nick started.

"But I've got no reason to think you are," Edge continued in the same even tone. "And nothing else in mind to do that would keep me from checking out that it's the truth."

Rankinn and the Comanche were the only prisoners who did not grin broadly or vent a harsh laugh at this—the white man continuing to despise the half-breed with his eyes, while the Indian expressed tacit and sullen mistrust.

"Just let us outta this cage and me and my brothers'll take you right to where the stuff is hid, mister!" Nick blurted out excitedly. "Art Cody's the one with the key for the locks! He's the fat tub of lard down there on the middle of the trail! It's one of a bunch hung on his belt!"

Edge gave an almost imperceptible nod and veered off his original path to halt and drop to his haunches beside the corpse of the twice-shot guard. Just a lone fly was disturbed now, buzzing angrily up off the crusting of congealed blood that surrounded the dead man's gaping mouth.

"Shit, Harlan, I reckoned we was done for and good when both Johnnie and Rod got themselves killed by that bastard Cody!" Ethan said, harsh laughter in his tone.

"Imagine, them two hotshots gettin' it from an old fart like him?" Nick added incredulously.

"We could've died out here," Billy-Joe Delany put in, voice and expression awed. "I figure hangin' has to be better than croakin' of thirst out in this godforsaken oven of a piece of country."

"For a time, I had my doubts about the desert heat getting the chore the hangman was being robbed of," Austin Gatlin contributed, his voice sounding oddly cultured in contrast with the others' harshly spoken tones.

"Don't you whites have a saying?" the Indian growled in an apathetic monotone that demanded the attention of the excited men and started to kill their joy. "To do with counting chickens before they are hatched?"

Both the Comanche and Rankinn had been the only prisoners to hunker down onto their haunches instead of crowding up to the bars while Harlan Price was negotiating for their release with the unresponsive Edge. Now they rose to their feet, in order to get an unobstructed view of the half-breed as he straightened up from beside Cody's corpse. And all eyes followed Edge as he unhooked a key from a large bunch of half a dozen and pushed it into a pocket of his pants.

"What's the idea?" Nick demanded, disappointment choking his voice.

"Your fault, I figure, big mouth," Chester Rankinn said, and his voice sounded as mean as his scarred face looked. His embittered gaze shifting from Edge to Harlan Price and back again while he clenched and unclenched his fists. "Yakkin' about us bein' shipped north for hangin' and tellin' this guy just why that's happenin'! Twenty grand and maybe double that! Half or all of it! What the frig?"

"While you're makin' with your mouth, Rankinn, Edge ain't givin' an answer to Nick's question!" Harlan Price snarled.

He and his brothers clenched their fists and did not

unclench them. And all three glowered their tacit intention to shut up the man forceably if necessary. Rankinn showed no sign of being afraid of the Prices, but an easy shrug of his broad shoulders revealed he was unaggressively resigned to whatever fate held in store for him while he was securely locked in the cage wagon.

"I, too," the Comanche said in his characteristic monotone as Edge moved around from the rear to the side of the rig, "have seen bounty hunters who have looked less like what they are. And I am not a criminal."

"Don't start with that innocence stuff again!" Gatlin growled in a tone of complaint, still sounding far more well bred and better educated than the others.

"Shuddup, all of you!" Harlan Price bellowed, and shoved aside his youngest brother, Billy-Joe Delany, and Gatlin as he swung away from the double-locked rear door and fastened a two-handed grip on the bars at the side of the cage where Edge was passing. "Don't be a fool, Edge! A lousy few hundred bucks! No more than a thousand for the whole bunch of us! And you'll probably have to wait for weeks, months, to collect it all! The Tucson office of Wells Fargo posted the reward on me and Nick and Ethan! Delany hit the bank in Lordsburg! The Indian claims he didn't screw and knife a woman in Douglas! Rankinn and Gatlin, they done what they did in Tucson!"

"Anyways, some of the reward money's already been paid, mister!" Ethan added. "And I don't reckon stage lines and banks and such like is gonna pay again for the same—"

"All right, keep us locked up in this stinkin' jail on wheels, Edge!" Harlan broke in on his brother as Edge stood looking up at the massed hatred being directed down at him through the bars—Not all the filthy, sweating, desperate, and defeated prisoners in the fetid cage expressed such clear-cut feeling: but each of them obviously experiencing it beneath the surface of what he showed. "I'll tell you where to drive this rig and you let us out when you've seen it was no lie about the deal?"

Edge touched the brim of his hat with a long forefinger

and answered: "Now we're thinking along the same line, feller."

"And how long is this line?" Austin Gatlin asked with a weary sigh, fanning his forage cap in front of his sun-punished face and looking in worse shape than ever now that the euphoria of expected release had proved ill-founded.

"In this heat, traveling the way we are, it oughta take around twelve hours," Harlan replied, endeavoring to conceal the full extent of his relief at the agreement reached. "Not includin' rest stops."

"Figure we spent more than enough time at this one!" Ethan snapped. "Climb aboard and get this thing rollin', why don't you, mister?"

"And hope that another of you white-eyes' sayings is not true," the Comanche muttered as Edge moved from sight beyond the solid partition at the front of the wagon.

"How's that, Injun?" Nick asked idly.

"That it is better to travel hopefully than to arrive."

"Hey, what you doin', Edge?" Harlan yelled anxiously, pressing his fleshy face tight against the bars. Then answered his own query aloud, so the other prisoners were put in the picture: "It's okay, he's just tendin' to his horse."

"Mister, we could use some tending, also!" Gatlin called.

Edge had uncinched his saddle and now dragged it free, heaved it up onto the seat of the wagon. Then led the gelding to the rear and hitched the reins to a bar—after the prisoners who had been grouped there backed reluctantly away in response to a head gesture.

"Even the guards made sure we had water when there was need," Gatlin went on, wincing as he interrupted his fanning to explore his painful-looking face with cautious fingertips.

"Cody and Nixon did, anyways," Ethan Price muttered sourly, and shifted his hate-filled gaze from Edge to the gunshot corpse of the most-resented guard. "That Mel Snyder would have sooner watched us die from thirst as swing from the gallows."

"Forget Snyder and dyin' any which way and all that stuff!" Harlan growled, a mirthless smile on his face as he watched their taciturn rescuer move back down the trail into the ravine, to where the dead men's quartet of horses were bunched in docile wretchedness in the expanding patch of shade cast by the north-facing wall of rock.

The men trusting in Harlan's leadership took their cue from the eldest Price brother and remained watchfully composed as the half-breed reached the group of animals, but the Comanche and Rankinn squatted down on their haunches at the front corners of the cage wagon and appeared to retreat into private worlds of sullen hopelessness.

"He's just bringin' the friggin' canteens, is all!" Billy-Joe Delany complained.

"I could find a use for one of those horses when we get to where we're going," Austin Gatlin muttered, disillusioned.

"I could use one of those rifles right here and now!" Ethan offered, then swept his angered gaze over the sprawled dead and added, "Or just a six-shooter would do it."

"Patience, brother," Harlan advised in a whisper that everyone aboard the wagon heard. But the unhurrying half-breed with eight canteens draped over his shoulders was out of earshot as he turned away from the horses in the ravine.

"Somethin' else you know about but ain't lettin' us in on?" Nick demanded reproachfully but realizing the need to keep his voice down. "Like Johnnie and Rod tryin' to bust us outta—"

Harlan glared his youngest brother into apprehensive silence and divided what was left of the censorious glower among the other prisoners who looked as aggrieved as Nick. Then rasped with sibilant harshness after a glance toward the returning Edge: "I didn't know where or when the boys would hit. Or how many of them. Just knew they'd try to spring us. But I know exactly where this tight-lipped sonofabitch is gonna get what's comin' to him!"

"You mean you plan—" the suffering Gatlin started.

Harlan directed another warning glare toward the element-burnished, blue-eyed face. Ethan, also aware that Edge was almost back within hearing distance, sidestepped and pressed the heel of his boot down hard on one of Gatlin's toes. And the man with the blotched and peeling face was silenced by the look for just a moment before pain caused a shrill scream to burst from his blistering lips.

"Gee, I'm sorry, Austin," Ethan apologized unfeelingly, as he again moved with the others to back away from the rear bars of the wagon.

"There's a water barrel lashed on at the side of the driver's seat, mister," Delany pointed out. "We figured you was gonna bring the horses up, so that when you set us free we—"

"He has seen the water barrel," the Comanche announced to the backs of the standing, sweating, stinking, tension-tautened men. "But he is wise enough to know that, as many as we are, in country such as this, we cannot have too much water."

Edge pushed the canteens between bars into the back of the cage, then backed off a pace and stroked the neck of his horse as he asked of Harlan Price: "Which way, feller?"

"Back through the ravine. Then we can cut across the desert. I'll holler out to you, okay?"

"Obliged."

"No more than we are to you."

Edge tipped his hat and started for the front of the wagon again, as all the captive passengers with the exception of the Comanche reached for a canteen. The Indian remained hunkered down on his heels, back pressed into the angle of the solid partition and bars: watching Edge with dark eyes that seemed to emanate a brand of palpable contempt. Then, for just part of a second, that powerful expression was gone, to be fleetingly displaced by an unspoken warning.

The half-breed had no opportunity to acknowledge the silent message before an expression of arrogant scorn returned to the Indian's face and he announced in his customary monotone, "I am innocent and should be freed at the earliest opportunity."

Edge neither knew nor cared whether the Comanche was telling the truth. He was certain, though, that the man had spoken merely to distract the other prisoners who may have been suspicious of his hard-eyed watch on their new captor.

"And I should have medical attention at the earliest opportunity!" Austin Gatlin added. And groaned in pain as he raised the unstoppered neck of a canteen to his puffed and discolored lips.

"You gotta get used to these two, mister!" Ethan Price snarled as the half-breed climbed up onto the seat in front of the solid partition.

"That's right!" Nick sneered. "This couple of jailbirds in a movin' cage ain't done much else but sing the same friggin' song ever since we started out from Tucson."

"And it's a lousy duet the rest of us are gettin' real sick of listenin' to!" Harlan growled.

"But we won't have to put up with it for much longer, huh?" Billy-Joe Delany suggested.

"Guess not," Edge rasped through clenched teeth bared in a grin as he flicked the reins to start the team and steered the pair of gray geldings into a tight about-face turn on the narrow boulder-flanked trail. "But for now," he added, "the malady lingers on."

Postscript to War

Edge made his first appearance, as Captain Josiah C. Hedges back from the War Between the States, in The Loner. *His experiences in that Civil War were extensively covered in the sequences of flashback stories that ended with* The Final Shot. *The story now to be told took place, chronologically, between the conclusion of* The Final Shot *and the opening of* The Loner.

THE LONE ride from war to peace was taking longer than ex–Captain Josiah C. Hedges would have wished. But even though many of his virtues had been corrupted during the bitter struggle between the Union and the Confederacy, one of those that remained intact, and was part of the basis on which he intended to rebuild his peacetime life, was a capacity for infinite patience. So, as he rode at an easy pace toward the Ohio River boundary between northwestern Kentucky and the southernmost tip of Indiana, knowing he had to cut a diagonal course across the whole of Illinois before he even set foot in his home state of Iowa, he harbored no futile regrets that night was falling fast through the warm twilight of the late May evening. And soon he would have to call a halt to rest himself and his mare before a new day's riding tomorrow.

It had been easy traveling today, along good roads on which he had met nobody who took exception to his presence—a man garbed in the uniform of a Union cavalry captain moving with a confidence approaching arrogance through a state that had never wholeheartedly been loyal to the Federal cause. Or, if anybody had openly or surreptitiously resented such a man in such a uniform, his lean but obviously powerful frame, the easy caution evident in his strong-featured face, his attitude in the saddle which suggested he was poised for instant reaction to attack—with fists, the Henry repeater rifle in the boot, or the Remington revolver in a holster—had dissuaded them from making an aggressive move against him. The way he wore the kerchief around his neck totally concealed all trace of the beaded thong and the pouched razor that hung from it at the top of his spine.

Full night descended on the verdant Kentucky countryside as he neared the fringe of an extensive stand of mixed timber. And he contemplated making camp within the now almost pitch blackness of the forest. But as he rounded a curve in the road to crest the top of a low rise, he saw the light of a half-moon glinting on the surface of the river he had known he was nearing. And he elected to ride on down what looked like a gentle grade so that he and his horse would be able to relish the taste of fresh rather than canteen water.

The trees thinned out and the light of the moon increasingly encroached on the darkness beneath their summer foliage. Then Hedges saw the house, after the road made a sudden turn to the left and dropped more sharply across the face of a sheer bluff of gray rock. A big, yellow brick house with a red tiled roof. It had five chimneys and more than a score of sash windows. Probably contained at least twenty rooms, spread over three floors. It was sited so that it's front faced the hundred-foot-wide, slow-flowing river, and its back an enclosed courtyard comprised of the cliff face and flanking outbuildings. There was an ornamental garden immediately in front of the house: between this and the riverbank, and stretched away to either side, were fenced fields. From the point where the public road reached the level of the river, a spur cut off from a gateway to angle toward the house.

The road that closed with the river and followed its course closely toward the west was as hard packed and well used as it had been for the many miles Hedges had traveled it this far. The private spur was as weed infested as the fields, which were separated one from the others by leaning or already broken-down fences. One half of a pair of wrought-iron gates at the start of the driveway to the house was rusting on the ground. Its mate was nowhere to be seen.

The closer Hedges rode to the house—and he felt drawn to turn off the public road and steer the mare along the spur—the clearer became the signs of dereliction in the wake of destruction. The house had been put to the torch. And, from the way that nettles predominated over all other weeds and wild grasses in the fields, so had the crops that had once flourished in the rich, riverside soil. Not recently, though. The taint of burning that he smelled faintly was probably more in his imagination than in the air, he guessed.

Swinging down from his saddle immediately out front of the stepped portico of the open door, Hedges could see that just some of the windows had been shattered while others were merely dulled by soot and smoke. Could see, too, that a great deal of paintwork was suffering from simple neglect rather than scorching. And very little of the exterior bricks and mortar and roof had been scarred by flames.

The mare whinnied nervously. And as an echo seemed to resound off the rock face out back of the house, Hedges shifted his perplexed gaze away from the building's facade and turned toward the horse: reached out a hand to stroke the muzzle of the uneasy animal. Which was when the gunshot cracked.

Fresh from the war that had honed his responses to a

peak of sharpness, the tall, lean, thirty-year-old man in the cavalry captain's uniform swung his hand away from the horse's head. Fisted it around the frame of the rifle jutting from the boot. Used the motion of the spooked horse lunging into a gallop to bring the Henry clear of the leather. Then dove for the ground where the mare had been standing, and powered into a side-over-side roll that carried him off the edge of the weed-choked area immediately out front of the house and down a three-foot drop into the grass of a onetime lawn at least a foot taller than that.

Two more shots were exploded in quick succession from the front of the house as the half-breed toppled from sight. Not from the doorway, though, where the first one had come from. Instead, out of broken windows on the floor above. Also, whereas the first shot had been triggered from a rifle, the others came out of the muzzles of revolvers. Although the men in the second story of the house had the shorter range and less accurate weapons, they had the advantage of elevated positions. And with the bright light of the half-moon beaming dangerously down on the deeply shadowed house and the sparsely featured terrain on three sides of it, even a man who had not lived for long and grueling years with the threat of violent death always close at hand would have realized the need for caution.

But only a man who had fought a bloody and bitter war against an acknowledged enemy while leading a group of men who would as soon have killed him as the Rebels would have been unable to check an impulse to time-wasting self-anger. Josiah C. Hedges, as he lay sprawled on his back between the ornamental retaining wall and the expanse of tall grass, both hands fisted white-knuckle tight around the frame and barrel of the twelve-shot repeater rifle, experienced this rage against himself for having allowed this vigilance to falter. For having been so intrigued by the strangely burned mansion that had withstood the attack of flames so well, he had failed to instinctively realize that he was under surveillance by menacing eyes.

"Yankee?" a man roared, his Southern accent turning the one-word query into a demand.

General Robert E. Lee had surrendered the Confederacy to Ulysses S. Grant at Appomattox Courthouse more than a month ago. Hedges had been there—had killed a Rebel sharpshooter on the morning of the day of the peace signing. All fighting on every scattered battleground of the Civil War had not ceased right then. But this particular Union cavalry captain had considered his war to be over. And a few days later, when he watched six of the meanest troopers ever to serve in any army ride out of sight with army discharge documents in their pockets, he had begun to reverse the dehumanizing process that the war had wrought in him. It would take time, he knew. What he had not realized was that he was making a mistake in assuming the North-South conflict was truly over. But how could he have been aware of what the future held?

"Yankee, you better listen to me!" the man inside the open doorway of the house yelled in a tone of impatience and rage as Hedges regained his own impassive composure and substituted positive action for negative thinking. "You hear what I'm saying?"

"He's not likely to answer you and give away where he's at, Ralph!" one of the men upstairs growled reproachfully.

"Maybe he can't, Lester!" another of the upstairs men suggested with a tremor of excitement in his youthful-sounding voice. "Maybe we killed the sonofabitchin' bluebelly!"

Lester, or somebody else on the second story of the house, vented a throaty sound of contempt for this theory.

"Your mount is back out on the river road!" Ralph announced. "Don't expect you to trust me enough to get up out of that grass and head on down to the animal! And, tell the truth, I don't know if I could keep Clay from trying to kill you again in that situation!"

"Damn right!" Clay snarled, excitement displaced by embittered eagerness. "Hadn't been for Lester spoilin' my aim, I'd have shot his ass off! Him being a bluebelly officer and all!"

"Goddamn you—" Ralph started.

49

There was a thud, then another sound that could have been a brief cry of pain. Next a scuffling noise that lasted for perhaps three seconds. All in an upstairs room. And a rasping whisper in the same area was curtailed by a new voice reporting tersely: "Clay won't be shooting off anyone's ass or his own mouth for a while, Ralph!"

"Bradley didn't have to do that to him, Ralph!" Lester complained.

"Goddamnit, who's in charge here!" Ralph snapped.

"Know how you feel," Hedges murmured through clenched teeth, his voice adequately masked by the chirping of crickets and the rippling of the river that were the only sounds to disturb the Kentucky night stillness while the men in the house were silent. "But you wouldn't expect sympathy from me?"

He had moved some twenty feet away from the place where he had dropped out of sight behind the retaining wall. Inching along on his back, feet first, to the right of the men in the house: the rifle resting along the front of his body as he propelled himself with boot heels and elbows. He could hear the tall grass rustling, and see the tops of it moving above him. He had to believe that at least somebody in the house could see the same movement on this early summer night in which not a breath of breeze was stirring, and were thus marking his painfully and sweatingly slow progress. He was unsure whether to believe in the apparent veracity of the discord among the men who should know exactly where he was.

"Yankee!" Ralph went on in a brittle tone of anger after tense silence greeted his demand. "Get to your mount just any way you want! And get in your saddle and be on your way! War's over and I've no intention of starting a private one! Shot I fired was meant as a warning, mister! Clay and Lester Beaudine, they fired instinctively when you took off like a scalded cat, way you did!"

In the peaceful night it was unnecessary for the man to shout. Hedges could have been three times his actual hundred-some feet away from the front of the house and still have heard clearly what Bradley interjected in an even-toned voice:

"Okay, Ralph. The captain's been told. He don't believe our word that he's got safe passage off the property . . ."

It was possible to visualize the shrug of shoulders from the tone and manner in which the man allowed the sentence to remain menacingly incomplete.

"You're right, Bradley!" Ralph agreed. "If that Yankee isn't willing to take the word of honor of a Southern officer and gentleman, then that's his lookout!"

The silence that was kept from being total by the crickets and the river descended once more, and endured for many stretched seconds. While Hedges lay utterly still except for the almost imperceptible rise and fall of his chest as he breathed: sensing the malevolence in the gazes that were swept back and forth over the tall grass of the neglected lawn as he waited to hear a particular sound.

The strain of this waiting while he forced his hearing to remain at the limit of its capability caused sweat beads to ooze from every pore in his body: the moisture standing out on his exposed flesh or pasting his clothing to his body. It was easy to imagine that his strength and energy were draining away from him to an extent where he could even doubt his ability to react as planned when the expected sound finally came.

Just then Clay Beaudine groaned at the threshold of regaining consciousness. And in the instant he recognized the tiny sound for what it was, Josiah C. Hedges became a total realist who refused to acknowledge that he possessed any imagination at all.

He powered up into a sitting posture and pumped the action of the Henry as he swung the rifle above the retaining wall. His mind was as blank as the inky blackness of the house doorway, into which he triggered a snap shot. The fear of dying caused the sweat on his flesh to turn ice cold. In these moments of retaliation against men who would have him dead, he no longer felt drained and exhausted. Relished instead an all too familiar exhilaration of battle as he used his elbows on the top of the wall to augment the strength of his legs and come up to his full height. This at the same time he was working the lever of the repeater again, ejecting a spent shellcase and jacking a fresh round into the breech. Imagination briefly flooded his mind with an image that it had harbored while he lay in perspiring stillness . . .

Of a man recovering from injury as his concerned brother and the indifferent man who'd caused the hurt turned instinctively toward him. Then the faceless—to Hedges— Bradley and Lester swung back to stare out the window in panic as the enemy rifle exploded. And then were momentarily in the grip of euphoric relief that the bullet did not find their flesh.

Because he was a realist who had been taught by harsh experience never to expect good when evil stood an even chance of being the truth, Hedges was not tempted to look with his mind's eye at a conjured-up picture of a faceless Ralph pitching to the dark floor beyond the threshold, hit by the blindly fired bullet.

Men shouted and Hedges had no way of detecting if one of them screamed with the agony of a fatal wound. He had leaped up onto the weed-carpeted, hard-packed area stretching from the top of the wall to the front of the house: the ready rifle aimed from his hip now. The main body of sound came from a long-ago broken window above and to his left of the flat roof of the portico. He couldn't be sure if he saw or merely sensed movement in the darkness out of which the barrage of voices came. He angled the rifle and squeezed the trigger a second time. Felt his facial flesh become involuntarily rearranged into a familiar killer's grin of naked brutality as he heard a scream. He didn't give a damn whether it was caused by agony or terror.

He lunged into a fast, crouching run, once more pumping the ejection and loading action of the Henry. Months, weeks, or so recently it could have been numbered in days, ago, he might have felt an undeniable compulsion to laugh aloud as gunfire crackled and bullets whistled through the air close to his rapidly moving form. But, like the man beyond the doorway had said, the war was over. There was no longer a cause to fight for and the knowledge of a whole military machine that ground inexorably onward without letup whenever a lone soldier died. Now he was just Joe Hedges, no longer entitled to wear the uniform he had on. Nor was he entitled—and neither did he expect—to be avenged if his decision to counterattack rather than retreat proved a fatal mistake. Hell, maybe in this fight he didn't have right and God on his side, but that didn't matter. The bastards were trying to kill him, and that was reason enough for him to enjoy striking back at them. But there was a natural damper on unbridled euphoria, born of the bald awareness that if he stopped a killing bullet he would not know why he died. And neither would Jamie, his kid brother who was waiting for him on the Iowa farmstead.

He reached the cover of the corner of the house and slithered to a halt. He was unable to mute the painful deep breathing of exertion and tension. But then the enemy surely knew where he was at the end of his unexpected dash through the open under the bright moonlight. He turned and leaned against the brickwork of the house wall, gazing across the neglected property to the glinting river, and worked at extracting the brutality from the grin that had become a fixed mask on his bristled, sweat-run face. Saw his horse down on the bank of the watercourse, calmly drinking. Felt his expression slowly transform itself into a smile of quiet satisfaction as he reflected upon the basic rule of war that had proved its validity yet once more: do the unexpected, and do it when the enemy least expects it.

"You okay, Ralph?" Bradley called, still sounding coolly composed in the wake of the outbreak of violence.

"Yes! You and the others?"

"Just me hurt from where he clubbed me!" Clay Beaudine snarled bitterly.

"The Yankee, Bradley?" Ralph wanted to know, anxious.

"If he was hit, it didn't keep him from makin' it to cover!" the other Beaudine brother growled before Bradley could respond.

"Lester's right."

"All right, Captain!" the man on the lower floor of the house yelled, raising his voice higher than ever to address the unwelcome visitor lurking outside. "I guess we have your answer! There is no longer any question of safe passage off the Engels estate! My offer is withdrawn!"

Hedges had begun to move again as soon as the exchange between the men inside the house got started. Faster than his inching slithering between the retaining wall and the tall grass, but slower than his hell-for-leather sprint across the open area. To the rear corner of the house, working hard to keep the sound of his respiration down as he crept stealthily toward his objective—a timber gate in an arch in the short length of ten-foot-high wall between the house and one of the outbuildings on this side of the courtyard under the cliff. He could both see and feel the rust on the door hinges and decided against even trying to see if it was locked or bolted. The iron handle was also badly rusted. But it was not so corroded that it failed to support his one hundred and ninety pounds after he had wedged the barrel of the Henry between the top of the door and the underside of the arch. He hauled himself up off the ground with one hand hooked over the frame of the rifle and one foot on the door handle. Then swung up onto the top of the wall, eased the rifle noiselessly free, and dropped to the ground on the other side.

More than one horse made small sounds in the stable on the far side of the enclosed area. But the animals were made uneasy by his intrusion for just a few moments before they calmed into a different brand of silence from that which gripped the men in the house: the horses sensing the visitor meant them no harm; the men knowing they were in imminent danger of being killed.

There were some broken windows in the moon-shadowed rear of the house, but Hedges found even easier access to the place: it was a warm night and the last man in from tending the horses in the stable had left the rear door wide open. The ex-captain of Union cavalry, breathing silently and easily now, went up two steps and across the threshold.

Where he stood stock-still and allowed the narrowed slits of his eyes beneath the hooded lids to become accustomed to the lower level of light. Very few aromas from the Kentucky countryside permeated into the atmosphere of the house, and now the smell of old burning was a good deal stronger in his faintly flared nostrils.

Within a few moments he was able to see his new surroundings more clearly. Saw that the room he was in had been stripped bare of everything that could be moved. And, from the blackened and decay-smelling heap of ill-defined shape in the center of the room, it was plain what had happened—the former furnishings, whether combustible or not, had been stacked on a pile and put to the torch. Months, or even years, ago: for at least one season's dampness had infiltrated the ravaged and abandoned-to-the-elements house.

Now, as he advanced across the room, setting his booted feet down as if they were bare and he was walking on broken glass, the house could never have been more silent—or so it seemed. But that was impossible. There were at least five men inside the place, and the living human body is never silent: in the ears of the individual who is desperately attempting to make no noise at all, its sounds are raucous. But, in many similar situations to this during the past four-plus years, the tall, lean half-breed who now peered cautiously around the jamb of a partly open door had learned how to ignore this internal pumping and murmuring while watching that he progressed as stealthily as he could and listening for any kind of giveaway from those he was stalking.

He had to cross another, larger room, which had been mistreated in the same manner as the first one, to reach another partly open door before his straining ears heard a sound he had not made:

A belch, followed by a low cry of shock.

"Clay, you stu—" Lester began to hiss.

"Quiet!" Ralph demanded.

"I couldn't help it," Clay defended in a childlike whine.

"Outside!" Ralph said, finding it difficult to keep his voice down as his temper rose. "A wagon. On the road."

"Just our luck," Lester groaned.

"Carry on, you two. There's no help for it. Quiet as you can."

"Sure, Ralph. Come on, Clay."

"I couldn't help it, honest."

Hedges had his back pressed hard to the wall on the opening side of the doorway, the Henry held in a double-handed grip and angled across the front of his body. Sweat felt hot on some areas of his skin and cold on others as his slitted eyes peered unblinkingly across the night-darkened room—as if he were watching the scene which, in fact, was taking place on the other side of the wall behind his back.

The scene was softly lit and in deep shadow—he knew this from the wedge of blue moonlight that fingered through the twelve-inch gap between the door edge and frame into this room. He knew, too, from the distance he had moved along the side of the house and the steps he had taken to backtrack through the interior, that he was on the threshold of the front hallway where Ralph alone had been waiting when he approached the place. His ears supplied the other, more important components of the scene.

Ralph had been joined by the Beaudine brothers from upstairs. The three of them in a group on the far side of the hallway at first. Then, on orders from Ralph, the brothers began advancing toward the area where Hedges waited in hiding. Obviously sent to search for him and to deal with him as silently as possible. While Ralph stayed watching the area out front of the house, paying particular attention to the wagon that even Hedges could now hear rolling down the same stretch of road he had traveled to get here.

"Hold it!" Bradley rasped, in a tone of voice that made no apology for assuming authority over Ralph. He sounded to be literally above the heads of the other three. Then, as he went on to explain the order, Hedges was able to follow with his mind's eye the progress of the fourth man down a staircase. The man spoke in a low-voiced rush, evidently intended to check any impulsive objections. "Watch and wait. We don't want to involve others unless we have to. If the captain forces us to, then no help for it. Meantime, let's wait until the wagon goes on by. What do you say?"

Only now did Bradley's tone moderate from one of command to inquiry. And, although Bradley did not raise his voice even to the level of normal conversation, Hedges received the distinct impression that his own agreement was also being sought.

"Whatever," Lester Beaudine allowed perfunctorily from just a few feet beyond the doorway beside which Hedges stood.

"Sure thing," his brother added, and this time almost succeeded in checking the belch of fear that emerged as no more than a gulp.

"Keep your voice down!" Ralph rasped with deep concern. Then, in a strangled tone, as if he might actually have been clutching at his own throat: "Goddamnit, it's him!"

Hedges folded away from the wall to push the barrel of the repeater between door and frame, leveled from his hip. And peered in the same direction as he inserted his leading foot in the same gap. Heard the clop of hooves and the crunch of wheelrims muted by the weed-covered earth as the rig turned off the hard-packed road and onto the neglected spur. Saw two men close to him, one at the foot of a staircase and another just inside the front doorway. Three of them staring at the fourth who was peering out through the doorway. The Beaudines with a revolver each, and Bradley and Ralph with rifles or carbines.

But it had never been the intention of the quartet of gray-uniformed soldiers of a defeated army to shoot the man in the approaching wagon. For a noosed lynch rope was hanging from the center of the hallway ceiling. And a four-foot-high wooden crate was placed directly beneath the rope, on an area once occupied by the fire-charred detritus that was now scattered haphazardly over the floor.

Hedges moved his leading foot sharply to the side, so that the door was kicked open. The Rebel soldiers gasped their shock as they whirled. Hedges took a single step forward and thrust the Henry at the most scared-looking Beaudine, so that the muzzle was just six inches from his twitching face.

"I'm as happy to trade words as gunshots, fellers," he drawled.

"Lester?" the thin youngster under imminent threat of death pleaded croakily.

"Okay!" Bradley rasped. Leaned his rifle against the fire-scorched wall at the foot of the uncarpeted and unrailed staircase. "All of you get rid of the guns!"

Bradley was the tallest and perhaps the eldest of the four. Ralph, who was close to the same age, was short and rotund, and he appeared almost painfully reluctant to follow Bradley's suggestion. Did so only after the twenty-year-old Clay had let go of his revolver and his stockily built older brother had returned his to the army issue holster on his gunbelt.

The Beaudines were enlisted men, Bradley was a sergeant, and Ralph a lieutenant.

"Why me first, mister?" Clay asked tremulously.

"Something good and bad luck have in common," Hedges answered and took a further step into the hallway. He kept the rifle muzzle half an inch from Clay's pulsing temple as he raked his narrowed eyes, glinting in the pale moonlight that entered through the open front door, over the faces of the other three men. "There's no accounting for it."

"We can account for the situation into which you have blundered, sir," Bradley said in his once again composed voice.

"Goddamnit!" Ralph rasped.

"Gonna string up a no-good sonofabitch that deserves it, is all," Lester muttered just as the wagon rolled to a halt immediately outside the house entrance.

And everyone in the tension-filled hallway spared the dangerous time to glance out through the doorway. To see that the pair of dark horses which snorted and shook at the end of a long haul were in the traces of a carriage rather than a wagon—a kind of post chaise with just the driver on the front seat while the rear seat was piled with the luggage that couldn't fit on the roof.

The four ex–Confederate soldiers wrenched their heads around to stare at the former Union army captain. Hedges remained totally impassive and kept the rifle in a rock steady aim at the head of the terrified Clay Beaudine. As this attitude was taken to mean he had no intention of starting further trouble, all gazes were returned to the area at the front of the house visible through the confining frame of the doorway.

The man who had been driving the travel-stained carriage and pair, climbed gingerly down from the high seat. He was of medium height, and medium build, a man of about fifty: the strain of a long journey rather than the number of his years probably causing the evident stiffness in his joints that slowed his movements. But it appeared to be the signs of mistreatment and decay visible from the outside of the once fine house rather than his own physical discomfort that caused a grimace to remain fixed to the pale, gaunt face of the dudishly dressed man who limped to the portico, climbed up the steps, and then became no more than a silhouette with a pale blob for a face as he halted in the doorway. Then, as if he were incapable of experiencing a greater degree of trauma than that which had assaulted his senses when he saw the house from the outside and could guess its interior condition, the man's demeanor altered not at all when he saw the five men standing silently in the fire-damaged room with the lynch rope hanging ominously from the center ceiling.

"General Engels," Bradley greeted him icily.

In a dull tone, the man in mufti corrected: "No longer a general, Bradley Dalton. When there is no longer a war, there's less need for—"

"You can't get rid of your evil by just takin' off your uniform!" Lester said accusingly.

"That the Beaudine brothers?" Engels asked, leaning forward from the waist a little as he sought a clearer view of the men at the rear of the hallway. Now revealed surprise in his tone as he added: "And a Federal captain, I do believe?"

"He's here by mistake!" Ralph snarled.

"And prepared to stay out of business that's no concern of his," Bradley Dalton said to Engels. Then made the statement a query by turning his head to look at Hedges.

"No longer a captain, Mr. Engels," the half-breed said. "But the war ain't been over long enough for that to matter if this is just another North–South skirmish."

"Merle Engels was CSA, same as we were!" Clay Beaudine explained eagerly, hopeful that this bald statement would get him out from under the threat of the unwavering rifle.

"That's right," Engels confirmed. "I served the Cause of the Confederacy and I'm proud to claim that."

"What do you claim about Cemetery Ridge south of Gettysburg back in July of 'sixty-three, Mister Engels?" Ralph questioned, stressing the civilian form of address to make it sound like a profanity. "When you were just a major?"

"In war, Lieutenant Ransom," Engels answered, a trace of tension sounding through his weariness, "soldiers of every rank up to and including the very top echelon are required to follow orders."

There was an abrupt flare of flame and all eyes looked toward it and blinked. The five former Rebel soldiers only now aware that Hedges had removed the threat of the rifle from Clay Beaudine's head—had the Henry canted to his left shoulder as he struck a match on its stock to light the cigarette angled from the side of his mouth. Once again, Bradley Dalton was the first man to recover from the unexpected.

"Gettysburg was a mess, mister," he said.

"I heard about it."

"We were part of Engels's brigade in the First Corps under command of Longstreet. Orders were to hold Cemetery Ridge against the Third Corps of your Army of the Potomac. For as long as it was possible to do so without losses exceeding acceptable levels. Isn't that how the order from Longstreet read, Ralph?''

"Quite correct, Bradley."

"An officer must exercise his own discretion—" Engels started.

"We had a hundred and seventeen men on that hilltop," Lester Beaudine cut in sourly. And peered into the middle distance as he recalled a day almost two years earlier. "Includin' Merle Engels. Five of us made it down from there."

"And you know what, mister?" Clay asked rhetorically, staring at the seemingly composed man in the moonlit doorway. "He got a commendation from Robert E. Lee himself and a field promotion. Can you believe that?"

"Sure, feller," Edge allowed. "Of war I can believe anything."

"Precisely," Engels agreed. "War is hell. And—"

"There was us taking orders from the friggin' Devil when hell was at its hottest!" Ralph Ransom spat out. And whirled into a turn away from Engels to face Hedges in a beseeching posture, his arms outstretched and his hands splayed. "We got leave, Captain. After Gettysburg and before they threw us in again under Longstreet at Chickamauga in September. Merle Engels had been transferred someplace else. We knew about him having this house and we came here that summer and—"

"Tried to burn it to the ground, appears to me," the weary homecomer cut in. And now he sounded resigned to whatever the fates had in store for him.

"No, we didn't try to do that," Dalton corrected. "We just burned everything you owned that would burn."

"That's not the way I heard it, from my people that you ran off and scared half to death, Sergeant," Engels countered, but he continued to appear uncaring of what was to come in this fire-ravaged room dominated by the unmoving lynch rope suspended from the ceiling.

"Can't blame them for not stickin' around to watch us, Engels," Clay said in an excited tone. "We sure as hell did scare them into runnin' like rabbits."

"We're sorry for that," Dalton hurried to cut off what the youngster was saying with such relish. "Your people couldn't help the kind of man you were. But we were so . . . so . . . consumed with hatred when we came here that first time—I think we would have stopped at virtually nothing to do what we were here for."

"Recallin' all those good men who died for frig-all nothin' on Cemetery Ridge!" Lester Beaudine growled.

Ransom plunged in as if he'd been waiting with mounting impatience to speak again. "They only died the once, of course. Same as anybody can. But a man who deserves it can be made to suffer in many ways before he gets to meet his Maker, Engels. When you heard what happened here, we expected you to have the place fixed up good as new again. So we could come back and destroy it all a second time."

"And if you moved elsewhere after that, to start afresh, there was a scheme to go there, too. And ruin whatever you built. Over and over until you were totally broke—financially and in spirit, too." Bradley Dalton was starting to sound as bone-deep tired as Engels. He shrugged his shoulders. "But then, when the war ended, we knew it would never work. We four each had to go our own ways. Separated like that, we wouldn't be able to sustain each other's resolve. Even now, time has already worked to dull the edge of our feelings against you."

"But we're going to hang you before we lose the will for that, Engels," Ransom averred.

"For those hundred and twelve guys that didn't all have to die south of Gettysburg," Lester Beaudine added.

"Right on," his younger brother agreed, but his enthusiastic words had a hollow sound.

Ransom, who was closest to where Merle Engels stood on the threshold of the house did not move. Dalton started away from the foot of the staircase, and the Beaudine brothers advanced after Lester had glanced at the silently smoking Hedges.

"There's nothing I can say to you men that will make you think again and—"

"Not a friggin' thing, Engels," Clay Beaudine cut in viciously.

Engels shook his head slowly. "Wasn't asking you anything. Was telling you."

Hedges took the cigarette from his lips, let it fall to the floor, and shredded the butt under a boot. And then took a backward step, needing to make a conscious effort not to bring the Henry down from his shoulder. This as he reached a decision about the attitude of the man who had come home. He was tired, that was for sure. But only from the long journey he had made to get here. He was not weary of living. So his composure was of confidence in, rather than resignation to, his immediate fate.

"Because there's no excuse for that many men being slaughtered. For victory, let alone defeat. Except for the existence of war. And in war, decisions are taken and orders are given and—"

"Mistakes are made!" Ransom cut in.

"Admitted," Engels allowed. "And for the rest of my life I'll be paying higher for that one than anything you men can—"

"Rest of your life is all gone, Engels," Lester Beaudine snarled. And snatched the revolver out of his hip holster.

"No you don't!" a woman who was not young said, her voice sharp in tone but lacking in tension. She stepped from the side to stand beside Engels. And squeezed the trigger of the revolver which she held in a two-handed grip at her belly.

"Lester!" Clay Beaudine shrieked as the bullet hit his brother and sent him staggering back against the crate beneath the noose.

"—do to me," Engels continued after pausing for the interruptions of voices and gunshot. "For I have a conscience that will never allow me—"

The silver-haired, darkly garbed, frail-looking woman thumbed back the hammer and exploded another shot. Like the first, its report was amplified in the unfurnished confines of the room. And the acrid taint of detonated black powder strengthened to mask the stale odors of decay and old burning. Which the second Beaudine was oblivious to as the bullet drilled into the back of his head and he sprawled face down on top of his brother's still form beside the overturned crate.

"—rest until the day I die. Not for a single second of any waking hour—"

Ralph Ransom swung his horrified gaze from Engels, to the woman, to the collapsed brothers, and then back to the man giving a rambling monologue out of a world of private desolation in which he was temporarily removed from the new slaughter taking place. Was so totally detached from his surroundings that he did not even flinch as Ransom lunged at him, arms outstretched and hands clawed.

The gun in the hands of the woman tracked to the side as the hammer was cocked. The trigger was squeezed and the bullet took Ransom in the throat while his curled fingers were still several inches short of fastening around the throat of Merle Engels. He gagged on his own blood and dropped heavily to the floor at the feet of his intended victim who was saying:

"—am I without anguish over the suffering I caused. And I may not sleep in peace for more than a few hours at a time—"

"Captain!" Bradley Dalton yelled, wrenching his head around as the third man dropped into a limp and inert heap on the floor.

"—without being awakened by a nightmare of such power—"

The doorway where Hedges had been standing was now empty. Dalton gasped with the shock of this new unexpected event. Heard the hammer of the revolver in the woman's hands click back. And then heard a more distant sound as he shifted his gaze again—saw his rifle and knew it was out of reach as he recognized the noise from out back of the house. The squeak of rusted hinges as the door in the side wall was swung open.

"—that I often plead for the good Lord to take me," Merle Engels finished.

Bradley Dalton was certain he was going to be killed.

And he opted to die in a futile attempt to achieve what he and the other three soldiers had come here to do. But he had a greater distance than Ransom to cover in order to reach the now silent man. And the bullet burst into his heart before he had completed a single pace. And when he fell dead to the floor, his outstretched arms were draped over the unfeeling corpse of Ralph Ransom, a long way short of his objective.

"Now, you mustn't talk that way, my dear," the woman chided softly. "You must keep in mind what the doctors said. You have a good wife and a once fine house that together we can restore to its former glory. And we shall do it, Merle. We shall—"

"The Federal captain, Dorothy?" Engels cut in on her anxiously as he emerged from the reverie that had insulated him from the fresh carnage.

"Over here," Hedges replied evenly from where he stood between the corner of the house and the parked carriage. The rifle was aimed from the hip at the couple up on the portico, its oiled barrel glinting only slightly less dully than his uniform buttons and the ice-blue slits of his narrowed eyes. "But anxious to be over there."

He gestured with his head toward the moonlit river with his horse silhouetted against it on the bank. Then he canted the Henry up to his shoulder with an almost inaudible sigh of relief as something thudded to the ground below the bottom step of the portico. The revolver.

"My husband isn't well, sir."

"I figured that out, after a while."

"Well enough to figure out a plan to trick these men when we heard the ruckus from the house back down the road," Merle Engels defended from out of the moon shadows that almost hid him and his wife.

"Yes, dear," she allowed, but if he detected the degree of condescension in her tone he chose to ignore it. Then her voice wavered, and in a suddenly weak voice she went on: "We owe you, Captain. For unwittingly warning us of the danger. And for not interfering in the way we handled it."

"My business was with the men you killed, lady. Couldn't have settled it better myself."

"Been practicing for the best part of two years, Captain. It was my home as much as it was his. You're on your way home from the war, son?"

"Yeah."

"Hope your homecoming turns out to be better than mine and Merle's."

"Me, too." He turned, to head on down the spur toward the road.

"Whatever, son!" the woman called after him, and there was a catch in her voice, as if she were struggling against tears. "Let it go! Revenge doesn't taste sweet at all!"

"If I've got that kind of problem waiting for me, lady," Josiah C. Hedges murmured, his voice no louder than the chirping of crickets and the rippling of river water, "I guess I won't know that for sure until I've licked it."

Chapter Three

AT night camp beside a low mesa where a patch of grass provided some feed for the three hobbled horses, Edge built and lit a fire and cooked a pot of chile beans from the supplies carried in a crate under the wagon seat.

During the slow trek through the heat of the afternoon and the rapidly cooling evening there had been sporadic bursts of angry complaints from the closely confined prisoners aboard the wagon. The men cursed the heat, the roughness of the trail, and then the desert floor when the wagon veered off the trail, the flies, the stink of themselves and each other, the legal system that had put them aboard the moving cage: and the man who did not represent the law but refused to give them their freedom.

Throughout this period the men in the cage and the half-breed were out of sight of each other on either side of the partition behind the driver's seat. And, apart from those times when he acknowledged Harlan Price's directions by altering the course of the wagon as the eldest brother instructed, Edge's continued presence was apparent only when the smoke from one of his infrequent cigarettes drifted aromatically through the bars.

Whether silently smoking or engaged in no other activity but driving the prison wagon toward an unspecified destination, the tall and lean half-breed maintained a cautious surveillance of the sun-parched terrain on all sides, not even neglecting the ground already covered. But, as the shimmering heat haze retreated to the extent that for several minutes in the cool of late afternoon overlapping early evening he could see as far as the distant mountains on every horizon, there was not a sign of man-made danger to be seen. While, of course, there was plenty of trouble in the making riding behind him—and never more than a few minutes at a time went by without one or more of the prisoners giving sour-voiced evidence of frustration simmering toward uncontrollable outlet.

But tempers cooled with the ambient temperature of the dwindling day. And when he called a halt under the rock face of the sandstone mesa and the travel-weary and heat-exhausted prisoners were able to sprawl out on the hard but no longer jolting wagon bed while Edge attended to the horses, the eyes that peered between the bars at him held perhaps a trace of gratitude for the part he'd played in bringing them such scant but blessed relief. Or maybe, the undemonstrative half-breed realized as he ignored the watching captives and went unhurriedly about the business of making camp, it was a matter of everything in the human experience being relative: the seven wretched men were not at the present venting profane complaints at him or any other aspect of their predicament and so appeared to be well disposed toward him and all else.

It was the young Billy-Joe Delany who told Edge about the provisions and cooking and eating utensils under the wagon seat. He revealed this information in a dejected manner, as if he did not expect Edge to do anything about feeding him and the rest of the prisoners. And for a few moments, as the half-breed started a pot of coffee to boiling, Delany's lack of hope appeared to have a sound basis.

Nick Price rasped bitterly through his clenched white teeth: "Don't want you to cook for us and wait on us, mister. Reckon all of us'd be happy to do our share of the chores . . . if we was let out of this cage."

"Some hope," the almost bald Austin Gatlin growled,

his sunburn not troubling him so much now. But the other discomforts expanding.

"While there's life there is, feller," Edge answered as he rose up from his haunches beside the fire.

"How do we know any of us is gonna have any life left after you get what you're after, Edge?" the scar-faced Chester Rankinn posed dully.

"He won't get what he's after until he lets me and my brothers outta here!" Ethan Price averred resolutely, fixing a hate-filled stare on Edge as the half-breed moved from the fire to the front of the wagon.

"You guys are wastin' your breath," Harlan Price said, sounding almost bored. "We ain't in any position to have him do anythin' we want. And he ain't of a disposition to do anythin' for us he don't want."

"He's fixing us some food," Gatlin pointed out.

"Not part of his plan to starve us, right Edge?" the eldest Price inquired, indifferent to having an answer.

"Gave up making plans a long time ago, feller."

The fire made crackling sounds as the tongues of flames threw animated patterns of light and shadow across the stalled cage wagon and the mesa behind it. This while the saddle horse and the pair from the traces tore hungrily at the dry scrub grass a few feet away. And the tension diminished in the fire-warmed night air of the desert camp as the prisoners relished the appetizing aromas—first of coffee and then of chile—infiltrating the evil-smelling atmosphere that was seemingly trapped behind the bars with them.

"We don't get to have coffee?" Chester Rankinn growled without hope to end a long silence as he watched Edge pour himself a cup from the steaming pot.

The half-breed sat on his saddle close to the fire and answered: "No coffee in your supplies, feller. Don't have too much myself, and no knowledge of when I'll be able to get fresh stocks."

"Stick it up your ass," Rankinn said. "But careful you don't poke your brains out."

The scar-faced man obviously had to make the effort to

get a tone of virulence in his voice. The prisoners were too hungry, the smell of the cooking food sharpening their appetites, to have the emotional energy to indulge in futile animosity.

After Edge had ladled the beans onto tin plates and pushed the food through the gap beneath the rear door of the wagon, only Billy-Joe Delany blurted an automatic thank you. The Comanche acknowledged his appreciation with a short, wooden-faced nod. The other five grabbed the plates and spoons and noisily began shoveling food into their mouths. And the kid and the Indian were not far behind the rest in finishing supper—as if they were afraid the greasy-jawed, lip-smacking faster eaters would claim a share of what they still had on their plates.

"Not enough for seconds?" Nick Price asked.

In response, Edge nodded to the cooking pot he had already taken out of the flames. Then went on eating.

"Sonofabitch, I'm still a growin' boy!" the youngest Price complained bitterly, and clanged his empty tin plate raucously back and forth along a row of bars.

"Quit it, Nick!" Harlan snarled. And snatched the plate from him.

"Don't fret, kid," Rankinn put in sourly. "If that guy out there is on the level, maybe one day you'll actually grow up."

"Hey, Ethan, did that rapist just say somethin' I oughta—"

"Quit it, Nick!" the fleshy Harlan repeated, in a softer voice but with more menace as he flashed a warning glare at his brothers and Chester Rankinn. Moderated his tone to ask: "Didn't you guys have enough sun all day, you gotta get hot under the collar now?"

"I surely had more than enough sun," Austin Gatlin confirmed. He pushed his empty plate out under the door and grimaced before taking a swig of stale water from a canteen. Then he looked aggrieved at Edge when the half-breed glanced at the other dirty dishes hitting the ground at the rear of the wagon, and defended: "Well, we don't have any cleaning facilities in here, mister."

"But if you let us out—" Nick began. Then curtailed it of his own volition with a sigh as he selected the spot in the wagon where he intended to sleep.

Others followed his example, the six whites segregating themselves from the Indian by at least two feet and the Comanche electing to remain in the front corner of the cage, sitting down in the angle of bars and partition with his arms wrapped around his drawn-up knees. Before Edge had finished his supper and cleaned and stowed his own utensils, most of the prisoners were deeply asleep and rumbling snores were the predominant sounds of the camp. Until a short but strident whistle pierced the night. And the stentorian noises faltered toward even breathing.

"They sleep like the animals they are," the Comanche muttered as Edge continued with the interrupted process of bedding down beside the lowering fire.

"A man can't help what he does in his sleep, Injun," Rankinn growled without rancor. "Right, mister?"

The half-breed tossed into the fire the butt of the cigarette he had been smoking.

"Sometimes when he's awake, too." He pulled the blanket up to his chin, sharing its warmth with the Winchester rifle that lay at his side under his draped right hand. And tipped his hat forward over his face as he rested his head on the pillow of his saddle.

"The guards—Cody and Nixon and Snyder," Rankinn said. "They allowed us a smoke after we was through with eatin', mister."

"Feel free, feller."

"We don't have no makin's!" Rankinn snarled sourly. "Cody or one of them others would give us the smokes!"

"You tell lies, too," Edge said from under his hat.

"Huh?"

"As well as commit rape and murder."

"Hard as they friggin' come, ain't you, Edge?"

"I should not be here," the Comanche said dully. "I was falsely accused of crimes I did not commit. That is no lie, man who sleeps with rifle."

"I believe you, feller," the half-breed drawled into the crown of his hat.

"But words count for nothing."

"Try sheep, Injun," Rankinn growled. "Countin', I mean. Kinda joke."

"Hey," Billy-Joe Delany put in sleepily. And giggled. "That rifle Edge sleeps with?"

"What about it, kid?" the scar-faced man asked wearily.

"You figure he sometimes cocks it?" He giggled again and blurted: "Another joke."

"You hear anythin', kid?" Rankinn asked in a tone of voice that frightened Delany into tense silence for stretched seconds.

Then the youngster replied anxiously: "No, I don't hear nothin'."

"Neither do I, so nobody else is laughin'. Go to sleep."

"Or maybe die laughin' at your own lousy jokes, Billy-Joe," Ethan Price burst out with weary ill-temper.

The silence lengthened, and after the fire had died to a heap of powdery gray ash it was kept from being perfect only by the varied breathing of men and animals at various levels of sleep. Edge, the Comanche, and Harlan Price slept more shallowly than the rest, and all three came awake together as the first shaft of brilliant light from the rising sun stabbed between two peaks in the San Mateo Mountains and splayed out across the San Agustin Plains.

"Earlier start we make, the better for all concerned, Edge," Price pointed out as he and the half-breed folded up off their backs at the same time. The Comanche had slept in the seated attitude.

"I've got nothing against agreeing with you when you're right, feller," Edge replied and spent just a moment or so flexing his muscles after getting to his feet. Then started to furl his blankets and stow away his already cleaned utensils.

"Fine," Price said in the same quiet, early morning tone of voice with which he had opened the exchange and the half-breed had chosen to match. While the others slept on, or elected to pretend they were still asleep. "Place we're headed for is called Cibola Draw. Over there in that high ground.'' He waved a negligent hand in the general direction of the rising sun. ''We make it at the same rate we did yesterday—and I know it'd be stupid to try to push the horses any harder—we should get there not too long after midday. Plenty of supplies there, so no need to waste time with loadin' all this junk back aboard.'' With another wave he encompassed the area of the camp.

This time Edge said, ''Fine,'' as he completed attending to his own gear. And the other prisoners began to be roused by the glaring light of the sun and the sounds of the quiet-voiced talk accompanied by the muted noises made by the half-breed as he prepared for departure. The other two Price brothers and Chester Rankinn came awake in ill humor, and Harlan Price allowed them to give vent to their feelings for perhaps a half minute before he broke in on their complaints to tell all his fellow prisoners what he had just told Edge. Did this while the men spat or urinated through the bars and the half-breed put the horses in the traces. Then, when Edge led his horse around the wagon to hitch him on at the rear, the eldest brother said:

''I don't figure we have to worry about the law startin' in to find us yet, Edge. On account of Art Cody and his sidekicks weren't scheduled to bring us to the new prison at Socorro Ridge until noon today. And even if some nosy parker rides by and spots them five corpses back on the trail, take time for the alarm to be raised anyplace it'll matter to us.''

''They were taking you to a new prison to hang you?'' Edge asked as he rasped the back of a hand across the bristles on his jaw and then spat into the dust among the discarded plates and spoons.

''Yeah, it's as crazy as it sounds!'' Ethan Price snarled. ''Because Charlie McMullen is a crazy man.''

''McMullen's the hangman for the penitentiary setup in this part of the territory,'' Harlan Price offered when his brother took time to direct a stream of saliva through the bars. ''Got some kinda political pull and can get away with whatever the hell he likes.''

"Somethin' like you, but you ain't no political—" Rankinn tried to interject.

"Not that it matters no more," Harlan growled to recapture the half-breed's imperturbably neutral attention as Edge rolled his first cigarette of the day. And Chester Rankinn did not even give the eldest Price a glaring look— accepting the fact that if and when the man outside the cage ceased to call the tune, Harlan would most probably take his place. "Unless me and my boys get a chance to give the bastard what he's got comin' to him. But McMullen enjoys his job more than most men. Started out by trade in England or Ireland or someplace like that as a hangman and never has done nothin' else to earn a buck. Had the gallows up at Socorro Ridge built special to his own plans and was fixin' to try them out . . ."

"*En masse,*" Austin Gatlin put in when Harlan seemed lost for a phrase.

"Yeah, try them out on a mass execution, Edge. Reason this stinkin' cage was sent around all over the south of the territory to pick us up for—"

"So it would seem, white-eyes, that you should be grateful to the hangman you hate so much," the Indian pointed out.

"Huh?" Nick Price grunted.

"Were you all not rounded up to be taken to the new prison, you would by now perhaps be already hanged?"

"Nah. Rod or Johnnie would've sprung us outta jail down in Tucson. Them or—"

"But none of that matters no more," Harlan broke in on Ethan again as the naming of the two dead men spread looks of scorn across the faces of the Comanche and Rankinn: and Edge listened more attentively. Harlan gazed fixedly out through the bars at the half-breed as the trailing rim of the new day's bright sun inched above the high, ragged ridges of the San Mateo range in the southeast. "We was gonna make an early start, right?"

Edge took out a match, struck it on a bar, and said with a nod: "For a half of twenty grand cash, I'll stay in an agreeable frame of mind, feller." He touched the flame to the tobacco.

"Plus the same share of the jewelry and stuff," Nick reminded eagerly.

"Easy, Nick," Ethan growled as the half-breed moved out of sight beyond the solid partition at the front of the wagon and climbed up onto the driver's seat. "The man just wants half the cash; he don't have to take anythin' else."

The brake blocks creaked away from the wheelrims, the reins were flicked over the backs of the two geldings in the traces, and the cage wagon rolled away from the night stop.

"Well, far as I'm concerned, that guy can name his own price," Nick came back happily. "Long as this one ain't sky high—strung up by the neck from Charlie McMullen's gallows!"

"Amen to that, whatever our names," Austin Gatlin said with feeling.

The lighthearted exchanges with an undercurrent of tension continued for a few minutes. Then, as the sun rose higher and the discomfort of its glaring heat worsened, the men's qualified good humor diminished. The Price brothers, Delany, and Rankinn cursed at the dust and the flies and the eye-stinging sweat and nostril-assaulting stench. While Gatlin claimed to be suffering the most because of his sunburn, and the Comanche every now and then maintained that as a wrongly accused and convicted man he should not be in the hellbox of a moving cage at all.

Then, as the day wore on, all talk was abandoned as the prisoners came to realize that nobody was listening to their tales of woe and that the mere effort of expressing personal grievances was serving only to intensify the suffering. And after little more than two hours of slow rolling toward the mountains which by then were shrouded in a slick-looking heat haze, the men in the back of the wagon were as close-mouthed as the half-breed who drove the rig.

During the talkative time Edge had listened effortlessly to the profanity-littered exchanges: paying particular attention to the Price brothers' words. But Harlan had not needed to cut in again to prevent either Ethan or Nick from unwittingly revealing that there were men other than Johnnie and Rod with a vested interest in turning the Price trio loose. And the half-breed's unanxious visual surveillance over the rock and cactus and brush of the sun-baked expanse of wilderness on all sides was as unproductive as his eavesdropping had been—he neither heard nor saw anything that would help him bring this situation to a successful conclusion: nor did he learn anything that indicated he had cause to be concerned about the outcome.

"Not so far now, I reckon," Harlan Price said, interrupting the pleasant train of thought that was running smoothly through Edge's mind. "You gotta swing to the south a little. Head into that cut between the rocks. Called Alamosa Canyon. Cibola Draw comes down into the canyon from the north no more than a mile from the mouth. You see the cut into the high ground I'm talkin' about, Edge?"

"Sure thing," the half-breed acknowledged as he abandoned wishful thinking about a half share—and even all—of what the Price brothers claimed was cached less than two miles from the spot where he now steered the wagon into a slight course variation. Such reveries had helped to pass the crawling time of morning and something over an hour of the afternoon while the San Mateo Mountains became more distinct in the shimmering heat haze. But now he emptied his mind of all side issues and concentrated his attention on the sandstone-walled canyon that could provide safe cover for a minor army of men behind the many outcrops and boulders spread across its rugged floor.

The tension that had sounded as a clearly discernible undertone in Harlan Price's voice was now a silent crackle in the stiflingly hot air of the canyon, and seemed to have the eerie effect of muting the sounds of the wagon's progress along a meandering, heavily signed path among the dangerous rocks. The sign in the red-tinged dust was primarily hoof- and footprints. Some horse apples and the remains of cigars and cigarettes as dry as the dust itself. But in such arid conditions it would require close-up investigation to determine whether this refuse was a few hours, days, or even weeks old.

Edge had to keep blinking salty sweat off his eyelids as his eyes swung back and forth along their glittering slits. His hands holding the reins felt oily as they remained ready to streak for the rifle jutting out of the boot on his saddle and the revolver protruding from his holster that was not tied down for riding a wagon seat rather than a horse. His muscles ached with the strain of being poised to lunge him into an instant response to danger.

Only the glistening beads of moisture on his heavily bristled face and the patches of wetness on his dark shirt might have revealed that he was not so unconcerned as his nonchalant attitude up on the wagon seat suggested. But it was blisteringly hot on the canyon floor anyway.

And probably it was not just imagination triggered by a sense of menace that made it seem even hotter as the canyon narrowed and the flanking walls rose higher. Where the draw ran into the canyon on the left, the cliffs towered to almost two hundred feet and the floor that was now clearer of rocks was no more than a hundred feet across.

"Avis, sweetheart!" Harlan Price yelled in high excitement.

"Ruby!" Ethan roared with equal enthusiasm.

"Jessica!" Nick sounded the most joyful of all.

The three brothers had been pressing their faces hard to the bars on the left side of the prison wagon: evidently hoping or even expecting to see friendly faces. And now the other four captives crowded to the same vantage point as the trio of women were named—to peer for the first time at the scene the half-breed had glimpsed perhaps a second before the Prices gave vent to their exhilaration.

Two blondes and a redhead, all about thirty, had stepped into view at the point where the draw joined the canyon when the horses in the wagon traces were perhaps fifty feet away. Not beautiful women, but not homely, either. All of them as well turned out as could be expected in the primitive, overheated circumstances: with painted faces, brushed hair, and wearing far from new but clean dresses that showed large expanses of bare flesh over the low necklines and tautly contoured much that was covered. The skirts of all three brightly colored dresses flowed voluminous from the nipped-in waists.

Each of the whorish-looking women flashed a bright-eyed, wide-mouthed smile of greeting. But none of the three spoke or made to wave until the wagon was brought to a standstill at the mouth of the draw.

"How you boys doin'?"

"Hell, you sure do stink!"

"You want us to pay off the driver, Harly?"

Each allowed the others to speak before she spoke her own piece. But all three acted in concert to raise their hands out from the bulky fabric of their bouffant skirts—to aim six revolvers of various makes at Edge. In common was the fact that all were cocked.

"Well, ain't that pretty as a goddamn picture?" Nick Price drawled, oozing confidence with every syllable.

"Hey, don't talk about pictures, man," Billy-Joe Delany blurted. "They get hung, and I don't wanna think about that no more."

"Whether they been framed or not, huh Injun?" Chester Rankinn taunted caustically.

"You gonna trust my word about the deal still standin', Edge?" Harlan Price asked with easy equanimity. "Or you gonna believe we Prices are as black as we're painted?"

"Appears I don't have much of a choice, feller," the half-breed answered evenly as he showed a cold grin to the three broadly smiling women. "Since these ladies have so artfully made me the only target in a shooting gallery."

Getting the Message

*During the previously unchronicled ride from
The Town With No Name in California Killing
to the Big Valley Station in Seven from Hell,
trouble broke Edge's journey on more than
one occasion. This was one of those times.*

THE MAN had been a long time dying and was a long
time dead. He had been stripped naked and then staked out
in the full heat of the California sun. But that wasn't all.
His tormentors had slashed cuts in his belly and chest and
sifted rock salt into the open wounds. Maybe the scavenging buzzards had appreciated the preserving action of the
salt, but probably not. The smell of approaching death
would have attracted them to the rim of the desert before
the man exhaled his final breath: and the birds would have
swooped down on their feast without waiting for the flesh
to decay. They would have gorged until satiated, then
soared away to roost in some sparse and uncool shade.

So as Edge reined his mount to a halt and looked down
at the corpse, it was only flies that buzzed angrily up from
the mutilated remains. And a small lizard scuttled out from
the dried, blood-crusted entrails in the ripped-open belly to

dart under a rock. The half-breed regarded the dead man with impassive eyes, and his only visible reaction was a wrinkling of his nose at the evil odor of decomposition rising into the hot air. And as he wheeled the roan mare away and continued on his fleetingly broken journey, there was nothing in his demeanor to suggest it was the gruesome sight which moved him on. For he rode easy and relaxed, as if nothing unexpected had entered his life that day, and ninety minutes later he passed the sun-bleached wooden sign marking the town limits of Caine.

It was almost dusk then, and the crudely constructed frame buildings of the town were squared with the flickering yellow light of kerosene lamps. Most of the citizens were in their houses eating the evening meal. But a low murmur of conversation trickling under the batwing doors of the Lucky Numbers Saloon indicated that at least a handful preferred to take their sustenance in liquid form.

The sheriff had maybe already eaten, and he lounged in a rocking chair on the sidewalk out front of the law office. The heat of the day hung heavily between the warped and peeling facades of the buildings lining the street, and the peace officer fanned his face with his hat as he watched the stranger approach.

"Passin' through, or stayin', mister?" he asked as Edge halted his horse out front of the law office. He was a man of middle years and had the spread to go with his age. He also had a barrel chest, arms that bulged his shirtsleeves with muscles, and the kind of burnished, deeply scored face that suggested he'd lived his years the hard way. His black eyes held a brooding expression as he watched the half-breed dismount.

"Depends."

"On what?"

"Maybe whether I like it here or not."

"Works both ways," the sheriff said.

"How's that?"

"Whether we like you or not."

The lawman continued to regard the stranger with an unblinking stare, but there was a sudden flicker of apprehension in the depths of his eyes and the thinned-out line of his mouth.

"Does the town take a vote?"

The sheriff shook his head as he continued to survey the stranger, the elderly Colt Walker revolver in the holster tied down at the half-breed's right thigh. There was a Winchester rifle in his saddle boot. If he saw the slight bulge of the shirt at the top of his spine as Edge half turned to hitch his horse to a rail, the man in the rocker had no way of knowing this was caused by a razor in a soft leather pouch.

"Man kinda decides it himself, mister. He acts peaceable and causes no trouble, the folks like him."

Edge slid the Winchester from its boot and held it in a loose grip, pointed at the ground. "Sounds reasonable, sheriff."

"Name's Smith. What's yours?"

"Edge."

Sheriff Smith blinked. "What kinda name is that?"

Edge smiled with his mouth. "My kind."

A shrug. "Okay. Just stay outta trouble, Mr. Edge."

"And if I don't, you'll stake me out in the sun for buzzard meat?"

The lawman stopped fanning himself and thudded his feet into the planking of the sidewalk to halt the rocking motion of the chair. "What's that supposed to mean?" he demanded, his expression indicating he might already know.

Edge gestured with the Winchester, out down the trail he had just traveled. "Five or six miles. Feller who won't cause any more trouble."

Smith got to his feet, his face suddenly pale. "Young man with brown and red hair?"

Now Edge shrugged. "He didn't have any eyes left. But I'd say he was young. And he had red hair."

The lawman reached out to support himself on the back of the chair. "Mike Croxley," he murmured. "The cruds did it. They said they would, and they did." He recovered from the shock and gazed at Edge with heavy contempt. "Why the frig didn't you bring him in, mister?"

"He smelled bad," the half-breed replied easily, turning away and looking toward the Caine Hotel across the street.

"And I bet you didn't bury him either?"

Edge shouldered the rifle and moved casually out into the street. Called back: "That isn't the kind of work I undertake, sheriff."

"Young Mike's old man ain't gonna like this," the sheriff rasped as he whirled and stomped hurriedly along the sidewalk toward the saloon.

At the hotel, the slightly built and watery eyed desk clerk told Edge there were no messages for him and accepted payment in advance for a second-floor room overlooking the street. He said he would arrange for the tub in the bathroom to be filled with hot water. And yes, he would let Mr. Edge know immediately a message was delivered for him. His horse would be taken from the rail out front of the law office and would be liveried.

Across the street, the owner of the Lucky Numbers Saloon listened in deep shock to the story told him by Sheriff Smith. Several patrons of the saloon heard the same news, for the painfully thin, sallow-faced Croxley had refused to acknowledge the lawman's suggestion that they talk in a back room. Instead, he remained seated with four others at a money-littered table, staring at the full house of his poker hand while Smith relayed Edge's account of finding the staked-out body.

"The yellow-livered skunks," the card dealer exclaimed hoarsely.

"I was goin' to pay what they asked," Croxley murmured absently, continuing to stare at the cards clutched in his trembling hands. "I figured Mike had suffered enough: I was only holding off awhile to teach him a lesson."

The other players and Smith stared at Croxley with a mixture of pity and scorn. They, like everyone else in Caine, knew of the man's disappointment with his son. The boy had been a no-account wastrel, constantly on the take from his father to finance his idleness: even—it was strongly rumored—stealing from him on the rare occasions when he received no for an answer.

So, when the young man had suddenly disappeared and a ransom note was delivered, there was a degree of sympathetic understanding for the elder Croxley's decision to hold off payment for a short time. But now, as the other poker players left the table and the saloon to circulate the horrifying details of Mike's death, every vestige of empathy evaporated. Whatever else the boy had been, he was Croxley's flesh and blood—and the father had stood idly by while the kidnappers subjected his son to an agonizing death.

When the sheriff finally left to instruct the town mortician to go and bring in the corpse, James Croxley went into the back room. By then the saloon was empty except for the morose-looking bartender, but Croxley did not want even him to witness the body-wrenching venting of his grief. He sobbed uncontrollably for a full thirty minutes, and only then could he begin to consider the situation with anything close to clarity. But even then, reason had little influence over his thought processes. For his mind was clouded by guilt, and this filled him with a burning desire to vindicate himself by revenge.

His movements jerky, almost mechanical, he removed his suit jacket and strapped on his gunbelt with the fully loaded Remington .44 in its holster. More than a hundred pairs of accusing eyes watched him as he pushed open the batwings and started along the sidewalk.

"Where you goin', Mr. Croxley?" the sheriff wanted to know as the mortician's buckboard started off down the road.

"The man who left my son out there like that has somethin' to answer for," Croxley announced coldly, staring straight ahead, ignoring the groups of shocked citizens who had been discussing the tragedy.

"You know the law about shootin' inside town limits!" Smith warned, stepping out of the doorway of the law office.

"Let him be. It's about time we had some excitement in Caine."

The lawman turned to look at the speaker. She was a

very pretty blonde, about twenty, with a provocatively curved body starkly outlined by the snug fit of a bright red dress. The neckline was cut low, exposing the powdered mounds of her thrusting breasts to a level just above the distended nipples. As the sheriff looked at her, her green eyes blazed and her vivid red lips parted to allow the tip of her tongue to coat them with wetness. Her breasts heaved as a further sign of her high excitement.

"Not this kind, Annabelle," the sheriff disagreed, tearing his gaze away from her body and looking at the man beside her. Smith knew him as well as the girl: the handsome and small-framed Teddy Tafts. The son of probably the richest rancher in southern California. He and Annabelle South had been sparking for better than six months.

"Sure this kind, lawman," a low voice argued. Added: "No, don't turn around!"

Annabelle, Tafts, and the half-dozen others standing on the sidewalk out front of the law office did not hear the urgent whisper. But Smith heard it clearly, and felt the hot breath of the speaker on his ear. He also felt the nudge of a gun muzzle against his spine.

"Back in nice and easy, lawman," the gunman instructed. "And close the door."

"Hey, you! Edge, or whatever you call yourself!" Croxley had halted in the middle of the street, directly opposite the front entrance of the Caine Hotel. His tone of voice and the manner in which his right hand hovered over his holstered revolver captured the attention of every eye on the street. Except for those of the sheriff, who stepped cautiously backward as instructed. Then closed the door of the office and drew in a sharp breath when the pressure against his back was relieved. But then the butt of the revolver crashed into the top of his skull and his head seemed to explode with white heat. His heavy body was caught in waiting arms and lowered silently to the floor. The man who had hit him dropped a folded sheet of paper onto the lawman's unevenly pulsating chest and then joined two others who were at the window, craning for a view of the action outside.

Edge was in the hotel bathroom when he heard Croxley's voice. The round wooden tub was almost brim full of steaming water, but he had undressed only to the extent of removing his hat. His eyes hooded and his lips set in a narrow line, he moved out of the room and down the hallway. There was a window at the far end, and he pressed himself against the wall as he looked through the dusty pane and down at Croxley in the middle of the street. Saw aggression in the stance of the thin man and hatred inscribed on his sallow features. The excitement generated by the watching crowd seemed to quiver in the warm evening air.

Edge raised a leg and shattered the glass with the heel of his riding boot. All eyes elevated their stare to the smashed window.

"You want me, feller?"

"If you're the no-account drifter who found my son's body, then didn't bury it or bring it in." Croxley's hand curled around the butt of his holstered revolver, but then swung away when he saw no silhouette in the square of light from the second floor of the hotel.

"That's what I did and didn't do all right," came Edge's flat voice.

"I reckon you done nothin' about it 'cause you got somethin' to hide!" Croxley accused.

Edge now knew all the details of the kidnapping of James Croxley's son. The hotel handyman who'd filled the tub with hot water had talked incessantly of it as he went about his chore.

"Go on home, feller," Edge called. "One death in a day is enough for any family."

Croxley glanced to left and right, seeking support for his belief in the faces of the bystanders. "You sound real mean, Edge!" he yelled. "Kidnapper mean!"

"Forget it. I had nothing to do with taking Michael out of Caine."

"Come down here and tell me that face to face!" Croxley demanded.

Edge sighed, and then his nostrils flared. The steam from the water in the tub smelled fresh and inviting. It had been a long ride from his last stopover to this one, and he relished the prospect of washing the sweat and trail dust from his body.

"Keep the tub hot for me," he muttered to the wizened old handyman as he started down the stairway.

"Please, sir," the watery-eyed desk clerk pleaded as Edge crossed the lobby. "Our sheriff doesn't approve of shooting inside the town limits."

"I'll try to keep him happy," Edge replied as he stepped out onto the sidewalk.

A gasp of expectancy rose from the watching crowd. Croxley jerked his hand a fraction of an inch closer to his gun butt, but resisted the temptation to touch it. Annabelle South vented a low moan and Tafts looked at her suspiciously, recognizing the sound as one of excitement. He noted the direction of her gaze and realized that it was the tall figure of Edge rather than the tension of the situation that had captured her imagination.

"A gunslinger," Tafts whispered derisively, trying to keep the jealousy from showing on his weakly handsome face.

"A *man!*" Annabelle said breathlessly, her attention riveted on Edge as the half-breed stepped down from the sidewalk and ambled casually across to Croxley.

Edge, his dark-skinned face showing not a hint of emotion, halted two feet in front of the bereaved father and allowed his long arms to hang loosely at his sides, the right hand a little below the butt of the holstered Colt. "What was it you wanted to hear from me, feller?"

There was an utter silence hanging over the town, as if every person except the two men in the middle of the street had drawn in a breath and was holding it. Croxley found his gaze a prisoner of Edge's hooded stare. His lower lip began to quiver, and a trickle of saliva escaped from the corner of his mouth and ran down his chin.

"A decent man would have taken care of my boy's body," he said tremulously.

"I figure you're threatening me," Edge countered softly. "That the way it is?"

He raised his right hand to scratch the back of his neck. His gun was further out of reach now. Croxley was attacked by doubts. He had no proof that Edge had been involved in Michael's death; and even if the man was guilty as hell, Croxley feared that killing him would do little to ease his own conscience or to mellow the contempt of his fellow citizens. But he had come too far to back down now. Giving vent to his grief had not relieved the anguish of his self-reproach. Killing this man might offer a brief respite. Or, perhaps being killed by him . . . that would be the complete solution.

Croxley went for his gun.

Edge's right hand streaked away from the back of his neck, the blade of the straight razor extending from his fingers glinting wickedly in the glow of the kerosene lamps. The watchers gasped at his speed. Then a woman screamed at the end result of the move. Croxley let go of his revolver and the gun slotted back into the holster from which it had been only half drawn. He stared down through terror-stricken eyes at the blood-oozing piece of flesh resting in a wagonwheel rut. And a moment before tears of pain welled into his eyes he recognized his own ear: sliced cleanly from the side of his head. Blood bubbled up from the gaping wound as agony took command of Croxley's brain and hurled him into unconsciousness. He pitched to the street in front of Edge, who stooped and wiped the blood from his razor on Croxley's shirt before inserting it back into the pouch.

Then his narrowed eyes raked the shocked faces of the crowd lining both sides of the street and his voice was soft but heavily loaded with menace when he warned: "Any man threatens me, he knows what to expect."

"You didn't have to do that!" a woman wailed.

"Wasn't what I intended," Edge answered, lightening his tone as he turned slowly and started back toward the hotel entrance. "But I was told there's a local ordinance against firing guns in town. So I had to play it by ear."

As he mounted the sidewalk, the crowd surged forward: some to gape at the dislodged flesh and awful wound, others to try to help the injured man.

"Hey, Mr. Edge?"

The half-breed turned and looked across the heads of the crowd toward Annabelle South standing on the opposite sidewalk. Her beau had left her to get a closer look at Croxley and she was a lone, exciting figure in front of the law office. She placed her hands on her hips and thrust her breasts forward in a provocative pose. And hung an inviting smile on her pretty face.

"Man wants to buy me a drink, I could sure use one."

Several men and women in the crowd forgot about Croxley as he groaned back to awareness, and found their attention divided between the impassive Edge, the coquettish Annabelle, and the anxiously disconcerted Tafts.

"What I could use is a hot bath, ma'am," Edge replied evenly. Then added: "And I figure what you need is a cold one."

As the half-breed went through the doorway into the hotel, several low guffaws rose from the crowd. Annabelle's face became purple with rage and her flashing green eyes swept over the street, seeking a target against which to vent her anger. But everyone realized her purpose and turned quickly away from her. Thus, when the door of the law office behind her opened, nobody saw it. And nobody saw a man's arm reach out, clamp a hand over the girl's trembling mouth, and drag her bodily across the threshold. The door was closed as silently as it had been opened. And when people chanced sidelong glances at the spot where the girl had been standing, it was as if she had been whisked off the face of the earth.

Upstairs in the hotel, as Croxley was carried to the physician's house and Teddy Tafts went in search of Annabelle, Edge stripped and sank his travel-weary body into the luxurious warmth of the water. He was soaping himself when he heard shouting out on the street, but paid no attention to the noise. Not until he heard heavy footfalls on the stairs, quickening to a run as they headed down the hallway, did the half-breed pick the revolver up from the floor and rest its barrel on the rim of the tub.

An ashen-faced Tafts pulled up short on the threshold of the bathroom when he found himself staring down the .45 bore of the Colt Walker. Blurted: "I mean you no harm, Mr. Edge!" He waved a sheet of paper in a shaking hand.

"That's a relief," Edge replied wryly, resting the gun back on the floor. "So what do you want?"

"Help!" Tafts shot back. "And I'll pay you for it."

"Only way you're likely to get it, feller," Edge told him, rinsing the soap off his chest.

"They've grabbed Annabelle! Knocked out Sheriff Smith and left this note on him!"

"So what does it say?"

Tafts looked at the paper and had to shake his head violently to clear his vision before he could read aloud: " 'To whom it may concern. By now you'll know what's happened to the Croxley boy. We don't get the ten grand delivered out at Murdo Canyon by sunup, the South dame will die worse than he did.' " He looked pleadingly at Edge and added, "It's not signed."

"What do you want me to do?"

"The bank's making up two packages of money, Mr. Edge. One of ten thousand dollars. One of a thousand. You can have the thousand if you'll ride out to the meeting place with me." He swallowed hard. "You seem like a man who can take care of himself."

"I've been an orphan a long time. You have yourself a deal."

In less than fifteen minutes, both men were mounted and riding out of town between sidewalks lined by curious and apprehensive bystanders. Among them was Sheriff Smith, his skull heavily bandaged; and James Croxley with a thick dressing on the side of his head.

"Reckon that's the last we'll see of them," Croxley muttered in disgust. "Exceptin', of course, somebody might come across young Tafts's corpse."

The lawman followed the progress of the two riders until they were swallowed up by the night. His eyes were troubled, and it was apparent that he more than half agreed with Croxley.

It was many miles to Murdo Canyon, and the gray light of false dawn was streaking the eastern sky when Tafts pointed out the narrow cleft in a towering escarpment.

"Widens out inside," he explained as Edge's hooded eyes raked the cliff face and spotted a dozen places from which they could be secretly watched.

They entered the canyon mouth just as the first rays of the new day's sun shafted across the almost barren wilderness of bare rock and sparsely scattered tenacious brush.

"You guys got a great sense of timing," a voice drawled.

The comment was accompanied by the ominous metallic scraping of three repeater rifles having shells levered into their breeches. The man who had spoken the menacing greeting rose from a cluster of rocks in front of Edge and Tafts. The others stepped out from cover on either side. All three were young, all moderately good-looking, and all dressed completely in black. The Winchesters they leveled were of an equally matching pattern.

"Teddy!" Annabelle cried in anguish.

"Dismount easy-like, gents," the spokesman for the trio ordered. "Then come and see how much we meant what we wrote in the letter."

Tafts looked desperately toward Edge, who shrugged nonchalantly and swung from the saddle with slow care. The rich rancher's son did likewise, and the gunman on his side moved in and smoothly unhooked the saddlebags. He peeked inside the bulky one and whistled his appreciation of its contents.

"They brought what we wanted, Sonny," he announced.

The spokesman nodded and maintained a steady aim at Edge. "This one's heeled," he pointed out. "Get his gun, Lew. Check the other guy, Andy. Then tie 'em—hands behind the back."

"Teddy, is that you?"

Tafts opened his mouth to reply to the woman, but no sound emerged from his fear-constricted throat. Edge, still covered by Sonny's Winchester, made no protest as his revolver was removed from the holster. Then his hands were tied. Tafts seemed to be in the grip of a paralyzing daze as he was searched and bound.

"This way, gents," Sonny invited lightly, leading the way.

The sides of the canyon mouth broadened by the yard and soon the men were on the rim of an enormous depression in the earth bounded on all sides by towering cliffs of red rock. As yet the early sun bathed only the western side, and the spot where Annabelle was held prisoner was in deep shade. Tafts gasped and made a move to run toward her, but Andy's Winchester was thrust forward and he tripped, pitching headlong to the ground.

The kidnappers had staked out the girl in precisely the same manner as the Croxley boy. She was naked and held prisoner on her back, the supine posture and the taut stretch of her arms almost flattening the brown-crested hillocks of her large breasts. Her legs, long and slender, were restrained in a wide splay of involuntary submission, the subtle down on her inner thighs and slightly concave belly thickening to a tangled forest of blondeness at her pubic triangle. Her pretty face was pale as the curving flesh of her body; but as Edge met her darting eyes and captured their gaze with his own, he thought her expression of relief was tempered with another emotion.

"You look like you're going to be a big help," she accused, sweeping her eyes from Edge to Tafts and back again.

"Did they hurt you, Annabelle?" her beau demanded hoarsely as he scrambled to his feet.

"What if they did?" she shot back contemptuously.

Tafts gulped and looked frantically around at the grinning faces of the kidnappers, realizing the futility of the threat that had been forming in his racing mind.

"We ain't done nothing—yet," Sonny supplied easily, moving to where three horses were tethered and sliding his rifle into a boot hung from his saddle. "Andy, count the money. Lew, blast either of them if they make a wrong move."

"No!" Tafts gasped as Sonny's grin became a leer and he swiftly unbuckled his gunbelt.

"That oughta be the lady's line," Lew put in as Sonny dropped his pants and kneeled between the inverted vee of Annabelle's naked thighs.

Lew's Winchester was rammed into the small of Tafts's back, freezing him into a pale-faced statue. Edge kept watching the girl's face. She raised her head, her eyes filled with hateful scorn as she saw the lust twisting Sonny's features into ugliness. But then her gaze dropped and focused upon the man's straining readiness. Tafts squeezed his eyes tight shut. Annabelle began to breathe faster and she arched her back as much as the ropes would allow, thrusting her open body toward Sonny's throbbing manhood. He angled his body to meet her eagerness. He entered her and she gasped.

Tafts snapped open his eyes and saw the pumping body of Sonny through a seething blur of revulsion. For an instant he was seized by a raging insanity and he leaped forward. Lew squeezed the trigger of his Winchester. The bullet smashed through Tafts's spine and was deflected into his right lung. He sprawled to the ground with a thin scream. Blood erupted from his mouth like vomited cheap red wine. He froze into the stillness of death.

Sonny climaxed with a groan and rose from the captive body which continued to writhe toward the threshold of ecstasy. "Any more riders for this high-spirited filly?" Sonny asked, yanking up his pants, then fastening his gunbelt back around his waist.

"Money's all here," Andy reported, hefting the saddlebags. "Reckon I can afford better than seconds."

"Me, too," Lew agreed.

Sonny nodded and moved toward the tethered horses, kicking Tafts's unfeeling head viciously out of his path. Andy and Lew followed him and the three of them mounted.

"You get loose, feel free," Sonny said, grinning at Edge.

"Never have paid for it," Edge replied as the trio heeled their horses forward and galloped out through the narrow mouth of the canyon.

Annabelle's face was still heavy with unreleased lust as she stared up at Edge and demanded: "Do something!"

Edge moved forward and stretched out on the ground beside her, rolled over on his side so that the back of his neck was close to her right hand. "Razor in a pouch," he explained.

Her fingers reached under his long hair and found the razor. Edge altered his position so that she could saw at the bonds of his wrists. The rope parted and he stood up and plucked the razor from her sweat-sticky hand.

"Finish me off?" she pleaded, her body arching once more.

The sun crested the eastern rim of the canyon and shafted down onto her anxious body and imploring face.

"I've been a long time from the well, lady, but I like my water sweet," he told her softly.

Her body went limp, but her face became taut with rage. "You bastard!" she snarled. "I'll tell them you killed Teddy, raped me, and stole the money!"

Edge nodded. "Reckon you would do that," he said, turning away from her. "Stick around."

"Where are you going?" she shrieked, suddenly afraid again.

"To get me some insurance," he answered as he retrieved his revolver and then went to mount his horse. "I'll be back."

He caught up with the three kidnappers in a stand of timber with a stream trickling through the trees. They were dividing up the ransom money while they waited for the coffeepot to boil on a small fire. He moved in to within ten feet of their camp, then stepped out from behind a tree, his Winchester leveled.

Lew spotted him first: so it was Lew who took the first bullet, screaming as his left kneecap was shattered. Sonny and Andy half stood and whirled, bills fluttering from their hands as they went for their guns. The Winchester cracked twice more. Edge aimed almost nonchalantly from the hip and both men vented their agony as their right kneecaps were shot away.

Even in their agonizing pain, each man knew the tall, impassive-faced half-breed could easily kill him, so no more did hands move toward guns.

Then Edge, his eyes glinting like slivers of blue ice under hooded lids, spoke not a word as he moved in closer. He disarmed the groaning men, then forced them to mount their horses and tied their hands to their saddlehorns. He linked the horses together in a line, and when he had gathered up the money he led his prisoners in a column back toward the canyon. It was almost noon when he rode through the narrow entrance. Flies buzzed away from the congealed blood crusting Tafts's back and zoomed in to feast upon the fresher supplies oozing from the leg wounds of the pain-wracked prisoners.

Annabelle, no longer attractive, was suffering some physical agony of her own now—her exposed flesh covered with red blotches and spotted by white sun blisters.

Edge cut her free and as she gingerly sat up, asked: "You still as hot as you look?"

"You're still a bastard!" she spat at him, crawling to where her clothes were heaped.

She groaned as the fabric of the dress chaffed her sunscorched skin. Edge loaded Tafts's body onto the dead man's horse and gave Annabelle the choice of riding with the corpse or walking. Hating the tall half-breed with every fiber of her punished body, she elected to ride.

Their approach was seen when they were still more than a half mile from Caine, and by the time they passed the town-limits marker every citizen was on the street. A stunned silence hung over the crowd as their eyes drank in the sight of Tafts's body slumped over his horse, the awful sunburns on Annabelle's once pretty face, and the blood-crusted wounds of the prisoners.

Edge, at the head of the slow-moving column, angled his mount toward the law office where Sheriff Smith waited. Said evenly: "Three fellers who'd like to be passing through, but I figure you'd prefer to have them stay."

The lawman nodded his bandaged head. Edge dismounted, hitched his horse to the rail, and crossed the street to the hotel. The clerk scuttled off the threshold and went behind the desk. He produced an envelope and passed it to Edge. The half-breed slid the envelope into his pocket without counting the money it contained. Knew it would be a thousand even.

"Did my message come?" he asked as a shout went up from the street. Many other voices were raised in anger, and the desk clerk glanced anxiously toward the door, eager to know the cause of the disturbance. But he found his gaze drawn inexorably back to the half-breed's impassive face.

"Oh, yes. Yes, sir, Mr. Edge. I almost forgot, what with . . ." He reached under the desk again and this time brought up a folded piece of paper which he thrust toward the half-breed before he rushed to the door.

Edge unfolded the sheet, which was a telegraph blank with a penciled message printed on it:

> WOMAN'S NAME ANNABELLE SOUTH. ONE
> THOUSAND DOLLARS IF LIAISON WITH MY
> SON BROKEN. JOHN B. TAFTS.

There was a great deal of noise out on the street now. A woman screamed and two gunshots sounded, but this only signaled an even louder din. Edge sighed, screwed up the telegram, and dropped it into a spittoon. There were no conditions attached to the assignment, but he doubted Teddy Tafts's father would pay the agreed fee under the circumstances. Not that it mattered, since, in a way, the younger Tafts had picked up the tab himself.

The town suddenly became quiet, and Edge's footfalls were loud against the stillness as he went out of the hotel. He halted on the sidewalk and began to roll a cigarette as he raked his narrowed eyes over the scene.

Sheriff Smith was still standing in front of the law office, but not willingly. Three men were forcing him to remain there under the muzzles of pointing revolvers. James Croxley sat on the seat of a buckboard, the reins of the team clutched in his eager hands. Standing unsteadily on their good legs in the back of the wagon were the terrified Sonny, Andy, and Lew. Their hands were still tied. Nooses were looped around their pulsing necks, the ends of the hanging ropes tied to the stout branch of a shade oak growing between the law office and the bank.

"Stop them!" the sheriff implored.

Everyone on the street turned to look toward Edge as he finished rolling the cigarette, slanted it from a side of his mouth, and lit it. He stepped down from the sidewalk and strolled across the street. The crowd parted to give him passage. He unhitched his horse and swung up into the saddle on the roan mare: glanced around and caught sight of Annabelle being helped by two fussing women into the house of the town physician. All eyes remained on him, and he sensed that a single word from his lips would halt the lynchings. Even Croxley, the ringleader of the plan to avenge his son's death, waited anxiously for the half-breed's verdict.

"Folks are riled up, Sheriff," Edge said evenly. "Look mad enough to raze Caine if they don't get what they want."

Croxley gave a yell and cracked the reins over the backs of the team. The buckboard jerked forward and the trio of kidnappers danced a fandango of death in heated midair. The simultaneous snapping of their necks was like a distant rifle shot. The crowd gasped and the guns covering the sheriff were lowered.

"You could've helped me!" the lawman accused as he sank down into his rocker. "I could've got them killers in jail so they could've been put on trial, legal and proper!"

Edge shrugged his shoulders as he arced the partly smoked cigarette to the ground, then turned his horse away from the hitching rail and replied: "Mostly people who die around me are either shot or cut or stabbed or like that, Sheriff. I haven't seen a lynching in a long time."

"So what?" the man in the rocker snarled bitterly.

"So a man gets tired of the same old things all the time," the half-breed answered wearily and heeled his horse toward a gap in the grim-faced crowd. "And a change is as good as arrest."

Chapter Four

THE redheaded Avis, who was the tallest, slimmest, most attractive, and perhaps youngest of the three women was also the acknowledged top hand of the gun-toting trio. Perhaps Ruby and Jessica accepted her as such because in the professional or otherwise pairings with the Prices, Avis was Harlan's woman and he was the dominant member of the family. But, this consideration apart, the two shorter and more thick-bodied blondes had probably gone along with Avis's leadership because they knew how afraid they would be when the guns posed their threat to a man's life: knew, too, how composed the redhead would remain.

They tried, but the two women flanking Avis were unable to conceal their uneasiness until the possibility of having to fire the guns at Edge was totally removed. Which took longer than everybody except Avis wanted.

"You boys and him ain't exactly kissin' cousins, huh?" the redhead asked, her smile hardening into a smirk as the other women's veneer of confidence began to blemish. "Me and them done right to get the drop on him, Harly?"

"You did fine," Harlan confirmed as the exhilaration of imminent freedom quickly diminished: all the men in the cage able to see that Ruby and Jessica were terrified while the third woman was perhaps dangerously overconfident. And, of course, they were unable to see how Edge was reacting on the other side of the solid partition. "Hey, Edge! No trouble, huh? A deal's a deal and—"

"You got the key to let them outta the back of this thing, big man?" Avis cut in on the apprehensively cajoling eldest Price.

"Sure," the half-breed answered, and slowly took the key from his pants pocket while his unblinking gaze and that of the woman remained locked. And the pair of guns in her long-fingered hands were held as utterly still as her dark eyes in their almond-shaped sockets. The muzzles were trained on Edge's chest, left of center: the Army Colt and the Navy Remington aimed from her hips.

Ruby's two Colts were wavering in a manner suggesting that the physical strain of holding the revolvers as much as the fear of having to fire them contributed to the sweat breaking out on her now frowning face. While Jessica, grimacing in a struggle to maintain her self-control, was like an inanimate statue as she thrust a Tranter and a Navy Colt at arm's length toward Edge. And it seemed as if she were in a world apart from this stiflingly hot canyon— withdrawn to such an extent that perhaps not even a threat against her own life would cause her to squeeze one of the triggers.

"Avis, don't—" Harlan began, sounding breathless. And the brand of silence that was clamped over the prison wagon suggested that all seven men trapped by its bars had been holding their breath.

"I'm handlin' it, Harly," the redhead interrupted him again. "Don't know what deal you got with him, but I can tell it don't call for me to blast him. I will, though, he don't toss that key down to us. Right now."

Still she and the half-breed did not break from the self-imposed trap of each other's stare: as he complied with her demand and arced the key down into the dust a foot or so in front of the ground-sweeping hem of Jessica's red skirts. All seven men pressed to the side bars of the cage were able to see the key land. And high tension was suddenly relieved. But embryonic joy was again dispelled when without attempting to pick up the key, Avis ordered:

''Now the pistol, then the rifle, big man.''

''Shit, Jessica,'' Nick started to snarl, ''grab that friggin' key and—''

''Ruby, Ruby, let me have them irons before you fall down and maybe kill some—''

''You boys shut up for a while, huh?'' Avis snapped. And, just for a fraction of a second, Edge thought she might shift her gaze to glare her anger at the men in the back of the wagon. His Colt was partway out of the holster then, but gripped by just a thumb and forefinger. And the woman urged: ''Just try it, big man.''

The half-breed was now absolutely certain that the dark-eyed redhead wanted to kill him. And so he took the utmost care to see that she had no excuse to do so when he tossed the Colt from its holster and his Winchester from the saddle boot over the side of the wagon seat.

''Atta girl, Avis!'' Nick exclaimed shrilly as the discarded rifle kicked up dust. And Billy-Joe Delany gave vent to a Rebel yell. Other prisoners who felt the need for vocal outlet confined themselves to gasps and sighs as Ruby gave a choked cry and let her arms drop to her sides as if the guns she held had increased to an unbearable weight.

''Get the key, Jess!'' Ethan urged.

But the blue-eyed blonde remained in the trancelike state of detachment that kept her deaf to extraneous sound and perhaps even made her blind to the man she was staring and aiming the guns at. It was the green-eyed Ruby who stooped and reached under the barrels of four revolvers to abandon one of her weapons and claim the key.

''At friggin' last!''

''About friggin' time!''

''Come on, sweetheart!''

''They're beautiful, all of them are friggin' beautiful!''

''Ain't this the best day of my life?''

Nick and Ethan Price, Chester Rankinn, and Austin Gatlin all contributed to the burst of eager talk as Ruby approached the rear of the wagon, still carrying one of her

Colts and with the key in her other hand. Billy-Joe Delany gave out with another Rebel yell.

Tense behind his apparent nonchalance up on the driver's seat of the rig, Edge was aware that the Comanche and Harlan Price were silent amidst the excitement. As silent as Avis and Jessica. One woman oblivious to what was happening while the other reconciled herself to the disappointment she felt. Watching these two women and listening to the sounds of unconfined joy from behind him, Edge elected not to try to guess what brand of emotions was causing the Indian and one of the Prices to be so subdued: beyond briefly acknowledging the unbidden notion that his own feelings doubtless were closer to those of the red than the white man.

"It's okay, honey, you can relax now," Avis said, and raised one of her arms to bar it across those of Jessica which were outstretched toward Edge. And then she bore down on the other woman, needing to exert considerable pressure to make an impression. But while she did this, and it served to snap the blonde out of her trance, Avis did not allow her gaze or the aim of her second gun to wander away from the half-breed. And then, as Jessica sank to her haunches, venting a sound that was half gasp and half sob, the redhead spread a smile that held more than a modicum of embarrassment in it across her face. "Goes for you, too, big man . . . far as I'm concerned."

"Hold it, you guys!" Harlan Price bellowed. And another tense silence descended in an instant over the wagon. It lasted for a stretched second before Rankinn shattered it.

"What's the idea, Price?" the scar-faced man demanded in a tone of matching harshness.

The prison wagon had shifted on its springs as the seven prisoners moved from the side to the rear: all of them desperately eager to get free of the cage at the first opportunity. But nobody sought to dispute Harlan Price's right to the position closest to the door. And, in the excitement of the moment, nobody saw what he did after he untied the reins so that Edge's horse could wander away into sparse shade—no one saw him reach a splayed hand through the bars, his blue eyes and the line of his wide mouth showing the eager-to-please Ruby a look that emphasized the tacit demand he was making. So that the woman gave him the gun without hesitation: and he was able to withdraw his hand and whirl around, to cover his fellow prisoners as he roared the order.

His brothers were as shocked as the other four men. And backed off with them: away from the Colt that Harlan gripped in his right hand while the heel of his left hovered above it in a threatened hammer-fanning attitude.

"Not you, cruds!" Harlan snarled, his eyes glittering with anger and excitement and dwelling for part of a second each on the uncomprehending faces of Nick and Ethan.

"Some of us indeed traveled hopefully," the Comanche said cryptically, watching the now grinning younger Prices move to flank their gun-toting brother as the first and then the second padlock was turned and Ruby swung open the door.

"Shit, we ain't done nothin' bad to you guys!" Billy-Joe Delany whined, his hollow eyes slick with imminent tears.

This as Ethan Price leaped out through the open doorway, and in his haste shouldered aside the again frightened Ruby so that she was knocked hard to the ground with a cry of pain.

"I don't understand the reason for what's happening?" Gatlin complained incredulously, looking at his fellow prisoners in turn: prepared to listen to any explanation.

"They're just natural-born sonsofbitches, is all," Chester Rankinn said in a husky tone of deep fear.

"I got 'em, Harlan!" Ethan Price yelled in triumph as he rose from snatching up Edge's Winchester. And he backed off to a point where by shifting the rifle just slightly to left or right he could cover the men in the cage as well as Edge on the driver's seat.

Nick was off the wagon by then, and now he snatched the key from Ruby's hand—and sent her stumbling over again just as she was to regain her feet. She began to wail her dismay as Nick swung away from her to fit the key in one of the padlocks and take a firm hold on the door.

"Out, Harlan!" the youngest brother snapped. "Shut your friggin' noise, Ruby!"

The woman choked herself into silence then could not hold back muted sobs.

Harlan turned and jumped to the ground. Whirled to cover Nick as the door was clanged closed and the key turned in the lock. But then he saw there was no need for concern.

The quartet of prison-garbed, shaven-headed, bristle-faced, sweat-run, and dirt-grimed men who remained in the cage had made no move to retaliate against those who moved to keep them still captive. In fact, with each second that passed, their will to resist was diminishing. They had failed to make a concerted rush at Harlan when he first got possession of the revolver, and now it was too late. As they huddled together in a comfortless group at the center of the wagon bed, each of them was probably more dispirited than at any time since sentence of death had been passed on him in some distant courtroom.

"What now, Harlan?" Nick asked, grinning happily.

His two brothers were abruptly grim-faced, Ethan taking his cue from Harlan.

"Maybe you didn't do nothing bad to us, Billy-Joe," the eldest Price allowed through his clenched, very white teeth. "But you ain't done us any good, either."

"Harly!" Avis said, a catch in her throat. Not looking at all like a woman disappointed at being denied the opportunity to kill a man. But not embarrassed to have harbored such a desire.

"Don't call me Harly, sweetheart," Harlan said, quietly but with menace. Not shifting his gaze away from the frightened men in the cage.

"Not in cold blood like this," the redhead pleaded.

Ruby forgot her own anguish now, to express silent horror for the plight of the helpless captives. While Jessica, also still down on the ground, screwed her eyes tightly closed and pressed clenched fists hard to her cheeks as she hung her head—like someone desperately trying to plunge herself back into a world removed from this new evil unfolding around her.

"You done fine, woman!" Ethan growled at Avis. "Now we'll take care of what's left of the chore to do!"

In acknowledgment of the order, and as a token of self-disgust at her inability to check the horror she had not realized she was starting, the redhead let the Colt and Remington clunk to the rock-hard ground as she whirled away from the wagon.

"You want reasons?" Harlan posed rhetorically to the men at his mercy. "Comanche, I just can't abide Injuns on principle. Billy-Joe, that Rebel yell of yours . . . well, kid, me and my brothers hail from New York State, and when the war was goin' on we was on the opposite side to you. Rankinn, you raped a woman before you knifed her. So you get it on behalf of these three sweethearts who set us free. And Austin Gatlin there—you sure have been gettin' on my nerves the way you ain't hardly ever stopped bellyaching about bein' sunstroked or whatever."

Tears were streaming down the gaunt face of the skinny young Delany. The red blotches on the sun-punished face of Gatlin now appeared more painfully vivid in contrast to the color-drained areas as he tried to plead for his life but was unable to gulp enough air into his lungs to power out the words. Both men darted entreating looks at Ruby and each of the Price brothers in turn. Rankinn glowered depthless hatred at Harlan Price. While the Comanche appeared to attain the state of waking daydream Jessica had found and then lost: his powerfully built frame relaxed and his strong-featured face set in a serene expression as his dark eyes gazed with seeming indifference into the middle distance of infinity.

"Edge?" Billy-Joe Delany croaked.

"Yeah, what about Edge?" Ethan wanted to know, and ceased raking the Winchester back and forth. Aimed it exclusively at the half-breed and looked as eager to kill him as Avis had a few minutes earlier.

"No!" Harlan snapped, anxious for the first time since taking control of the situation, as he glanced at his brother and recognized Ethan's almost irresistible desire to use the repeater against the half-breed. "A deal's a deal! We didn't promise nothin' to these guys!"

Edge saw the threat of imminent death recede as the grinning killer face of Ethan Price and the aim of the rifle in his tight grip shifted toward the rear of the wagon. As this happened, he considered the possibility of hurling himself down off the seat and retrieving his surrendered Colt. But such a move would still have been suicidal, so he waited, tensely ready behind a shell of unconcern, for the odds to shorten in his favor.

"Oh God, no!" Austin Gatlin wailed.

"You can't!" Billy-Joe Delany screamed.

"Sonsofbitches!" Chester Rankinn bellowed.

If the Comanche vented a vocal reaction to summary execution within the cage wagon stalled on the floor of this oven-heated canyon he did not make it loudly enough to be heard by the half-breed, who continued to watch Ethan with apparent indifference and await his opportunity.

On the periphery of his vision Edge saw that Avis was compelled to whirl around and stare into the rear of the wagon. And Jessica, unable to remain trapped in the self-imposed confinement of her detachment, continued to fist her cheeks but found herself forced to raise and turn her head and snap open her eyes. And out of his view, Ruby was unable to tear her horrified gaze away from the scene; while, breathless with fascination, Nick Price did not want to.

Harlan Price fired the first shot, his left hand dropping to his side as the well-placed bullet drilled into the chest of the scowling Rankinn. Ethan exploded the next two while his brother deliberately thumbed back the hammer. One of these ricocheted wildly off a bar and another smashed through Billy-Joe Delany's right ankle.

"Watch the friggin' bars!" Harlan snarled. Glowered angrily at Ethan, then spread a cold grin of evil across his element-burnished face. He gripped a bar with his free hand, as if to steady himself, then thrust the barrel of the revolver between two others and took careful aim at the trembling and weeping Austin Gatlin. Placed a shot in the man's belly.

"That don't sound like the Johnnie Reb yell no more, Billy-Joe!" Ethan roared as he ran to the side of the wagon and pressed the rifle barrel between bars. Triggered a shot into the youngster's other leg.

Edge, blind to the carnage, struggled against the near compulsion to concentrate his entire attention on the Frontier Colt that lay on the dusty ground beside the offside front wheel of the wagon. Forced himself to listen to every violent sound from behind the solid partition—and to watch for a first sign that the two women in his sight were not oblivious to his slow move along the seat.

"Don't torture them!" Avis shrieked against two more gunshots and the screams of the men hit by the bullets exploding amid acrid spurts of black powder smoke.

There were six revolvers scattered on the ground between the wagon and the two shocked women: the one surrendered by Edge, one discarded by Ruby when she snatched up the key, and the two each abandoned by Jessica and Avis in disgusted protest at what was about to happen. As he counted the third shot to blast from the barrel of Harlan's gun, the half-breed decided he could ignore the blonde Jessica, who had now unfisted her hands and was pressing the palms to her ears. But the redhead might well regain her composure and go for one of the other revolvers when she saw him make his move.

In the gunsmoke-swirling rear of the wagon, Gatlin took another bullet in the belly and sat down hard on the corpse of Rankinn: clawing both hands to his wound and bending his head to gaze at the blood squeezing between his fingers. Harlan allowed the man to sit and suffer while he cocked the Navy Colt and tracked it to cover the as yet unhurt Indian. Hatred cut deep lines into the flesh around his narrowed eyes and slightly parted lips as he shot the Comanche in the crotch. The powerfully built man thudded back against the partition behind the driver's seat and began to slide down it, his expression of wooden resignation gradually altering to a look of even deeper hatred than that displayed by his executioner.

Billy-Joe Delany, his legs shot from under him, was down on the wagon bed, writhing in the slickness of his own blood as the roaring with laughter Ethan exploded more bullets into his skinny frame. Just this demonic shrieking and the tortured youngster's agonized screaming competed with the crackle of gunfire. If there were any other sounds, Edge was not able to hear them.

The fourth chamber of the Navy Colt was emptied of a live bullet and the half-breed heard a dull thud and a subdued pattering sound: had no way of knowing that this was caused by Gatlin's body sprawling to the bed of the wagon while blood and tissue and bone splinters from the fatal head wound splattered across the partition.

Three shots were fired rapidly from the Winchester, and again Edge was unable to see the resultant death behind him—as the pain-wracked, blood-sodden body of Billy-Joe Delany was at last stilled by a bullet in his brain.

The repeater made an empty sound as Ethan pumped the lever action, and Edge experienced a momentary surprise as he realized that the Price with the rifle was the first one to run out of shells—had blasted a dozen shots with merciless and hysterical glee at the helpless men in the cage. Then Harlan Price fired a fifth shot from the Colt, to send a bullet into the center of the Comanche's heart: killing the man instantly where he sat with his back against the partition.

Edge was a fraction of a second away from powering down off the wagon seat on the other side of that partition. Knowing for sure that the rifle in Ethan's hands was empty and that Harlan's Colt had just one live bullet in its cylinder. But then, in another fraction of a second, the half-breed lost his opportunity. For Nick Price leaped into view after racing along the side of the wagon. He stooped and snatched up Edge's Colt. On his face an expression of bitter ill-humor as he whirled and tracked the gun. Then he snarled a curse when he saw that there was no life left to end behind the bars on three sides of the cage. With his lips still open in the shape of the obscenity, he moved the gun back to draw a bead on its owner.

"Kill him and you'll live to regret it, little brother!" Harlan warned coldly.

The blue eyes of the youngest Price came close to spilling tears of frustration as he lost the battle of wills with Harlan, who then allowed in an almost tender tone:

"But you can plug him somewhere it'll hurt real bad for a long time if he don't get down off that seat and come around to the rear of this here wagon, Nick."

A grin of eager anticipation spread across the young man's face as he backed away a couple of paces and jerked his head to the side. With his brother moving away from the wagon, Ethan had to swing wide to go around behind him and out of the firing line when he went to pick another handgun up out of the dust. Edge took extreme care not to give either man an excuse to shoot him as he climbed down off the seat.

"Give him the key so he can unlock the door, Nick," Harlan instructed.

Nick backed off another two paces, and tossed the key into the half-breed's splayed hand. Because the youngest brother was breathing so fast and noisily with excitement, it almost seemed as if Harlan and Ethan and the three women were holding their collective breath.

"One thing about ridin' with a bunch of dead men," Harlan said evenly as Edge swung open the door and heaved himself up into the rear of the prison wagon, "a person don't have to bother with polite conversation."

The half-breed raked a bleak-eyed gaze over the sprawled corpses on which nature's scavengers were already feasting. Growled: "And the flies are less bothersome, feller."

While his brothers moved in closer to cover Edge through the bars, Harlan clanged the door closed and turned the key in one, then the other, padlock. And the threat of the aimed guns was not removed until the key was in the pocket of the man's prison uniform tunic.

"Some deal you made with him," Avis said sourly.

"Promised Edge here a half of our stake, sweetheart," Harlan answered with a grin as he moved along the side of the wagon. "And if a man don't keep his word . . ." He paused and shrugged. "Well, I just intend to keep mine, that's all."

"Keep mine, too," Edge said as he squatted in the barred corner of the cage that was in the uncool shade of the afternoon sun.

"What'd you promise us, Mexican?" Nick demanded with a sneer.

"Giving you fair warning now. If anybody here ever points a gun at me again, him or her better shoot to kill. Because I'll sure as hell kill them."

"Big talk from a big guy who can't do frig all to anyone," Nick countered and aimed the Frontier Colt at Edge again.

But then the youngest brother rasped an obscenity as Harlan struck a blow across the wrist of his gun hand.

"Time enough later, little brother. After he's a rich man." The scowl he had shown to Nick started to become a consoling smile, and then developed into an evil grin as he turned to look at Ethan and the woman and finally the half-breed. "Gonna make you that, just like I said I would, Edge. But I can't guarantee you'll have much time to enjoy the wealth."

"Some deal," Avis reiterated dully.

"Guess I always knew there'd be a price tag, lady," Edge drawled.

Harlan laughed and his brothers took their cue from him in the manner of men following an example they did not quite understand. Then they listened intently, eager for comprehension, as Harlan said happily:

"What you think of the deal, Edge? At least you get to die a rich man, huh?"

"It gives me the needle, feller," the half-breed answered evenly, "but then I guess I never was bound for heaven."

The Vengeance Guns

Memories of Emma Diamond were still fresh in the mind of Edge and he had yet to have his run-in with a fat man called Sullivan when the following events took place. Thus, they occurred while he was heading away from the Rio Grande where it flows south of the Santiago Mountains in Texas (Ashes and Dust) *and toward Fort Waycross, Territory of Arizona* (Sullivan's Law).

THE half-breed dismounted from the trail-weary black gelding in the front yard of the big house at the eastern end of the street and went to the well. The rusted handle squeaked when he cranked it, and he could hear that the bucket leaked as he winched it up the shaft. But it was still more than half filled with cool, clear, sweet water when it reached the surface.

He drank with cupped hands, and when his thirst was slaked he held the bucket out for the horse.

At no time since swinging down from the saddle did he relax his cautious surveillance of his apparently deserted surroundings. Seeing at close quarters the community he first spotted two hours earlier. Then just as a blurred image in the far distance of this piece of desert on the New Mexico–Arizona border. A huddle of dark shapes gradually becoming more distinct as the slick-looking heat shimmer of midmorning retreated before the advance of the slow-riding man. No smoke smudged the perfectly blue sky above the town as he approached it from the east; and at midday, when he rounded the corner of the two-story house which faced along the single short street, he was convinced that no one lived here anymore.

But that did not necessarily mean he had the place to himself, so he continued to mistrust the utter silence and total lack of movement that a man with imagination might regard as eerie. And the glinting slits of his ice-blue eyes missed nothing, while in back of his seemingly casual attitude he was constantly poised to respond in an instant to the first sign of danger.

Like the brief, fast series of metallic clicks that he recognized as the sounds of a shell being levered into the breech of a repeater rifle. His eyes raked toward the source of the sound and he saw the sun-glinting barrel of the rifle as it was jutted through the glassless window of the weather-ravaged Golden City Saloon, three hundred feet down the street to his right.

He saw the puff of white muzzle smoke as he fisted a hand around the frame of his own Winchester where it jutted from the boot hung on his saddle. Heard the report of the gunshot as he flung himself backward: away from the gelding and onto the ground in the cover of the three-foot-high wall encircling the well shaft. His rifle was clear of the boot and he had a double-handed grip on it: needed only to thumb back the hammer because there was already a shell in the breech.

The crack of the gunshot masked the thud of the bullet's impact. The horse snorted and shook his head violently. Droplets of moisture spattered Edge's cheek and the back of a hand. But not water. Blood. The forelegs of the horse buckled and his neck hit the ground. Then the animal rolled down onto its side and its flesh quivered. The half-breed lay still: and for a stretched second all that moved in the area of the well was the blood oozing from a hole just beneath the gelding's right eye and the sweat beads which squeezed from the pores of Edge's heavily bristled face.

Then the half-breed let out his pent-up breath in a soft sigh and began to breathe normally again. Heard the sound of the repeater's lever action as the spent shellcase was ejected and a fresh bullet was jacked up from the magazine.

"Hey, you in the saloon!" Edge called.

"There's three of us, so you don't stand no chance, saddletramp!" The voice sounded young.

"I'm talking to the feller with the rifle!"

"That's me! What d'you want?"

"Want to know what my horse did to you, kid!"

"I was aimin' at you, saddletramp!"

"You better pray you get lucky next time! Or that your buddies are better shots than you are!"

Edge looked back over his shoulder, along the length of his prone body, and across twenty-five feet of hard-packed and dusty ground to the porched doorway of the big house.

"You moved, saddletramp!" There was a whining tone of petulant excuse and vindictive accusation in the voice. Which drew a gruff, low-toned response from another man in the dilapidated saloon.

"Yeah, I'm real sneaky when somebody's trying to kill me!" Edge called and rolled onto his side, pulled his knees up to his chest, and shuffled around without exposing any part of himself beyond the curves of the well wall.

"Help me! Please help me!" The woman's voice was shrill with fear.

"Shut that bitch up!"

After the jolting shock of the rifle shot Edge experienced only mild surprise at the abrupt intrusion of the woman's plea. And welcomed it as the unexpected bonus of a diversion: capturing as it did a part of the kid's attention and then stoking his anger. Edge powered up onto all fours, then lunged forward. The kid cursed and triggered another shot. The half-breed veered sharply to the left and saw splinters of wood explode from one of the porch uprights. Heard again the lever action of a repeater.

A man shrieked: "Drop the bastard, Kelly!"

Edge leaped up off the dirt and partly turned himself in midair. Tucked his head down and pressed his cheek against his right shoulder a moment before his left one crashed painfully hard into the crack where the double doors of the house met.

He had counted on an abandoned house in a ghost town not being locked up, but applied enough force with the flying dive to take account of a wrong guess.

A third rifle shot cracked and he saw the bullet imbed itself in the door to his right. Then his shoulder hit the timber and not for the first time in his life he was philosophically prepared to face death without knowing why it should be ordained to be in this place and in this manner.

But the doors were flung inward and he was falling. Gritted his teeth against a fresh wave of pain as he crashed to the boarded floor, but refused to indulge himself in a vocal outlet and the luxury of remaining still until he had rolled into the cover of the room wall. Where he lay on his back in a frozen attitude, face contorted by a grimace while he vented a string of curses from between curled-back lips. This as a fusillade of rifle shots peppered the double doors with bullets to swing them open again as they started to close after bouncing off the flanking walls.

"Sneaky's damn right!" the kid shrieked in righteous anger.

"You missed him, Kelly! Now what the hell we gonna do?" This was not the same man who had urged the youngster to drop Edge.

"Shut your big mouth, Harry!"

There was a hard silence that lasted perhaps three seconds before the woman began to sob.

"And I told you guys to shut her up!"

Heavy footfalls thudded across a floor and then came the crack of a hand striking flesh. A shrill cry that curtailed the sobs and then more silence.

Edge rose painfully up onto all fours and then came

erect against the wall, using his rifle as a crutch. His body ached all over, with his left shoulder giving him the most discomfort. He massaged this and waited, the grimace leaving his face as he listened for the slightest break in the hot, bright silence that was clamped over the town.

''Hey, saddletramp?''

A minute had slid into history before Kelly called to him. Edge continued to massage the painful area and to breathe regularly as he gazed across the large and once grand hallway of the house. For a lot of years it had been tightly sealed by the closed doors and the boarded-up, glassless windows. But enough sun-warmed fresh air had now entered so that it longer smelled of decay and his own sweat-run flesh.

''Answer me, damn you!''

Edge ceased tending his injury and took out the makings. He rolled a cigarette as he heard an exchange of voices which reached along the street and into the house as no more than indistinct whisperings. Until Kelly snarled in a rage:

''You guys think he's dead, you go check him out!''

Against the challenging words, the men in the saloon failed to hear the striking of a match on the rifle stock. But the stream of gray smoke that Edge blew out was seen in the sunlight shafting through the doorway.

''The sonofabitch is havin' a smoke!'' As he completed this, Kelly sought greater release for his frustration with another shot. And the stairway with a broken and leaning bannister directly across from the threshold showed another hole.

''You're wastin' time and breath and lead, Kelly!'' Harry accused.

The youngster shrieked an obscenity and then there was a loud crash, as if he had slammed his rifle against unmoving timber. Another silence followed by a period of harsh-toned discussion which Edge heard as mere scratchings on the heat of the day. He folded away from the wall and did not need to stoop to place his eye to a crack between the boards across the window.

Apart from the horse carcass with the desert flies gorging on the rapidly crusting blood, the single street looked exactly as it had when he first rode up to the front yard of the house. He used a hand to take the sweat off his forehead and bristled cheeks and wiped the salt moisture on his pants leg, below the tied-down holster with the Frontier Colt jutting from it. His expression did not alter when, a few minutes later, he saw shadowy movement at the batwinged entrance to the saloon.

"Hey, saddletramp!"

Now Edge turned his head to blow a stream of tobacco smoke across the open doorway of the house.

"I was wrong! Takin' that shot at you! You weren't sent here by Seth Adams, was you?"

"You got something right, kid!"

"Didn't figure he'd put his pretty little wife's life on the line that way! But hear this, mister! If I have to kill her on account of you, your life won't be worth a plug nickel! If you know Seth Adams—"

"I never heard of him." Edge dropped the cigarette butt to the floor and its smoke continued to drift across the doorway.

"So I'll tell you, mister! He's the richest, most important, and meanest man in this piece of country and—"

"You want to bring me a horse down here, kid?"

"What?"

"You killed my horse. I need another one."

Kelly responded on a shrill, rising note. "You listen to me, saddletramp! If you don't toss out your guns and surrender to me and Harry and Floyd, I'll drill Rose Adams right between her big blue eyes! And when her husband reaches Golden City, I'll let him know it was you made me do it!"

The rich man's wife vented a choked sob.

"Knew my horse, kid. Never did hear of any Rose Adams before."

Now the woman screamed again. And was silenced by another open-handed blow against her bare flesh.

"I want you to listen to me!" Kelly shrieked, then

forced himself to moderate his tone. "Look, we got no reason to want you dead, mister. I was all screwed up when I took that shot at you. All you gotta do is fold your hand and wait for the rest of us to finish the game."

"Do it! Please do as he says! He'll kill me, I know he will!" The woman sounded on the brink of hysteria.

"She knows it!" Floyd yelled. "And you know this, mister! Kelly ain't just spoutin' off about Seth Adams! He finds out you got his wife killed, you better start countin' your breaths. Because any one of them could be your last!"

"Could just be it's the tobacco that counts, feller," Edge murmured softly so that he alone heard, as he saw the discarded butt finally go out. And then he began to roll a fresh cigarette.

"Look, there's a lot of money ridin' on this deal!" Kelly continued. "And with Adams bein' such a hard sonofabitch, I was all tensed up when you come ridin' into town! Lost my damn head and . . ."

The kid went on talking. First making excuses for his hot-headed action in blasting at a total stranger. Then giving promises that Edge would not be harmed if he surrendered. Next enlarging what he had already revealed about the nature of Seth Adams.

For a while, Edge remained by the boarded-up window, listening to Kelly and watching the street. But then, after lighting the fresh cigarette, he inserted the saliva-dampened end in a crack between two boards and moved away. Did not need to pass the open doorway to reach a door beside the stairs. Which gave on to a passage with an arch at the end opening into the kitchen. An unlocked rear door allowed him to leave the house and step out onto the back lot.

From there he could still hear Kelly's voice clearly, speaking into the otherwise total silence that gripped the ghost town and the encircling desert: a dusty pink area in the immediate vicinity of Golden City, monotonously flat, sparsely featured with sagebrush and mesquite and cactus.

The kind of terrain that was easy to watch from the abandoned mining community at its center.

But the trio of men in the saloon had failed to realize Edge was approaching until he emerged at the front of the big house. Which maybe meant they were not expecting anybody to arrive for some time and had not yet started keeping watch. Or, more probably, Seth Adams was due to reach town from the west—riding in on the just discernible trail which began at that end of the street.

". . . and so you better make up your mind quick, mister!" Kelly continued. "To take your chances that I'll keep my word and everyone gets to keep on livin'! Or I blow out Rose Adams's brains, which puts you right away on borrowed time!"

"He's runnin' outta patience, mister!" Harry urged.

"And you're changing the game, feller," Edge growled to himself as he reached a corner of the house. "A while ago he was talking poker."

There were just a few feet of open space between the building line of the big house and the cover of the livery stable on the other side of the street. And Edge traversed this without being seen while attention continued to be focused on the doorway across which the blue tobacco smoke was slowly drifting.

"Well say somethin', damnit!" Kelly snarled.

"Hey, the sonofabitch is comin'!" Floyd yelled.

Edge's palms were suddenly greasy with sweat as his hands fisted tighter around the barrel and frame of the Winchester. This as he reached the side wall of the livery and shot a glance back over his shoulder—saw the dust of his passing settling back into the impressions of his booted feet.

"All right! All right! Keep it down! let me friggin' think!"

Floyd had sounded panicked. Kelly was simply enraged.

Edge advanced along the wall to the street-facing corner of the livery and removed his hat: risked a fast glance along the unsidewalked street and out on to the west trail.

"He'll see the dead horse!" Harry said huskily. And

confirmed what Edge had suspected a moment before his eyes proved it.

It was not his own escape from the big house Floyd was concerned with. Rather, the advance out of the distant heat shimmer of a horse and buggy. And now Edge withdrew his head into cover, replaced his hat, and glanced at the open doorway of the house. The cigarette had gone out, but it had already served his purpose.

"I said to shut up and let me think, damnit!" Kelly screamed.

They were amateurs. That had been plain from the outset. The youngest with the brains and the other two content with his leadership until the stranger intruded and the smooth running of their plan began to hit snags. Then Harry and Floyd becoming more dissatisfied with Kelly by the moment, realizing he was as afraid as they were—had triggered this dangerous situation by his jittery act of firing a shot at the stranger. And missing the target.

"Hey, mister! I want you to listen real good to me! And I swear I'm tellin' the truth! Seth Adams owes us. From way back in the war. He was a Yankee major. With Sherman on the march to the sea. Him and his cavalry troop hit our place. Mine and Floyd's. I was just a little kid. Floyd, he was away fightin' with the Confederacy. There was just me and Ma and Pa and our sister Louise at home. Louise was engaged to be married to Harry. Harry was away at the war, too. Ma and Pa hid me when Adams and his Yankees hit the place. Adams had them shoot Pa in the belly and made him watch while they took my Ma and Louise. All of them had the women in turn. And when they was done they tossed Ma and Pa and my sister into the house. Set fire to it. And didn't take off until after my folks stopped screamin'. For God's sake, mister! I spent my life huntin' for that sonofabitch! Don't you do nothin' to keep us from—"

"They'll kill Seth!" Rose Adams shrieked. "The money doesn't matter to them! They've tricked him into coming out here alone so they can—"

This time it was something heavier than a hand that

117

crashed against the head of the hysterical woman. It made a sickening thud and she was plunged into unconsciousness before she could utter a response to the instant of agony from the blow.

As Captain Josiah C. Hedges of the Union cavalry, Edge had taken part in Sherman's infamous march to the sea. A campaign of death and destruction that had sent the Confederacy reeling toward inevitable defeat. He could not recall any Major Seth Adams, but in an army the size of the one commanded by Sherman, that was hardly surprising. It was no reason to disbelieve Kelly's story. And the merciless brutality of the events the kid recounted rang true to the half-breed, who had witnessed similar atrocities during that time of which Kelly spoke.

But, as he moved closer to the saloon, listening to the youngster's voice, which was by turns bitterly angry and whiningly pleading, Edge's impassive expression was a true reflection of his actual lack of feeling.

He was advancing across the back lots of the abandoned and derelict buildings. First the livery stable, then a store, a blacksmith's forge—and had reached the rear of a bakery separated by an alley from the saloon when the woman's shrill entreaty was so harshly silenced. It was then he heard a horse whinny softly and peered through the open doorway of the bakehouse which had been stripped bare of apparatus. And curled back his thin lips in a cold-eyed grin when he saw the three horses standing in the hot shade.

"All right, saddletramp!" Kelly snarled into the brief silence that followed the stunning of Rose Adams. "We're outta time now! But you better stay quiet as the woman and keep your nose outta our business!"

"That's enough, Kelly!" Floyd rasped, and if Edge had still been in the big house at the end of the street he would not have heard the soft-spoken warning.

Then the clop of hooves and the turning of wheelrims reached his ears as he selected the strongest of the three horses in the bakehouse—a gray gelding—and began to saddle the animal. Content that the saddle, accoutrements, and bedroll were newer and of better quality than his own gear on the dead gelding.

He had fastened the cinch and was adjusting the length of the stirrups when the horse and buggy rolled onto the west end of the street and came to a halt. Seconds of silence slid by. Then:

"All right, you bastards! I got your message and I'm here! Let's deal!"

Adams sounded weary and angry. Perhaps he had driven a long way to reach Golden City, or maybe he was emotionally rather than physically exhausted.

"Come on up the street to the front of the saloon, Major!" Kelly demanded.

"Where's Rose?"

"She's right here! Do like I tell you to!"

While he rolled another cigarette and hung it unlit at the side of his mouth, Edge heard the creak of springs and timbers as a heavily built man climbed down from the buggy. Then footfalls advancing along the street.

"I don't see no money, Major!" Kelly snarled.

"I don't see my wife," came the less raucous response.

"You better damn well have it!"

Under cover of the exchange, Edge left the bakehouse and, treading quietly, crossed the alley to the rear of the saloon. He elected to enter by swinging over the sill of a glassless and unboarded window rather than trusting the closed door to open silently. He was just bringing his trailing leg inside when the revolver shot cracked. The footfalls on the street came to an abrupt halt, a man grunted and then dropped heavily to the ground. Seth Adams screamed:

"You murderin'—"

"You ain't dead yet!" Kelly growled across Adams's accusation. This as the batwings were pushed open, feet rapped on the floor of the saloon, and something was dragged across it to be hauled outside.

"Rose!" the injured man blurted in horror as the batwings flapped closed.

And Edge took long, silent strides across the room in

the living quarters and went down a short passage that ended at an arch behind the counter of the now empty saloon.

"Remind you of anythin', *Major* Adams?" Kelly demanded with pointed emphasis.

"Dear God in heaven!" the injured man gasped.

There was just one table and two chairs in the saloon. One of the men had used a crate to sit on. The woman had been on the floor, surrounded by the tattered remains of the expensive clothing that had been ripped from her body. A trail across the accumulated dust of many empty years showed where she had been dragged to and through the batwinged entrance and out to the sun-bright street beyond.

"If you've so much as—"

"We stripped her bare-assed naked and then had to quiet her naggin' is all," Harry put in coldly to silence Adams. "It's now we get to give her what you and your lousy troopers give to Floyd and Kelly's Ma and sister back in the war."

The sun had shifted across its zenith and was beginning to slide down the southwestern sky now. So the interior of the saloon was in deep shade. Edge reached a point short of the batwings where he could look out over them and clearly see the area at the center of the street where the group was gathered.

The sixty-year-old, fleshily built, gray-haired, city-suited Seth Adams was sitting in the dust, clutching with both hands at a bloodied area of his belly. On his time-lined, pain-wracked, colorless face there was an expression of despairing comprehension. Sprawled out naked on her back in front of him was a slender, blonde woman of no more than twenty-five years. With classically beautiful features marred by a purple bruise on her left temple. Her wrists had been tied in front of her, but now her arms lay on the ground above her head at the limit of their reach, showing that she had been dragged unceremoniously out of the saloon by a man hauling on the rope that bound her. She was still unconscious, her nude breasts rising and falling regularly as she breathed easily.

Kelly and Floyd shared a striking family resemblance in their good-looking faces, although there was about a fifteen-year age difference between them. Harry was a match for Floyd in age—thirty-five or so. All three were dressed like cowhands which, judging by the kind of accoutrements carried on their saddles, they were. Each packed a revolver in a hip holster and toted a Winchester rifle. Kelly and Harry flanked the gunshot man and the unconscious woman, while Floyd had his back to the group: watching the big house at the eastern end of the street. He held the repeater rifle in a two-handed grip across his chest.

"That was war," Adams choked, tearing his gaze away from his wife to rake it between the embittered faces of Kelly and Harry. "Things like that happen in war. Both sides were guilty of them. Ten thousand dollars. Just like you asked for. I brought it. In a bag back in the buggy."

He was obviously suffering a great deal of pain from the bullet imbedded in his belly. But it was the anguish of anticipating that which was yet to come that commanded his expression and intonation.

"Me and Floyd's Ma and Pa and the girl Harry was gonna marry, Adams!" Kelly spat out. "Gut-shot and raped and then buried alive. Ain't enough money in the world to pay for what you done."

It was evident that Adams's mind was racing in what he had to realize was a vain attempt to fasten on some reasoned argument that would sway his captors from their plan.

"Get to it!" Floyd urged, and sounded and looked almost as frightened as the wounded man. "We're sittin' ducks for that saddletramp—"

"Wake her up, Harry!" Kelly instructed tersely.

Harry dropped to his haunches, rested his rifle across his thighs and began to slap the cheeks of the woman until a groan trickled from her throat.

"You're dead and you have to know that!" Adams blurted suddenly. "I came out here alone, just like I was told. But there's no way you're going to get more than a few miles out of this godforsaken place. If I'm not back on the spread before five o'clock—Rose and me both—a hundred men will be riding out here."

"You think we didn't figure on a double cross, mister?" Kelly sneered. "You think we didn't count on Mr. Big Shot Seth Adams plannin' on gettin' back his money? Hell, we knew you'd fix it for your men to come after us. So we got nothin' to lose by makin' you pay more than money for what you done back in the war. If we're gonna die, it might as well be happy as well as rich."

The woman had groaned her way back to awareness and now she swung her head to and fro, fear-filled blue eyes widening and losing their glaze as she saw the extent of the terrifying situation into which she had been thrust.

This as the relentless singlemindedness of the three men finally convinced Seth Adams that there was no avenue of escape from this waking nightmare in the full glare of the blistering sun on the single street of Golden City.

He was despair personified.

"Help us!" the woman pleaded at the top of her voice, forcing herself up into a sitting position so that her bound wrists fell between her naked thighs. "For pity sake, help us!"

She tore her tear-filled, red-rimmed eyes away from the wretched sight of her wounded husband to stare between Kelly and Floyd at the big silent house dominating the eastern end of the street.

"Rose!" Adams cried. "There's no one here can help us, my—"

"There is, there is! There's a man in the house down there! He was riding that horse that's dead by the well!"

Now Adams snapped his head around to look along the street with hope blazing in his widening eyes.

Kelly vented a harsh laugh and taunted: "A tough-talkin' saddletramp is all he is, Major! Who ain't got no reason to risk his neck on your account!"

"I'm a rich man, stranger!" Adams shrieked. "I'll pay you anything you ask if you'll—"

Edge's ready-cocked Winchester had been canted to his right shoulder. Now he swung down the barrel and fisted his free hand around it: as he brought the stock to his shoulder and squeezed the trigger. Took three strides to bring him up to the batwings as Kelly, blood gushing from the entry and exit wounds in his neck, pitched sideways to the ground with a dying sigh. The lever action was worked and the ejected shell was spinning through the hot air when the half-breed snarled:

"Don't aim those rifles at me!"

Floyd and Harry had both whirled to face the saloon entrance, but only after the shock of seeing Kelly's death had frozen them into immobility for a vital second.

"Best you just toss them away," Edge went on, less stridently, but with equal menace.

The men's eyes found Edge ahead of their rifle muzzles and they saw he was aiming the smoke-wisping Winchester between them. They obeyed the first order, but not the second.

"You killed my kid brother," Floyd accused, voice pitched unnaturally high with emotion.

"And we'll be next!" Harry rasped. He let his rifle drop to the street and raised his hands shakily above his Stetsoned head.

"Your kid brother killed my horse." The half-breed's Winchester raked to the side to draw a bead on Floyd as he argued his point.

"Blast them, mister!" Adams commanded. He tried to rise but was forced to drop back again with a groan when a fresh wave of pain exploded in his belly.

"Damn you!" Floyd said bitterly and hurled his rifle away. Kept his arms down at his sides as he struggled to fight back tears of grief or frustration or both.

"Now the handguns, fellers."

Both men eased the revolvers gingerly out of their holsters and threw them several feet to the side. Then Edge canted the rifle to his left shoulder and delved for a match in his shirt pocket. Struck it on the doorpost and lit the cigarette as he came between the batwings. Everyone watched him in bewilderment mixed with fear. All of them were sweating heavily. The flies which had earlier fed on the blood of the horse now swarmed to gorge on the more recent wounds of the dead Kelly.

"Mister, this ain't none of your concern," Harry complained.

Edge nodded. "I know it, feller. The kid and me have finished our business. Like for you to go into the bakehouse out back of the bakery across the alley there. A horse inside is ready saddled. Bring him out to me, will you?"

Incredulous shock showed on the faces of Seth and Rose Adams now.

The woman asked huskily: "You're just going to leave us here with these evil men?"

"Go get the horse like he told you, Harry," Floyd urged, excitement rising within him.

Harry moved away from the group cautiously, not trusting Edge and not taking his suspicious gaze off him. But once in the alley between the saloon and the bakery, he was heard to break into a run.

"Name your price!" Seth Adams shrieked. "I'll pay anything! There's ten thousand in the buggy! On account! However much more you want I'll—"

"Like for you to go along the street and bring the buggy, feller," Edge said to Floyd.

"Sure. Sure thing." He started to run at once.

"You're just going to take the money and leave us here?" Adams accused, contempt mixed in with the pain in his eyes. Then a plea filled them. "Will you do just one thing for me, stranger?"

"What's that?"

"Take Rose with you, please? She didn't have any part in that rape and slaughter in the war."

"Wondered if you'd ask that."

Floyd climbed up onto the buggy. Released the brake and cracked the reins. Then yelled: "Get the hell out, Harry!"

This as he jerked on the reins to demand a fast, tight turn from the horse in the shafts of the buggy. Pumping hooves and spinning wheelrims billowed up a great cloud of dust.

"The sonsofbitches are running!" Adams roared.

Harry heard Floyd's call and whatever had been in his mind when he went for the horse, he now elected to follow his partner's frenetic suggestion. The hoofbeats of the saddlehorse being ridden at a gallop sounded above the noise of the racing buggy for a few moments. Then merged with it.

Edge drew once more against his cigarette then spit it out. He ignored what the wounded man and the naked woman were yelling at him as he gazed along the street and out at the open trail to the west. Where the buggy was cloaked by the dust cloud billowing behind it. And then another elongated dust cloud showed, streaming out in the wake of Harry astride the galloping gray gelding as he rode from behind the final building on the street and angled on to the open trail.

Seth and Rose Adams curtailed their demands when the Winchester barrel fell away from the broad shoulder of the tall, lean man. The bullet was triggered from the muzzle amid another spurt of acrid-smelling gunsmoke. Harry was pitched sideways from his saddle and sent bounding and rolling across the trail. The horse, unburdened of his rider, galloped a few more yards and then began to slow. There was no slackening of the buggy's pace.

"What about the other one?" Seth Adams snarled when he wrenched his gaze away from the distant trail to stare at Edge: and saw the impassive-faced man was calmly canting the rifle back to his shoulder again.

"He ain't stealing anything that belongs to me, feller. Harry was taking my horse."

The half-breed went to stand over the naked woman.

She blurted: "Oh, my God, so you're going to . . ."

Her voice trailed off as he delved a hand into the long hair at the nape of his neck. And came into sight again clutching an open straight razor that was carried in the pouch concealed under his shirt at the top of his spine.

"You're a beautiful woman who deserves better than him, maybe," Edge told her and stooped to cut through her bonds with the razor. "But you are his, and there's an end to it."

"Thank you. Thank you so much." She looked and sounded near to collapse.

"Best you go and get dressed now, ma'am."

"Seth, you need to be tended to and—"

"Do like the man says and get some clothes on your nakedness, woman," her husband ordered. Then, when she looked down at herself, she gasped, swung around and staggered into the saloon. And Adams shook his head as he directed a bewildered look at Edge. "You got to be crazy, stranger. Allowing that bastard to ride off with ten thousand bucks. I wasn't lying when I said you could have it. And more if you wanted. For taking a hand in this."

"Figured you weren't lying about those hundred men, either."

"Damn right I wasn't!" Suddenly his pale, pain-wracked face showed a brief grin. "Hell, you're smart, mister. My boys'll see him driving my buggy . . . and even if they don't blast him there and then, they'll find the money and figure the worst happened."

His wife came out of the saloon, clutching the torn bodice of her dress to her breasts and carrying a wad of something white and frilled in her free hand.

"We have to stop the bleeding, Seth," she said anxiously as she crossed to him. "And get you to a doctor fast."

"No, Rose. A doctor will have to come to me. I won't survive a ride back with this bullet inside of me."

She was down on her haunches beside him, gently easing his clothing away from the wound. Then she cried out in horror at the sight of the gory hole in his bulging white flesh.

"Mister, I don't know what to do for Seth. Can't you help?" she pleaded.

Edge was gazing out along the street and open trail beyond, where some half mile from the western limit of town the saddlehorse had halted. The moving dust of

Floyd's frantic departure was now merged with the distant heat shimmer.

"Only know how to put a bullet into a man, ma'am."

"Well, at least help me to get him in out of the sun?"

From far to the west came a crackle of gunfire, which drew the eyes of Seth and Rose Adams to gaze in the same direction as Edge. And what they saw was a large group of riders emerging from the hazed distance.

"Thank God the men didn't wait until the time you told them, Seth," the woman blurted.

Her husband's grin of relief was short-lived and then he glowered at Edge. "I ought to tell them you were one of the bastards, mister! If you'd made your move earlier, maybe I wouldn't have this lead rotting my insides!"

"No, Seth! You can't! How was he to know they'd—"

"I said I ought to, Rose. But I'm not going to. He kept things from being a lot worse than they are. On your way, stranger."

Edge touched the brim of his hat, turned, and started to walk unhurriedly along the street.

"One more thing, mister!"

Edge paused without turning around.

"I'm obliged to you for what you did do."

The half-breed reached the loose horse in time to catch hold of the reins before the animal was spooked into a bolt by the great mass of men galloping their mounts along the trail. Cowhands like Kelly and Floyd and Harry. In the center of the group was the buggy with one of Adams's men driving it and the bullet-shattered, blood-run corpse of Floyd slumped across the passenger seat. The bulk of the men rode on by, but in the settling dust of their passing a trio slowed and brought their horses to a halt beside Edge as he swung up astride the gray gelding.

"Where the hell you think you're goin'?" one of the three demanded.

"Away from here."

"Says who?"

All three of the grim-faced men dropped hands to drape

the butts of holstered revolvers. But Edge slid his Winchester smoothly into the saddle boot.

"Seth Adams, feller. And it happens to be what I want to do."

"The boss okay?"

"He's got the kind of bellyache a man could die of."

"Mrs. Adams?"

"A bump on the head and the start of an all-over tan is all."

"And what you got to do with all this, stranger?"

The front riders of the group had reached the ghost town. And now one of them came galloping back along the trail, reined in his mount two hundred feet away, cupped his hands to his mouth, and yelled:

"Hey, you guys! The boss says to let him be on his way!"

"Me, I'm just passing through," Edge said to the confused men. "Got so thirsty I came close to dying for want of a drink."

One of the three spit to the side and growled as he shook his head: "I swear, sometimes there just ain't no understandin' what gets into that Seth Adams."

"Well," Edge muttered as the three cowpunchers heeled their horses to ride on by him toward Golden City, "there ain't no doubt about that today. It was a forty-five-caliber bullet."

Chapter Five

AFTER The brutal slaughter of the caged men and the imprisonment of Edge in the wagon, the Price brothers and the women ambled noisily out of sight into the draw. They went two by two, each man with a proprietorial arm draped carnally around the shoulders of his woman. Harlan, Ethan, and Nick attempting with good humor and underlying impatience to snap Avis, Ruby, and Jessica out of their varying states of shock.

Soon, the evilly elated men and the women who seemed to be recovering from the horror of their experiences were far enough into the side cut off the canyon for the sounds of their laughter and talk to be beyond earshot of the single living prisoner: and the half-breed had time to roll and smoke a cigarette in wooden-faced silence before the return of the group was signaled. When, from out of Cibola Draw there drifted into the furnace-hot air of Alamosa Canyon the clop of slow hoofbeats, low talk, and some muted laughter—both male and female—just a few seconds before the Prices and their women reemerged.

Harlan, Ethan, Nick, and Ruby were astride a horse apiece, while Avis and Jessica were doubled up on another. The brothers had changed out of their prison garb into Western-style trail-riding clothes. Neither they nor the women had taken the time to wash up. There was about the women an unkempt and disheveled look, more noticeable maybe because they had appeared so unexpectedly well-turned-out against the rugged backdrop when they'd first showed themselves with the aimed guns. The men looked replete and satisfied with every aspect of their lives.

"Want you to know somethin', asshole!" Nick announced as he and then Avis swung down to the ground at the rear of the wagon where Edge continued to sit in the shaded corner.

"You got yourself a captive audience, kid," the half-breed growled, and it elicited smiles or laughter from everyone except the youngest brother, who scowled resentfully, as if suspecting the joke might be on him.

"I just wanted you to know!" Nick snarled across the sounds of mirth, "that me and my brothers ain't usually through so soon with gettin' off our rocks, you know what I mean?"

Avis had gone to get Edge's chestnut gelding from the shaded area under the canyon wall where the animal had wandered when he was freed from the wagon. This as Nick hitched the reins of his mount to the barred door and slid a Winchester from the saddle boot.

"Been a long time since the last time, and we got other things on our minds, you know what I mean?" Nick pressed on, going to the front of the wagon. "Things to do that can't wait."

"What's with you, little brother?" Harlan rasped, his short-lived merriment giving way to impatience. "You tryin' to make him horny jealous or somethin'?"

Nick pushed his rifle along the seat and hauled Edge's saddle and gear off the footboard—dumped it on the ground with a spit and a grimace. "Hell no, Harlan. But some guys, you know—and he's one of them kind, seems to me—they figure a man who ain't able to keep it up for hours on end . . . well, he ain't so much of a man. I ain't never come across a Mexican who figured any other way."

Nobody offered to help the straining Avis saddle the big gelding with the heavy gear.

"You can sure as hell keep up the talk for hours on friggin' end," Harlan told his youngest brother caustically.

Ethan vented a short, harsh laugh and growled: "He's only half greaser, Nick, so he's likely only half as good as—"

"Mexican, feller," Edge put in.

"Huh?" the perplexed Ethan grunted.

"Half Mexican is what I am. Riles me to hear my Pa's nationality insulted."

Ethan's blue eyes blazed out of a face that was suddenly contorted into animalistic ugliness by the roiling rage deep inside him. He made to snatch the half-breed's Winchester from his saddle boot, but Harlan jerked out a hand and fastened a painful grip on the wrist of the younger man.

"Frig it, Harlan! We ain't nothin' but half-witted if we let this half-assed, half-baked, half-Mex get away with bad mouthin' us like—"

The accepted head of the family withdrew the restraining hand and patted the pocket of his freshly donned shirt which was apparently where he'd transferred the key to the padlocks. "The sonofabitch get away, Ethan? Let him talk if he wants. Say any friggin' thing he wants. He's half everythin' you say. Plus half dead, on account of havin' one foot in the grave. And the more he bad-mouths us, the more fun we'll have killin' the rich sonofabitch and claimin' our inheritance off him, huh?"

The eldest brother's grin of anticipation bore a close resemblance to sexual lust as he outlined his intentions for Edge. Up on the wagon seat, out of everyone's sight, Nick vented several inarticulate sounds of gleeful relish. While Ethan and the three women expressed tacit reluctance to condone Harlan's plan.

There followed perhaps a half minute of near silence while Avis finished readying the gelding for riding and then hauled herself wearily up into the saddle. During this period, Harlan's good humor rapidly diminished into the anger of impatience while Nick whistled a cheerful tune and the others became frowningly resigned to following their older brother's lead.

"Okay, turn this shit-stinkin' rig around and let's move outta here!" Harlan snarled when Avis was ready.

And nothing more was said by anyone—the happy whistling of Nick the only human sound to rise above the clatter of turning wheels, the creak of springs, and the clop of hooves—until the moving cage and its five trailing riders were clear of Alamosa Canyon. Heading due south among the western foothills of the San Mateo Mountains at the same easy pace as always.

Edge moved to the front corner of the wagon opposite the spot where the Comanche had spent so much time. He picked up two canteens from between the sprawled and starting to stink corpses as he altered his position to stay in the sliver of shade provided by the front partition and the roof.

"You won't have time to die of thirst, Edge, so feel free to drink all you want," Harlan offered, spreading a grin back across his fleshy face as he watched the half-breed drink frugally before pushing the stopper back into the neck of a canteen.

Harlan was riding immediately behind Nick's horse. Ethan and Avis rode to his right, and Jessica and Ruby were on his left. The five of them maintained a fairly straight line of advance in back of the wagon that set such an easy pace.

"He's right, mister," Avis confirmed "We don't have far to go."

"Who asked you to butt in?" Ethan snapped.

Avis shrugged. She and the other two women had now dropped all pretense at being in tune with the moods of the Price brothers. Ever since the ride out of the canyon had commenced with Nick concentrating on driving the wagon while his elder brothers gave their gloating attention to Edge, the women had felt it safe to drop their guards and indulge their true feelings. Which ran the gamut from shock and revulsion, remorse and self-pity, to despair and varying degrees of fear that sometimes altered by the moment.

"Cibola Draw was our bolt hole, if you know what I

mean," Harlan explained. "A place for me and my brothers and the boys to come when the strain of earnin' a crust got to be too much." He laughed and leaned forward to look across Ethan at Avis, then glanced to his left at the other women as he sat straight in the saddle again and accepted the cigarette his brother had rolled for him. "Got ourselves an adobe place there filled with all the comforts of home. Women to love, food to eat, tobacco to smoke, liquor to drink. Shelter from the elements—and the friggin' law." He scowled but then grinned. "Even books to read, would you believe? That Rod Grant—him that tried to spring us along with Johnnie Shute just before you butted in and started to screw up, Edge—he used to read a lot of books." Harlan shook his head pensively, then shrugged. "Still, different people got different interests. Anyways, like I was tellin' you . . . Cibola Draw was the place we used to head for when the pace started to get hot and we needed to head for the hills. Me and Ethan and Nick, and whoever we was runnin' with at the time."

He broke off to have his cigarette lighted by Ethan, who had now finished rolling one for himself.

Nick spoke into the pause without glancing back along the side of the wagon: "And you said I could talk for friggin' hours, big brother!"

This said, he started in to whistle again. And sounded more gleeful than before, as if he thought he had scored a point off his dominant brother.

"Harlan's tellin' how smart we been, Nick!" Ethan snapped. "Ain't makin' no excuses to this no-account half-greaser for the goose gettin' cooked soon as it was put in the oven!"

He roared with laughter and reached out to slap Avis's thigh instead of his own.

"Couldn't ever be sure we'd make it to the draw free and clear of the law or bounty hunters and could never trust them we was runnin' with to be so careful as me and my brothers," Harlan put in quickly and testily while Ethan was still enjoying the joke his older brother did not appreciate. "So we never stashed more than day-to-day cash there. The money and other stuff that's gonna buy us a good and easy future, Edge, that's hid some other place. Not far off.''

Harlan began to enjoy himself again, as he concentrated his steady gaze on Edge's bristled, sweat-beaded, dirt-streaked, inscrutable face. The half-breed was sitting on his haunches braced in the angle of the corner, swaying with the motion of the wagon rolling over uneven ground. This guy was like the Comanche and like Rankinn and like himself, Price reflected. But then revised that estimation, because of factors it irritated him to admit. Like the Injun was all. Chester Rankinn and himself and thousands of that ilk sometimes came close, but they were never entirely a match for Edge and the Injun and the handful who shared their capability for hiding their true emotions behind an impenetrable mask of impassivity. Perhaps because, Price pondered with a grimace, there was no pretense involved: such men might actually feel the nothing they showed whether they be enduring the worst of privations or engaged in the utmost of pleasures. Shit, if that was so, he sure had no reason to envy such coldhearted, unfeeling, emotionless sonsofbitches. And now he rekindled the warmth of feeling that came with a sense of dominance over lesser beings and melded it with something akin to contempt for his prime victim as he went on to explain:

''Knew when Rod and Johnnie showed up that the women would still be at the draw, Edge. See, Avis is Rod's sister. Wouldn't take off until she was sure somethin' bad had happened to Rod. And Ruby and Jessica, well them and Avis have always stuck closer together than most families—except for this one, of course. Knew the females would be watchin' real anxious for us to come home. And wouldn't trust what was happenin' when they seen a stranger up on the driver's seat.''

The ice-blue eyes moved fractionally between the narrowed lids as Edge looked fleetingly at the redheaded woman. And saw again, for an instant, a glimmer of apology in her dark eyes. She offered no response to his almost imperceptible nod—a gesture meant to convey his understanding of her fervid eagerness to kill him at the start, when she had immediately assumed Edge was responsible for her brother's absence.

"And the beautiful little sweethearts did just like I figured they would!" Harlan crowed, and spread a patronizing grin over the trio of gloomy-faced women. And it was only then that he became aware of their uneasy despondency. The volatile man's grin was swept off his face as he snatched away the cigarette from his mouth, hurled it at the ground, and snarled: "What the frig's the matter with you people? The friggin' bad times are over and the good times are gonna start to roll! We're all through with this lousy piece of dried-up, half-dead country! Them bastards that planned on hangin' us can have it all to themselves! We're gonna get us our stake from where it's hid, and then we're gonna head for where the livin's easy! Gonna travel first class and live so high off the friggin' hog we'll get dizzy just lookin' down on all them assholes that'll be runnin' around doin' what we pay them to do!"

"*Yyyiiiippppeeeee!*" Nick yelled, drawing out each letter and raising his tone to a higher pitch.

"You bet, and how!" the slightly more articulate Ethan rasped through teeth clenched in a grin of gleeful excitement.

"There ain't nothin' we Prices can't do! For ourselves . . ." Harlan grinned again now, an expression of pleasure but with an underlying glint of warning deep in his blue eyes as he glanced at each sullenly dejected woman in turn before adding: ". . . and for them that are with us."

"And maybe we'll even stand treat for one that ain't with us, huh Harlan?" Ethan rasped, and blew a stream of tobacco smoke between teeth that were now displayed by lips drawn back in the line of a scornful sneer. "Our jailbird, here? Real mean and quiet, ain't he? You reckon he'd get happy and sing if we bought a gilded cage to put him in?"

Ethan roared with laughter. And Harlan found himself caught up in the euphoria that his brothers had generated out of his calculated attempt to brighten the women's mood. And staring through the bars and across the sprawl of foul-smelling, fly-infested corpses at the taciturn Edge with much the same brand of joyfully triumphant condescension as the brother riding at his side, he growled:

"Hey, we sure should do that, Ethan! Wouldn't want it to get put around that when we got rich us Prices were cheap: Cheep-cheep—you get it, huh?"

Now Harlan tossed back his head, turned his face to the cloudless sky, and vented a gust of harsh laughter. Uttering a sound that for perhaps a full second was loud enough to blot out all others in the immediate vicinity of the sluggishly moving wagon. Before, as Ethan gaped his mouth to join in the laughter but kept his brutal gaze fixed on the impassive face of Edge, the blast of a shotgun exploded and reverberated within the tension-walled confines of this shifting tableau. And one laugh ended and another failed to start when the youngest brother toppled off the side of the seat and fell hard to the ground beside the wagon that did not stop. The corpse came to rest on its back, to reveal to all watching eyes that its face had been reduced to a crimson pulp that seethed and bubbled for several seconds, pieces of dark-colored shot and starkly white shards of bone floating in the blood. Flies swarmed away from the old dead to forage ravenously on the fresh corpse.

"Nick sure got it," Edge drawled.

The Quiet Gun

At the conclusion of The Guilty Ones, *Edge rode out of the middle-western town of Greenville. In the next book of the series,* The Frightened Gun, *he has reached the Sarcobatus Flats region to the east of present-day Nevada's state line with California. His journey took him far to the south of the direct route between these two points and a part of the trip was made by stage.*

IT was three o'clock in the afternoon, and old Miles Moran who had control of the six-horse team hauling the Concord coach of the South-Western Territorial Stage Line was trying to make up lost time. He was yelling at the team and cracking his whip above their backs to demand full speed along the high trail that cut through the Mule Mountains above the Arizona Territory border with Mexico.

The red-bearded, watery-eyed Moran was grim faced as he strove to make good the thirty-five minutes wasted by a delay in Bisbee. Up on the box seat beside him, Rick Reese grinned his enjoyment of the high speed which caused the ancient Concord to roll and pitch and raise the gray dust that stretched out behind in a long cloud. With one hand gripping the rail and the other fisted around the frame of a double-barrel shotgun, the good-looking young guard chewed tobacco, every once in a while spitting a stream of dark-colored juice over the side of the speeding stage.

"You're doin' fine, Mr. Moran!" Reese yelled as a landmark on the Bisbee—Benson trail—a grotesquely eroded pinnacle of rock—showed ahead.

"What's that you say?" the old driver shouted.

"Keep goin' like this and we'll get to Hunter's Pass right on time!"

Moran nodded and brushed his sweat-beaded brow along a forearm. "Just hope the passengers appreciate what I'm doin' for them, Rick!"

There were four people enduring the discomforts of the ride inside the stage. In the left corner seat facing forward was the black-haired, blue-eyed, and beautiful Linda Goodman. She was in her early twenties, and the only thing she was appreciating as the wheels of the Concord seemed to jolt into every pothole on the trail was the reassuring grip of Lieutenant Sherman Jackson's hand over her own.

The army officer at her side wore the uniform of a cavalryman with the insignia of the Fifth Company stitched to his tunic sleeves. About five years older than the woman, he stood five feet ten inches tall and had a well-built frame. His hair was light brown—almost blonde—but the neat moustache that decorated his sun-burnished, pleasant-featured face had grown gray. While he held the woman's hand with his left, his right pressed with greater force against the two bulging sacks marked PROPERTY OF THE UNITED STATES ARMY that rested on the seat beside him. There was a look of disapproval on his face which deepened each time Linda vented a low-voiced response to a jarring lurch of the stage. But he never verbalized his feelings—perhaps since it was his late arrival at the Bisbee stage line depot that had caused the delayed departure for which Moran was now attempting to compensate.

On the right rear-facing seat was an eighteen-year-old Chinese girl, Lee Tu. She sat with her arms akimbo, pressing her slender body hard into the angle of the corner as she peered fixedly out the window at the dust-blurred panorama of barren ridges which restricted the view from her side of the coach. Her round, drab-complexioned face was expressionless; and she seemed to accept the rigors of the hell-for-leather race through the mountains with indifference.

In much the same manner as the tall, lean man seated directly across the aisle from Linda Goodman perhaps. But Edge's expression could not be seen, since his black Stetson was tilted forward to conceal his face. He was slumped in his corner seat, feet braced on the bucking floor, hands interlocked under the long hair at the back of his neck. He rode easily with each roll, pitch, and lurch of the Concord: as if he were asleep and comfortably unaware of the frenetic motion and harsh sounds of the hurtling stage.

"Good grief!" Linda exclaimed, her voice close to a scream, as she pressed her sweating face to the window. "Look, Sherman, we could all be killed!"

The lieutenant leaned across her to peer at the reason for her fear. As Edge pushed the Stetson back on top of his head and glanced down into the boulder-strewn bottom of a 150-foot-deep gorge which cut through the mountains less than six feet away from the thundering hooves of the horses and the spinning wheels of the Concord.

"Just think how often a stage must plunge off this cliff!" the woman gasped.

"Figure it would just be the once, lady," the half-breed told her evenly. And rasped the back of a hand over his bristled jaw as he shifted his gaze away from the chasm.

"I'm sorry, sir?" Lieutenant Jackson said. "I didn't catch what you—"

Linda Goodman interrupted with a grimace: "The *gentleman* attempted a joke in poor taste, Sherman. Any stage that went off this cliff would, of course, never—"

She curtailed the rest of her thought with a choked cry as a fusillade of gunshots sounded above the clatter of hooves, creak of timbers, and rattle of wheelrims. And then this din was increased as new elements were added to it—the screech of brake blocks and the shouts of men.

"Sherman!" Linda screamed, clinging to the soldier like a child to its mother as the abrupt halting of the stage caused it to veer violently from side to side on its skidding wheels.

And the fear which was plain to see on her suddenly colorless face was even more blatant on Jackson's features as he struggled to shake free of her and fumbled at the fastened flap of his holster. This as Lin Tu clutched at the window frame with one hand and crossed herself with the other moving her lips in silent prayer.

Edge yelled, "Leave it be, Lieutenant!" The stage came to a halt, the springs creaked, and the horses snorted. And into the stretched second of tense silence that followed, the half-breed added softly, "For now, huh?"

"Everybody out from inside!" a man ordered.

"Ain't aimin' to hurt no one!" another assured.

"Easy up there, you guys!" a third warned.

The Concord had come to a standstill with its left side tight to the base of an escarpment, some thirty feet from the lip of the sheer drop down to the gorge. Into this area between the coach and the precipice, as the dust from the frantic halt settled, rode three masked men holding cocked Winchesters. Two of them leveled their rifles at the windows of the stage while the third angled his up at Moran and Rich Reese.

"Oh, good grief!" Linda Goodman gasped.

Edge pressed down on the handle, swung open the door, and stepped down from the stage. Then he turned to help out the American woman.

"No, old-timer!" the central of the three mounted men snapped. "You and the guard stay up there!"

"We ain't shippin' nothin' that—"

"Shuddup, old man!" the rider on the right snarled as he raked the barrel of his rifle away from the men on the high seat to aim it again, like the others, at the door of the Concord. This as Edge reached inside the stage to grip the forearm of the reluctant Linda Goodman. He jerked her outside, then had to encircle her waist with an arm to keep her from pitching to the trail when her booted feet thudded down beside him.

"What the hell?" the centrally placed masked man snarled as the woman screamed her pain and alarm.

Edge released his hold on the woman and delved into a shirt pocket for the makings. Said evenly; "Figure her beau won't risk pulling his gun with the lady out here in the open."

The obvious leader of the trio nodded, and his green eyes above the kerchief mask lit with a smile of approval. "You're smart, mister."

"Part of the reason I got to be thirty-eight, feller."

"Stay smart and maybe you'll make it to thirty-nine. Ease the gun outta the holster and toss it over to the side."

"Rest of you people inside, get the hell out like you already been told!" the man on the right ordered as he once more swung his Winchester across and up to aim at the two men on the high seat.

Lieutenant Jackson emerged from the stage, venom sparking his brown eyes as he shifted his unblinking gaze from the masked men to Edge and back again.

"The gun, soldier," the man on the left said pointedly, as Lin Tu climbed down from the Concord, her face set in its familiar expression of resigned acceptance of whatever destiny might hold in store for her.

Tight-lipped, Sherman Jackson copied Edge's action of sliding the revolver from his holster and arcing it ten feet off to the side.

"Where is it, Lieutenant?"

"Where's what?"

Edge glanced up at the high seat and saw that Moran and Reese were in rigid attitudes, arms raised above their heads. The young guard's shotgun was resting across his thighs.

"That your ring on her finger, soldier?" the man on the right growled, and again altered the aim of his Winchester.

"Please don't take it!" Linda Goodman pleaded. "We've only been engaged for a week."

She clung more tightly to Jackson and brought up her left hand to press the diamond ring on its third finger to her full lips.

"Jewelry we don't want," the man in the middle said coldly. "The army money we do."

"And if we don't get it, you'll have a real short engagement, lady," the man on the right warned, emphasizing the threat by bringing his rifle up to his shoulder and sighting along the barrel at the woman.

"No, Dan! Pete said no killin'!"

All eyes darted to stare at Rick Reese as he blurted the entreaty.

"You crazy bastard!" the leader of the masked men snapped at the guard as the youngster expressed abject fear.

"Go bring the money, Ross," the man on the left ordered, gesturing with his rifle. "You people, move away from the door."

"Be inside, I reckon," the holdup man in the center added.

Dan Ross slid from his saddle, canting the Winchester confidently to his shoulder as he swaggered toward the stage. The four passengers moved out of his path.

"You're right, Pete," he called as, without entering the stage, he reached inside and dragged out the pair of bulky sacks with U.S. Army markings that Jackson had been gripping so tighly. They were obviously weighty, and they clinked as he hefted them.

"Why, boy?" Moran asked throatily, as if it required a great deal of effort for him to pose the query to Reese.

"Because!" the young guard replied, and the force of the word shot the wad of tobacco out of his mouth. Then he stared anxiously down at the masked men to demand: "Pete, you'll have to take me with you now!"

"Like frig we will!" Ross countered.

Reese, his anxiety expanding, suddenly stood up. His hands were still held high, as if he had forgotten about them. The shotgun slid off his thighs and thudded to the ground, exploding a billow of dust. "But you gotta! Now they know I was the one what told you—"

"You opened your big mouth, Reese!" Ross yelled. And vented a string of obscenities as he stumbled under the weight of the coin-filled sacks and dropped them and his rifle.

"Ain't got a horse for you, Rick," the leader pointed out flatly.

"Then I'll take one of—"

Reese went for the Army Colt in his holster rigged for a left-handed cross draw. The two men still astride their mounts hesitated; aware of the fact that in moving from the doorway of the Concord, Edge and Jackson had stepped closer to the spot where their discarded guns lay in the dust.

Staring wide-eyed at the men in the saddles, Reese failed to see Dan Ross get his hands on the shotgun that was closer to him than the fallen rifle beside the sacks. Lying full length on the ground and with both arms at full stretch, Ross angled the shotgun skywards and squeezed both triggers the instant the two hammers were cocked.

Reese was dead when a nervous spasm of his finger sent a bullet blasting from the muzzle of his revolver: the crack of the Colt's firing hardly discernible in the wake of the double-barrel gun discharging both loads in unison.

As the twin reports resounded among the ridges of the Mule Mountains, the buckshot ripped flesh from the chest and face of Reese, sending a shower of blood and tissue toward the sun-bright Arizona sky. Sheened white bone showed through the crimson pulp of Reese's torso and head; then his unfeeling corpse crumpled and tipped forward as his killer rolled clear.

"Pete, I'm hit!" one of the two mounted men cried, capturing all attention from the shattered remains of Reese. The man continued to aim his rifle, but one-handed now, the other clutched to his belly. Blood erupted from the wound of Reese's dying shot, squeezed out through the cracks between his fingers.

"Sonofabitch!" his mounted partner groaned.

"A gutshot, Pete," the injured man moaned, swaying in the saddle. "I can't ride."

Pete's eyes above his mask were momentarily clouded by indecision. But he never shifted his gaze away from the quartet of passengers grouped at the rear of the stalled stage.

"A horse you can't ride, maybe," he muttered. "Put the sacks back aboard, Dan. Get down off there, old man."

"We takin' the stage, Pete?" Dan Ross asked eagerly.

"Damn right. Help Jeb inside. Then grab the loose guns and load them. Hitch the horses to the rear. Move again, you people."

Once more, Edge was the first to comply and the other three passengers followed him. Then were joined by Moran, who seemed stunned by Rich Reese's guilty revelation and violent death.

A trail of blood spots marked the painful progress of Jeb from where he had been shot to the side of the Concord. Insignificant compared with that which had poured from the corpse. But Jeb was obviously badly hurt.

In less than a minute, Ross had done as instructed; then he climbed inside with the wounded holdup man. Pete got up on the box seat, kicked off the brake lever, and urged the team into movement. He was no longer concerned with the group of five people on the ground who cracked their eyes and compressed their lips against the assault of swirling dust that rose in the wake of the departing stage.

"Damn it to hell!" Lieutenant Sherman Jackson snarled as the Concord clattered out of sight around a curve in the cliff. "I'm responsible for that money!"

"I told Rick's Pa on his deathbed that I'd look out for the boy," Moran murmured miserably.

Eyes blazing with fury and hands trembling as she clenched and unclenched them, Linda Goodman cried accusingly. "Good grief, he fixed for us to be held up! And we could all have been killed because of that!"

The sounds of the stage faded from earshot, as Moran,

his eyes more watery than usual with tears that threatened to spill from them, shook his head and countered: "Rick must've had good reason, miss."

For the first time since she had seen the blood and tissue explode into the air, Linda looked at the spread-eagled body that was now infested with flies gorging on the rapidly congealing blood. "You can't make excuses for a rotten, low-down—"

She choked on the words, then suffered a violent reaction to the gruesome sight and whirled away, staggering to the base of the cliff where she bent double and began to vomit.

"Linda!" Jackson choked, and lunged toward her.

"Not just speaking ill of the dead," Edge murmured as he took a match from a shirt pocket and raised a foot to strike it on his boot heel. Lit the cigarette angled from a side of his mouth.

"He has been severely punished for the disgrace of his misdeed," the Oriental girl said, seemingly as unmoved by the violence as the tall, lean man at her side. But she crossed herself in the Catholic manner.

This as Edge glanced at the pulpy mass of Reese's face and spat into the dust and Miles Moran sighed and murmured; "He sure enough lost face, lady."

The half-breed asked of the stage driver; "We still closer to Bisbee than anyplace else, feller?"

A shake of the head. "The Hunter's Pass way station is only about ten miles up the trail, mister."

"Is there a telegraph there?" Jackson asked, his concern for Linda Goodman replaced by a greater anxiety now that his fiancée had finished retching.

"No, sir. There ain't. But there's food and water and shelter while we wait for the Tombstone depot to send people lookin' to find out where the hell our stage is."

"How about horses?"

"Mendez has a fresh team at the way station, but—"

"No buts, mister," the lieutenant cut in. "I have to get word to the army or the law about this robbery as fast as possible. If that money isn't recovered on the double, all hell will break loose. Let's go. Come on, Linda, pull yourself together.''

"First I gotta bury Rick," Moran announced flatly.

"The hell with that. The buzzards and coyotes will take care of him." Jackson turned to look at Edge and posed: "Sir?"

"Don't ask him for help!" Linda snapped as she rubbed at her vomit-run jaw with a handkerchief. "He was worse than useless when we were held up."

"I figure over the side will suit everyone who cares, Lieutenant," the half-breed answered. "He won't exactly be buried, but he'll be under this patch of ground."

Jackson looked at the old-timer, commanding rather than requesting approval, as Edge moved to grasp the corpse's wrists.

Moran thudded a boot heel against the rock-hard ground and reluctantly allowed: "Reckon it's the best we can do for him."

"Better than he deserves," Linda snapped.

Her fiancé picked up Reese's ankles, and then he and Edge carried the sagging corpse to the top of the gorge, swung the dead weight twice, and hurled it out and down. Neither man remained to watch the body corkscrew through the hot air and impact with bone-crunching force on the rocks at the base of the drop.

"Shouldn't we say somethin'?" Moran asked.

Edge glanced over his shoulder and growled, "Wherever you're headed for, Reese, have a good trip."

Lin Tu crossed herself once more and spoke a few words of what might have been a prayer in the Spanish language.

"Right," Jackson announced. "Now if everybody's ready to move, let's go."

He took Linda's arm to urge her along the trail between the tracks of the Concord's wheelrims in the dust. Edge and Moran fell in behind the couple, and the Chinese girl brought up the rear.

"What kind of hell, Lieutenant?" the half-breed asked after perhaps five minutes of silence during which they rounded the curving cliff and began to climb a gentle grade.

"Excuse me, sir?"

"If it's too long before the money's missed . . . what kind of hell will break loose?"

"That's confidential information, sir."

"Good grief, it's hot," Linda complained, fanning a hand in front of her face.

"It'll get hotter, and then it'll rain hard as it can in this neck of the woods," Miles Moran warned her absently, peering morosely eastward.

The mid-afternoon sky was still a brilliant blue with just a few scattered flat-bottomed clouds overhead. The sun inching across the western dome of the sky was as harshly glaring as it had been all day. But beyond the eastern ridges of the Mule Mountains where Moran was looking, a cloud bank was building up. Gray and forbidding.

"Let it be soon," the hatless woman in the high-necked, long-sleeved green dress said with a sigh. And, judging from the way the skirts of the dress flared and the manner in which her upper body maintained its impressive curves, it was not just the outer garment that was causing her discomfort.

In his full walking-out uniform, the lieutenant was also unsuitably attired for a long trek across unshaded country on a hot afternoon.

Except that Lin Tu, like Linda Goodman, had left her hat aboard the stage, the Oriental girl was better prepared for the hardships of the trail. She was wearing a simple, white, loose-fitting garment. When it did contour her slender body and limbs as she moved, there seemed to be nothing between its fabric and her skin.

Miles Moran, like Edge, wore a wide-brimmed hat, shirt, and pants.

"That why so much army money was sent by stage, Lieutenant?" Edge asked as he arced the cigarette butt away after another long period of silence.

"What?" Jackson was again nudged out of his private world of anxiety by the half-breed's voice. "Yes . . . Yes, sir. Even at Fort Buchanan only a privileged few know about the money and the reason for it being sent north.''

''Silver dollars, I guess? Figure about five thousand in each sack?''

Jackson sighed. ''That's right, sir.''

The lieutenant had not turned around when he answered Edge. Now Linda swung her head to show the half-breed the grimace set on her sweat-tacky face.

''Why are you so interested, mister?'' she demanded. ''Did you have designs on the money and get beaten to the punch. Or do you—''

''Linda!'' Jackson censured.

''No, lady,'' Edge answered, his voice evenly pitched but his slitted blue eyes glinting dangerously. ''I never have been in the robbery business.''

''I'm sorry, sir,'' the cavalryman apologized, taking hold of Linda's arm and forcing her to face front again.

''Well, why *is* he so interested?'' she muttered, disgruntled. And drew no response.

It was the Chinese girl who ended another long silence when she said, ''I think you are part Mexican, Mr. Edge?''

''A country you know? You pray in the language.''

She nodded and her short black hair did not move, hugging her head like a peakless cap. ''My father, he was the only Chinese Christian priest in Mexico. I was born and grew up there. Far in the south. Chiapas. You know that part?''

''Priests ain't supposed to marry and have kids,'' Miles Moran growled.

Edge resumed his interrupted surveillance of the surrounding hills, aware that this was Apache country. Aware, too, of his empty holster. And, naggingly conscious, also, of the mistake he had made in trusting the stage guard to watch for a surprise attack. By Apaches or whoever.

''My father was not converted to the faith until after my mother died, sir,'' Lin Tu said to Moran.

''You're a long way from home,'' Edge said.

''I have no home, sir. My father was murdered by bandits. I came north to look for a husband.''

Linda Goodman laughed. "Hey, Edge, I think maybe you've just had a proposal!" she snorted.

"I ain't no seconder to that kind of motion," the half-breed growled.

"I am just speaking to fill the time," Lin Tu added quickly.

"Then best find another subject, Lin dear," the American woman suggested as she directed a mocking grin at Edge.

"Tu," the half-breed said.

"What?"

"Orientals reverse first and second names, lady. It's Miss Lin or, if you want to be friendly, just Tu."

"Pardon my ignorance," Linda snapped, with a defensive sneer of annoyance and contempt.

"No sweat."

"I'm drenched in it."

"It's just a manner of speaking, my dear," Jackson offered placatingly.

"Well, I don't like his manner!"

Jackson glanced back at Edge and this time confined his apology for the woman to an expression of mild helplessness.

Linda ran a hand across the nape of her neck under her hair and muttered, "When's that damn rain you promised coming, driver?"

"About nightfall, I reckon," Moran answered with a glance toward the slowly building cloud bank in the east. "And when it comes, Miss Goodman, you'll wish it hadn't. If we're still out in the open."

The bearded old-timer's weather forecast proved correct. The sun remained hot and glaring for the rest of the afternoon as the group penetrated further into the mountains, infrequently stopping to rest at the insistence of the constantly complaining Linda Goodman. But, as evening approached, the cloud bank suddenly spread, to catch up with and overhaul the sun before it dipped beyond the western ridges. Then the sky was blanketed with gray and the belt of torrential rain was quick to lash at the arid ground.

Initially the storm was welcomed by the hot, weary, and

thirsty group. But as full night came to the Mule Mountains, the cold and the incessant beat of the downpour caused as much discomfort as had the blistering sun of the day. The needling drops stung their flesh, soaked their clothing, and turned the once rock-hard trail into a morass of clinging mud that sucked at their booted feet. And finding shelter from the rain turned out to be more difficult than locating shade from the blazing sun.

As they left the cover of a rock overhang, the half-breed made to follow Jackson and the two women who were now breathlessly eager to reach the Hunter's Pass way station which the old-timer had said was just about a mile distant from here. But the morose Miles Moran caught hold of his shirtsleeve.

"Mr. Edge?"

"Yeah?"

"I been thinkin'. Money interests you, don't it?"

"What it can buy does."

"I ain't got much in the Bisbee bank. Drivin' a stage don't pay real well. But I could give you a thousand dollars."

"Obliged."

"It's my life's savin's, mister."

"Dead or alive?" Edge asked as he moved out into the full force of the downpour.

Moran hurried to catch up with him. "You ain't takin' me serious, mister. Rick's old man and me, we was the best of buddies. Rick done wrong, and ain't no one more shocked by that than me. But, like I already said, he must've had good reason. I didn't look out for him the way I promised his Pa, and it's on account of that I want to see them fellers that killed Rick brought to justice. I'm too damn old to do it myself. But you . . . you're the kinda feller that could do it. The army money—payroll or whatever the hell it is—you got that on your mind. And them killers got it. I'm just sayin' that if you go after it, I'll pay you an extra thousand for gettin' the killers to boot."

"Ain't payroll money, feller."

They had caught up with the other three, and, as if ashamed of the offer he had made to Edge, Moran fell silent. Nobody else spoke until Lieutenant Jackson yelled excitedly:

"Look, isn't that a light?"

"Be the way station," the bearded old-timer muttered as Jackson, Linda Goodman, and Lin Tu broke into an awkward run through the mud. "Some hot grub and coffee will go down well," Moran said and added a stream of saliva to the sodden ground as the three moved out of earshot. Then added: "I reckon the lieutenant stole that money, Edge. Figured to desert the army and set up house with the woman. Reason he's so damn nervy and she's so grouchy. Had it made and now it's all gone. What do you think, mister?"

"That some hot grub and coffee will go down well," the half-breed answered as he peered at the long, low, single-story adobe building sited to the left of the trail at the base of a fifty-foot-high cliff. There was just one lighted window, to the right of the door where Jackson and the two women stood, the man banging the side of a fist against the panel.

"Go to hell," Moran snarled.

"Been headed in that direction for a long time, feller."

The half-breed and the old-timer joined the group in front of the way station just as the door was swung open and a wedge of yellow light shafted out into the night.

"Been expectin' you folks," Dan Ross growled in greeting. Then sneered as he added: "Mr. Cannon says I have to invite you in."

If anyone felt any trepidation at the sight of the now unmasked Ross swinging the dead Reese's shotgun in their direction, it was quickly overcome by the prospect of warmth and shelter behind the forty-year-old, short but well-built man.

"Cut the cackle and get 'em inside!" Pete Cannon snarled from where he sat beside a makeshift bed comprised of an armchair and a bench on which the wounded Jeb lay.

"You figured there was a good chance they'd be here, didn't you?" Miles Moran rasped at Edge from the side of his grimacing mouth as the sodden group moved into the way station.

"Horse or stage," Edge muttered, eyes raking the scene, "a man with a forty five-caliber slug in his belly can't travel far."

The room was a public one, with a glowing stove in a corner and tables and chairs scattered over the bare floor. The roof was made of timber and the walls of whitewashed adobe. It was just a place where stage passengers could rest up and perhaps eat a meager meal during the brief time it took for a team to be changed.

The unconscious Jeb, who looked enough like Pete Cannon to be his elder brother, had been made relatively comfortable close to the stove. Both men were in their early forties, close to six feet tall, and lean of build. Jeb was balding and had a small black moustache, while Pete still had a lot of slicked-down hair of the same color. Jeb seemed to be naked to the waist under the blanket which draped him, but Pete Cannon and Dan Ross were still attired in the black shirts, pants, and kerchiefs they had worn at the holdup. The only gun in evidence, apart from that stolen from the dead Reese, was the Army Colt in the tied-down holster of the uninjured Cannon. Ross did not wear a gunbelt.

Juan Mendez was unarmed. He was a broad-shouldered, pot-bellied man approaching fifty. A little over five feet tall, he had a receding hairline above a round face set in a scowl of resentment as he watched the newcomers enter. He wore a white shirt and pants.

"Howdy, Juan," Moran greeted the Mexican as he headed for the stove, rubbing his hands together and then extending them toward the heat.

Mender grunted: "These *hombres* got guns so I give them what they want. But I don't run no charity place here. Anythin' you want, you pay for."

"You can see why he's called the Miser of Hunter's

Pass,'' Moran muttered as all the new arrivals except Edge gathered at the stove.

"Coffee and hot food, feller," the half-breed said as he dropped into an armchair just inside the doorway.

"Hey, *I* got the gun, mister!" Ross snarled, and swung the twin muzzles at Edge. "You don't give no orders!"

Edge looked from Ross to the Cannon brothers and dug the makings from his shirt pocket, the tobacco and papers and matches dry inside their pouch. "Feller with the bullet in his guts is going to die pretty soon, so he doesn't matter. You and you"—he stabbed a brown-skinned finger at Pete and Ross—"had better not aim a gun at me again. Unless you squeeze the trigger. Try to warn people. Both of you made the mistake once. Don't do it again."

"Why, you—" Ross blurted, and thumbed back both hammers.

"Quit it, Dan!" Pete Cannon snarled. "Tough talk don't hurt no one. You some kinda doctor, mister?"

Edge lit the cigarette. "No, feller. I just have a nose for infection. Ain't the first time I've smelled gangrene in a wound."

"Edge is right," Jackson agreed. "I had two years medical training before I enlisted in the army and—"

"Right," Pete Cannon cut in, and rose to his feet. "You take care of my brother, soldier boy."

"But I—"

"I ain't askin' for no miracles," Cannon growled. "Jeb's gonna die for sure. I didn't need him to tell me that. But you oughta be able to doctor him up so it don't hurt so much while he's cashin' in."

Jackson vented a sigh of relief. "I don't have any drugs, of course, but I can do my best."

As the cavalryman moved toward the patient, Linda Goodman turned to Mendez. "What about the hot coffee and food?" she demanded. "I'm chilled through to the bone."

"I got a rule," the Mexican answered, the scowl still firmly in place as he stared at Lin Tu. "I don't ever serve no colored people here."

"That's fine, because none of us are cannibals, feller," Edge said. "Animal meat will be good."

Chile beef was what the others had eaten, and the smell of its cooking still permeated the air along with the stink of decomposing flesh from Jeb Cannon's wound and the new odors from the rapidly drying clothes of the latecomers to the way station.

"Do like they want, Mendez," Cannon ordered, watching with a grimace as Sherman Jackson started to remove the bloody pus-encrusted deressing from the belly of his brother. This as Ross dropped heavily into a chair against the wall that gave him an unobstructed view of everyone in the room. His displeasure with the situation was plain to see on his bristled face.

"How long before Jeb kicks off?" he asked as the Mexican shuffled out of the room and Linda and Tu sank gratefully onto chairs. Moran remained standing in front of the stove, his rigid back turned toward everyone.

"He won't make it until morning is my opinion," Jackson answered, gingerly uncovering the festered bullet wound and flinching at the sight of it.

"You got the rest of your life to spend the money, Dan," Pete Cannon said sourly. "For the half share of Jeb's part, allow him the little time he's got left without begrudgin' it him."

Ross snorted.

Jackson said, "I need boiled water, clean rags, and some whiskey if there's any."

"You hear that, Mendez?" Cannon called.

"I hear. Whiskey, it costs money." This from the kitchen, where the Mexican had lit a kerosene lamp.

"They can afford it, Juan," Moran yelled. "They got ten grand. Nearly as much as you, I reckon."

Ross laughed at the stage driver's sarcasm. Then: "You sound jealous, old-timer. Maybe sorry it was your partner and not you that—"

Moran whirled to glare at Ross and counter: "Jealous of a stupid dead man?"

"Stupid enough to get himself killed," Ross taunted.

"He would have got his share if he'd done as he was told," Pete Cannon growled. "It wasn't planned for anyone to get hurt."

The effort of stoking his hatred for Ross and Cannon seemed to drain the bearded old man who sank into a chair and croaked: "Why?"

"Because he was fixin' to blast me, lunkhead!" the man with the shotgun snapped.

Juan Mendez brought a pail of steaming water into the room, slopped some over the brim as he set it down, and muttered, "I'll bring the other stuff you want."

"I mean why did Rick help you?"

"He needed the money, old-timer," Cannon answered, and sat down with a nod of approval at the gentleness with which Jackson had begun his treatment of Jeb. "More than the stage line paid him. Somethin' about a girl."

Moran shook his head reflectively. Then glared at Linda Goodman and rasped, "Quite a coincidence, I reckon."

"What the hell's that supposed to mean?" the woman flung at him.

"Moran's one of the great thinkers of our time, lady," Edge put in. "Figures the lieutenant stole the money from the army so that you and he could lead the good life."

"He's wrong!" Jackson snarled as Mendez delivered the bandages and whiskey.

Edge directed his glinting gaze at Cannon, who shrugged and said: "Just heard from Reese that the army was shippin' some hard cash by the civilian stage. Details didn't matter."

"Tell them, Sherman," Linda instructed.

"It's a military secret," he answered as he began to bathe the wound.

"What's the whiskey for?" Ross asked.

"If he comes to, it'll help ease the pain."

Talk finished and the beat of the rain on the roof of the way station became less forceful. Juan Mendez clattered pots and pans in the kitchen, from which came the appetizing aromas of brewing coffee and cooking chile. Jackson completed his work on the wound, covered Jeb Cannon with the blanket again, and straightened up with a sigh.

"Just where will all hell break loose, feller?" Edge asked, crushing out his cigarette on the arm of the chair.

"Just why are you so interested?" Jackson said wearily as the Mexican entered the room carrying a tray loaded with cups of coffee. And Jeb Cannon recovered consciousness with a shrill scream of agony; drawing all eyes except those of one man toward him as the sound from his throat blotted out every other.

The exception was Miles Moran, who leaped from his chair with the agility of a man half his years, lunged across the intervening space, and got a one-handed grip on the shotgun before Ross realized what was happening.

"Pete!" Ross shrieked.

Cannon wrenched his eyes away from his pain-wracked brother, half whirled, drew his Colt, and fired. But it was not Moran who took the bullet. Juan Mendez had backed into the line of fire as he attempted to get clear of it. And he vented a Spanish curse as he dropped the tray and was sent into a half turn by the impact of the lead tearing into his upper arm. This while the bearded old-timer went down under a cracking blow from the twin barrels of the shotgun as Ross regained control of the weapon.

Then Ross, his face contorted by fury, hit Moran again as he rolled to the floor. And was about to follow it with a third clubbing blow when Cannon roared, "Quit it, Dan! Get the friggin' woman!"

For a stretched second, nobody moved. Jeb Cannon was unconscious again. Moran, blood oozing from a gash in his temple, was also out. Mendez was in a half crouch, clutching at his wounded arm. Edge and Tu looked at each other with expressionless eyes—both having seen, as the blanket slid off Jeb, the Colt in his holster. Jackson and Pete Cannon stared at the open door of the way station, through which Linda had powered under cover of the shooting of one man and the clubbing of another.

"I'll get the bitch!" Ross yelled, and started forward.

"No!" Cannon countered.

The Chinese girl posed a silent query with her dark

156

eyes, and Edge responded with an almost imperceptible nod.

"What the hell can she do?" the calmed-down Cannon asked the still-enraged Ross. Then both men turned their guns on Tu as she stood up.

"He should not catch cold as well," the Oriental girl explained as she moved to the improvised bed and covered Jeb again with the blanket.

"Linda could get lost and die of exposure on a night like this!" Jackson yelled. "I'll go and bring her back!"

"Stay there, soldier!" Ross ordered, leveling the shot-gun at him. Then he displaced his scowl with a grin to add: "You find her, maybe you and her'll take off and try to make it without the money. How about the hard man goes, Pete?" He jerked his head toward Edge. "Give him, say, thirty minutes? Then start blastin' people if he ain't back by then. One every fifteen minutes to keep it interestin'?"

"The hell with that," Cannon muttered. "She can't do nothin' to hurt us out there."

"She can do somethin' back here," Ross countered. And he scowled at Tu who was crouched beside Jeb Cannon. "Ain't a lot of difference between the chink and a boy. But that other one, she's a whole lot of all woman. Plain to see."

"You lay a finger on—" Jackson started.

"You ain't in no position to tell me what to do, soldier!" Ross hurled at him. "And you neither, Pete!" he went on as Cannon made to continue the argument. "I've agreed to stay in this stinkin' place until Jeb kicks off. Only thing that made it worthwhile stayin' is gone now. And if Edge don't go bring her back, I'm takin' off, Pete. And I figure you'll have some trouble ridin' herd over this bunch on your own."

Cannon was angry, then frustrated, finally resigned to losing out to Ross. He sighed, glanced up at a large clock on the wall, and allowed: "All right, Dan. It's a deal. On your way, mister. Thirty minutes is all you get. If I even think you're tryin' somethin'—the chink girl gets it first."

"Edge!" Jackson groaned. "You can't bring Linda back for what Ross has in mind for her!"

The half-breed rose slowly from his chair, knowing there was no way he could get Jeb Cannon's revolver from Lin Tu without being seen. He told Jackson: "There ain't no fate worse than death, feller. And the one he has in mind can sometimes be a pleasure."

"You bastard!" Lieutenant Jackson yelled at Edge as he stepped across the threshold and closed the door behind him. "You bastard! You're all bastards!"

The door, the falling rain, and then distance diminished and at length masked the cavalryman's hysterical shouts and whatever was said or done to quieten him. Which did not include the firing of a gun, for Edge would have heard that as he followed the trail of Linda Goodman's footprints.

The tracks she had left were plain to see in the wedge of light that streamed from the misted window across the sodden ground. The intensity of the storm had lessened so the indentations of the woman's booted feet were not washed out as soon as she made them. Beyond the reach of the light, tracking her might have been more difficult, except that her objective was obvious—a boulder-strewn area on the far side of the pass from the way station at the base of the cliff. The footprints marked a running, wavering course toward this patch of cover shadowed under the brightening sky and Edge strode that way without even glancing at the ground once he was certain he knew where the woman had gone.

Although the hiss of the rain against the ground was less noisy than before, he failed to hear Linda Goodman until she gave an involuntary gasp of fear when she saw him and knew she was trapped. He was in among the boulders then and spotted her cowering at the side of a large rock.

"Please!" she rasped hoarsely. "Please don't take me back. Leave me here. I promise I won't—"

"It's Edge," he interrupted, standing stock-still as he recognized the note in her voice that warned of hovering terror.

"I can't take any more. God, I've tried to put a brave

face on it. I could have taken it like the rest, I know I could. Except for that man. He kept looking at me. The one with the gun. It was like I had no clothes on and his eyes were crawling over my bare skin. It was horrible. Please, I promise I won't—''

She curtailed what she was saying with a sharp intake of breath. Edge advanced a pace and she threw her hands up to her face. Another pace and she screamed. But the terror constricted her throat and the volume of sound she vented bore no relation to the wideness of her full lips. Then she sucked in a deeper breath, ready to scream again, half rose and pressed her back against the rock. But Edge's right hand, clenched into a fist, struck her hard on the side of the jaw. She collapsed into a heap, a sigh of escaping air sounding as an anticlimax in her throat now.

"I won't lie to you, lady," the half-breed muttered as he looked back at the way station for a sign that the sound of her strangled scream had been heard there. "That hurt you more than it did me."

The single lighted window showed solid yellow with not even the shadowy silhouette of a curious watcher to partially obscure it. Then, as he turned back to check on the woman, he froze in a half crouch, peering up at the top of the cliff above the way station. A man sat a horse up there, so still that the mount and rider looked like a statue carved out of unmoving rock, Then, to either side of this horseman, others showed. Two at first. Next, as he continued to watch, they were joined by others. Eleven in all. Dark shadows against the clearing sky. All naked above the waist and wearing head feathers. In this part of the country, they were certainly Apaches,

He could not see their eyes, but he knew the braves were watching him. Saw or perhaps only sensed the menace in their fixed surveillance of him. But there was no sign of aggression . . . not yet.

He rested fingers on the firm, warm neck of Linda Goodman and felt a strong pulse. Her breathing was deep and regular. "Keep sleeping quiet, lady," he murmured and then stood up, moved out of the boulders, and gazed up at the bunch of Apaches for several seconds. Finally raised a hand to acknowledge that he had seen them, before breaking into a run.

He was out of their sight for no longer than three minutes, lost in the shadows of the stables and the parked Concord at the rear of the way station. Then, when he and they were in a position to see each other again, he paused to look directly up at them, but this time made no sign before he returned to where the woman was slumped, scooped up water from a puddle in the cupped palms of both hands and flung it in her face.

She groaned and spluttered, then became rigid with fright as he fastened a tight grip on both her shoulders. Told her softly: "Lady, it's Edge, remember?"

Her mouth gaped to vent another scream. He shook her violently by the shoulders.

"Shut up, lady. Unless you can tell me who I am?"

She squeezed her eyes tight closed and whispered through compressed lips: "I know who you are. You've come to take me back inside that place. That man, I—"

"Listen. You're going to be all right. Ross won't hurt you. But unless you go back inside, he'll kill the others. Including your lieutenant, lady."

She caught her breath. "No, I didn't mean for anybody to—"

"Shut up and listen. I'm going to ask you to do something. And if you start screaming again, what Ross had in mind for you will be like a Sunday school game. And it won't be me who is playing it with you."

"You're hurting my shoulders."

"Look over my left one."

"What?"

"Look over my left shoulder, lady."

She did so, and immediately saw the line of Apaches up on the top of the cliff. Gasped: "Oh, good grief, it's starting."

Edge gave a low grunt, satisfied with her positive response to his order and the knowledge that his hunch had been proved correct. "Seeing them scares you, but it doesn't surprise you, lady?"

"I don't know what you—"

Edge shook her once more. "Come on," he said harshly. "It's no coincidence those Apaches have shown up here tonight. A while back you told your lieutenant to open up about the money. Tell me about it now."

"Sherman says it's a secret and I can't—"

Edge let go of her and unfolded to his full height. "All right, lady. I've got nothing to lose except some reward money, and when I got aboard the stage at Bisbee I didn't know I'd be in line for any kind of payoff. I figure I can get safe passage away from here in return for handing you over to those Apaches. And after they've had their fill of you, they won't have too much trouble getting what they really came here for."

"You wouldn't!"

"You're betting your ass on that, lady. Mescaleros place a high value on white women who are old enough but not too old. So if—"

"All right," she broke in. "You're the most—"

"I know what I am, lady," he said as he dug the makings from his shirt pocket and began to roll a cigarette. "It's information of a different kind I want."

She hugged herself, as if she were cold, then sighed.

"Two weeks ago a troop from Fort Buchanan ambushed and massacred more than twenty Apaches down near the border. They were heading for the fort and might have razed it and killed every man there if the colonel hadn't been warned of the attack. That was the most significant incident, but there have been others over the past three months." She glanced up at the braves atop the cliff. "Those Apaches, or at least their chief, gave the warning. The silver is to pay for past favors and ensure there are more in the future. It's purely a private arrangement between the officers at Buchanan and the Indians. Using army money meant for other purposes. That's why Sherman was taking it up to Tombstone by the stage. From there he was supposed to ride with it out to a meeting place—''

"That's enough, lady," Edge interrupted as he lit the cigarette which had been made and hung from the corner of his mouth as he listened.

"The fellers up on the hill can raise a lot of their brothers to break loose some hell if they don't get their payoff?''

She nodded miserably and did not bother to brush away the strands of lank, wet hair which fell across her face. Then, with soft-voiced intensity, she told Edge, "It's completely unofficial, of course, but it has got results. It can get more. And Sherman will be in line for promotion.''

"Let's go back inside.''

"Please?'' She scrambled to her feet. "I listened to you, now you listen to me. Sherman was supposed to deliver the money to the meeting place at dawn tomorrow. Those Indians must know the stage didn't reach Tombstone and they've come looking for it. If you can get the money away from the Cannons and Ross, Sherman will see you get a reward.''

She brushed the hair off her face, darted out her tongue to moisten her lips, and regarded Edge coyly through her long eyelashes. "And if you see that nothing bad happens to me, I'll reward you, too.''

"Sounds like highway robbery, lady," Edge said as he took her arm and steered her out from among the boulders. She eyed him quizzically as his lips drew back to show his teeth in a mirthless grin that did not touch his eyes. Added: "I make a stand and he delivers. His money and his wife . . . to be.''

"You picked a lousy time to make a joke," she accused sourly.

"It was a lousy joke," he answered as he looked up at the clifftop and saw that the Apaches had vanished.

"Do you think they'll wait until dawn?'' she asked.

"Apaches are like women. Unpredictable. When we get back inside, you haven't seen any Indians. And you got that bruise on your jaw when you tripped and fell.''

When they reached the way station he banged a fist on the door.

"Edge?" Pete Cannon yelled.

"You got it, feller. I've brought the woman."

"Oh, my God," Lieutenant Jackson rasped. He made to rise from where he was seated beside the wounded Jeb Cannon as Edge opened the door and urged Linda Goodman over the threshold. But he sat down quickly again when the shotgun was aimed at him.

Juan Mendez and Miles Moran were slumped in chairs beside the stove, both conscious again. Lin Tu was bathing their wounds. Pete Cannon stood beside Jackson, and Ross was once more seated in the chair with his back to the far wall. Everyone showed signs of the tension draining out of them as Edge closed the door—except for Ross, who expressed frowning suspicion as he got to his feet.

"Watch them, Pete," he growled, moving toward the kitchen doorway. "Maybe he found her in a couple of shakes and used the rest of the time doin' somethin' else. I'll check."

"Sherman, I'm sorry, darling," Linda Goodman gasped tearfully. "I don't know what came over me. I was suddenly so frightened."

"Sit down and keep your mouth shut, lady," Pete Cannon instructed, abruptly made anxious by Ross's wariness and watching Edge with nervous eyes. This as the half-breed lowered himself into a chair and momentarily locked eyes with the Chinese woman but read no message in her dark irises.

Edge did note over the next few minutes, though, subtle signs of a relationship developing between Mendez and Tu—the Mexican smiling and speaking soft words of appreciation for the way she ministered to him.

The bearded Moran noticed this, too, and rasped through teeth gritted in pain: "Someone should have put a bullet in you years ago, Juan. If that's what it takes to improve your disposition."

The Mexican scowled and vented a curse in his native tongue. Ross reentered the room wearing an even deeper scowl as he reported to Cannon: "All like we left it, Pete. He talks tough, but I reckon he don't have the guts to try nothin'."

"The lieutenant made it clear the money is army business, feller," Edge said, smoke trickling from a corner of his mouth.

"You mean you don't mind about bein' cooped up in this dump, mister?" the man with the shotgun taunted as he sat down in the familiar chair.

"Beats being outside on a night like this," Edge said as the sound of the rain on the roof was reduced to the gentle pattering of a light shower.

This as his clothing and that of the woman steamed from their recent soaking and the heat of the room. Ross eyed Linda with a leer as the wet fabric of her gown clung closely to her full body. And she groaned her misery.

Edge said to Pete Cannon; "The lady ran off because of your partner's interest in her, feller. It ain't welcome."

"I'll kill him if he tries to touch her!" Jackson blurted, his eyes shifting constantly from Linda to Ross and back.

"Quit it, Dan," Cannon growled, obviously anxious about his brother's deteriorating condition. "Soon now, you'll be able to buy all the women you want."

"Lookin' don't hurt, damnit!" Ross complained. Then gave a short laugh and raised the gun. "But don't nobody have to be concerned on that score. I was just kiddin' around. I wouldn't touch her—even with this."

"So no sweat," Edge said as he crushed out his cigarette, and Ross laughed again. "How about the coffee and food now?"

"Yeah, Juan, I could eat a horse," Moran agreed.

"I will serve you," Tu offered quickly, straightening up from the Mexican as she knotted the sling in which his arm rested.

"You I wouldn't touch with Pete's gun," Ross snorted.

"Go ahead, chink," Cannon told the Chinese girl wearily.

She went out into the kitchen to finish cooking the meal Juan Mendez had started, and came back a few minutes later to give coffee to everyone while they waited for the food. There was little talk after this, as night entered the small hours of morning and the rain stopped. The bearded Moran slept and was perhaps close to unconsciousness as a result of the clubbing he had taken. Jackson and Pete Cannon continued to sit by Jeb, whose breathing became shallower as each long hour slid past. Linda Goodman seemed to be in a trance as she sat very erect and stared into infinity. Lin Tu either sat on the floor at Mendez's feet or undertook the chores of adding logs to the stove and then making more coffee as dawn's light entered through the window to pale that of the lamp. Then Jeb Cannon made a croaking sound deep in his throat and died.

"He's gone," Jackson said softly in response to Pete Cannon's desperate look, speaking as he lifted his hand away from the still neck pulse of the corpse.

"So let's go," Ross growled, getting to his feet.

"First we bury Jeb."

"Damnit, Pete!"

"Won't take but a few minutes," Cannon said coldly, drawing his revolver as he stood up. He raised his voice so that the Chinese girl in the kitchen could hear him. "Forget the coffee, chink! Go out back and bring some shovels. The rest of you, out front."

Edge went first, his narrowed eyes glittering dangerously as the revolver and shotgun tracked to cover him. Linda followed him, and then came Jackson. Moran was crowded by the resolute Cannon and the disgruntled Ross.

"Over there'll be a good place," Cannon instructed, gesturing with the Colt to a patch of turf on the far side of the trail, a few feet short of the rock-littered area where Linda had attempted to hide in the night.

Tu appeared with a long-handled shovel in each hand as Edge looked up at the lightening sky where it touched the clifftop. There was no sign of the Apaches this morning.

"You, Edge, and the soldier boy!" Cannon commanded. "Dig. Six feet long and deep. I want a proper grave for Jeb."

As the work commenced and the false dawn gave way

165

to the true one, the half-breed could sense he was being watched from a distance. Linda, too, probably: since she had seen the Apaches in the night. The rest might have been warily conscious of the same sensation had they not been so concerned with other matters: Moran with his painful failure to extract revenge, Jackson with the loss of the money and its repercussions, Mendez and Lin Tu with each other, Cannon with grief, and Ross with impatient eagerness to be gone from Hunter's Pass.

The sun was up and hot by the time the grave was dug, and as Jackson sweated over displacing the final few shovelsful of dirt, Cannon waved his gun toward Edge and Moran.

"Go get Jeb," he demanded.

He went with the tall, lean half-breed and the bearded old-timer and stood on the threshold of the way station, watching as they lifted the blanket-draped corpse. Then he walked alongside the body as it was carried toward the group at the freshly dug grave.

"Put him down and wrap him up in the blanket," Cannon ordered. "That's enough, Lieutenant. Up outta there now."

Then the grieving man froze as he reached down to give Jackson a hand out of the grave. This as Ross shouted and also came to an abrupt halt close to where Edge and Moran were down on their haunches beside the body.

"You were with him all night!" Cannon snarled at Jackson as he and Ross dragged their wide-eyed stares away from the empty holster that was revealed when Moran pulled the blanket off the dead man.

Edge locked eyes with Lin Tu and nodded as he reached into the long hair at the nape of his neck. Cannon whiplashed upright and aimed his Colt at the terrified Jackson, thumbing back the hammer. While the Chinese girl, her face as impassive as Edge's, jerked her hands out from the loose sleeves of her dress. The Colt in her right fist was already cocked, and she blasted a bullet into Cannon's heart from a range of four feet.

The gunshot and the sight of his partner staggering

backwards with a bloodstain blossoming on his shirt front captured the horrified attention of Ross. But, a fraction of a second later, he uttered a shrill curse and made to swing the shotgun in Juan Mendez's direction as the Mexican snatched the Colt from the Chinese girl.

Linda Goodman covered her face with her hands and let out a piercing scream. Jackson struggled to scramble out of the grave, his blazing eyes fixed upon the revolver still clutched in Pete Cannon's dead fist. Miles Moran hurled himself face down on the ground, desperate to get under the line of fire.

Edge's right arm moved in a blur of speed, the blade of the razor flashing in the sunlight. Then he dived across four feet of turf and felt warm wetness on his hand as the honed metal slashed deep into Ross's left wrist. As he felt the blade touch bone, he twisted the razor and peeled a great flap of flesh from the back of Ross's hand.

The injured man's scream of pain rose to the shrill height of fear as the half-breed got a grip on the shotgun and wrenched it from his weakened grasp. Then, as he whirled away from Edge, Ross collided with the petrified Linda Goodman.

Juan Mendez had got Jeb Cannon's Colt away from Lin Tu by then, and Jackson was out of the grave and had claimed the matching revolver from the second dead brother. Edge dropped the razor and started to bring the shotgun to bear on Ross. But abruptly Ross was in control again. He grabbed a bunch of Linda's hair in his injured hand, stepped behind her, and drew a knife which he pressed into the flesh at the side of her neck.

"Drop them guns, you bastards!" he yelled.

Sherman Jackson was the only man in a position to get a clear shot at Ross. But he did not trust his aim. The woman was squarely in the line of fire of Edge and the Mexican.

"Please," Linda gasped.

Two revolvers and a shotgun thudded to the rain-softened ground.

"I oughta kill her to make you pay," Ross snarled at

167

Edge. "And I will, if you don't back off from them guns!"

He dragged his gaze away from the half-breed to look at Mendez and then Jackson. The Mexican and the cavalry officer complied with the order, but Edge held his ground.

"Kill her and you get it next, feller. Just get the hell out of here."

Ross, blood pouring from his badly cut hand, teetered on the brink of mindless fury while everyone else stared at Edge with dumbstruck shock.

Then Ross blurted, "Not without the money, you sonofabitch!"

Edge nodded. "Moran, go saddle a horse for him. And load the sacks on it."

"No!" Jackson snarled.

"Please, Sherman," the woman with the knife at her throat pleaded. "Let it be over."

"Do it, old-timer!" Ross commanded as Moran got unsteadily to his feet. "And no tricks, or . . ."

The knife blade moved fractionally closer to cutting the sweat-beaded flesh. And the stage line driver hurried away to do as he was ordered. There was a tense silence at the graveside while the chore was completed, with runnels of sweat coursing down every face. Then the gray gelding was led across the trail, and Moran released the reins and moved away from the horse. Ross forced his hostage to accompany him to his mount, but then, with a yell of triumph, he shoved her aside, dropped the knife, and slid the Winchester from the boot.

"You figure you can kill us all before one of us gets a hand to a gun, feller?" Edge posed evenly.

Linda had fallen hard to the ground. Now she rose to her knees and cried, "You've got the money! All of it! For God's sake, go!"

Ross aimed the rifle at her and warned: "Back off from that shotgun, Edge, or I'll blast her for sure."

The half-breed nodded and did as he was told. Then, when Edge was ten feet away from the twin-barrel gun, Ross swung up into his saddle. He still held the Winchester and there was an evil grin on his heavily bristled features.

"You folks done me a favor," he said. "Like the dame said, with Pete dead I got all the money for myself now." The grin became a scowl as he stared at Edge. "But you cut me bad, you sonofabitch!"

He aimed the Winchester at the half-breed's head and squeezed the trigger. But the hammer clicked hollowly behind an empty breech. Fury gripped him as he pumped the action and tried again. Then he screamed, "You sneaky bastards!" He hurled the rifle to the ground, jerked on the reins to wheel his mount, and thudded his heels into the animal's flanks.

"What happened?" Moran forced out from his constricted throat as everyone else stared after the galloping horse.

"Unloaded the rifles last night," Edge answered as he moved forward to pick up his razor, wiped the blood off the blade on the shirt of Pete Cannon, then replaced it in the neck pouch.

"Shoot him, Sherman!" Linda shrieked as she snatched up the shotgun. "Before he gets clean away!"

"Out of range," Edge said flatly as he picked up the Winchester and Jackson dived for Pete Cannon's Colt.

Both the lieutenant and his woman fired, but the buckshot and the bullet fell far short of the galloping rider. This as the half-breed took a single shell from his pants pocket and fed it through the loading gate of the rifle. But he made no move to aim at the retreating Ross, and everyone at the graveside stared at him incredulously.

"Why do you not do anything to stop the man, sir?" Tu asked.

"Figure I've already done it all," he answered, and shifted his narrowed, glinting eyes to the top of the cliff. Where the line of Apaches heeled their ponies forward and halted.

Then, a moment later, the seams in the money sacks— weakened by Edge's razor while he was in the stable during the night—broke under the weight of the contents.

And sunlight glittered on the silver dollars which spilled out and laid a metal trail behind Ross's galloping horse.

With a whoop of delight, Jackson powered into a run as Ross realized what was happening and reined his mount to a skidding halt. But the Apaches drew rifles from their saddle boots, took aim, and fired. The cavalryman came to a stop, and everyone else froze when they saw Ross and the gelding sprawl to the ground, blood spurting from bullet-holed flesh. And everyone except Edge remained motionless as two braves swung their rifles to cover the group at the graveside while the other Indians withdrew from sight.

Out back of the way station, the half-breed did not hurry. Took his own gear from the roofrack of the stage and saddled Pete Cannon's gray gelding. Then he fully loaded the Winchester from the cache of hidden shells. As he led the horse out of the stable, Linda Goodman hurried up to him.

"The Indians are collecting the money. You did what I asked, but you won't want to—"

"I don't reckon he did so much!" Miles Moran growled from where he was checking over the stage. "The Oriental girl shot one of them thievin' bastards, and the Injuns took care of the other sonofabitch!"

"I have what I figure it was worth," the half-breed said as he swung up into the saddle, and the move caused the coins in one of his saddlebags to jingle. "Don't plan on taking anything else. From anybody."

He heeled the horse into a walk, glancing out to where the Apaches were frantically scooping up the scattered silver dollars. The two braves had left the clifftop vantage point now, confident the white-eyes would cause them no trouble.

"Sherman!" Linda yelled as Edge dismounted to claim one of the discarded Colts. "Sherman, he's stolen some of the money!"

Edge holstered the revolver and climbed back into the saddle. "A hundred dollars, Lieutenant," he told the frowning Jackson. "Little enough." He nodded toward the busy

Apaches. "And maybe they'll figure they just didn't find it all."

The cavalry officer nodded and sighed. "Whatever you say, mister. Appreciate your help. And so will every white person who lives in the Fort Buchanan area."

"You ain't ridin' the stage no more when I get her ready to leave?" Moran asked.

"Nor me, sir," Lin Tu said from where she stood on the threshold of the way station with Juan Mendez. "I think I have perhaps found what I was searching for."

"So some of us will live happy ever after, maybe," Edge muttered, looking from the corpses of the Cannon brothers to where the just as dead Dan Ross lay sprawled by the carcass of the horse. And felt no pang of regret that he had not personally killed two of the men for twice pointing guns at him.

"Well, how about that?" the bearded stage driver growled. "That miserly old skinflint Mendez is gonna share what he has with somebody else. Never ever thought I'd see the day!"

"Maybe he figures it's true what those that believe in life after marriage say, feller," the half-breed drawled as he turned his mount toward the departing Apaches and touched the brim of his hat in the direction of the whites.

"What's that?" Moran asked, puzzled.

"That Tu can live as cheaply as Juan."

Chapter Six

THE prison wagon rolled to a halt and the riders reined in their mounts. There was a stretched second of utter silence, then Ethan Price said in an incredulous tone:

"Sonofabitch, Harlan, they shot young Nick!"

"Shot the kid stone dead, so he won't ever grow up to have the Devil in him, huh?" a man yelled gleefully. "Won't ever get to be old Nick, if you see what I mean?"

He laughed as raucously as had the Price brothers a few moments ago. But curtailed the sound abruptly, even before another man warned without a trace of mirth:

"Anybody got an itch, scratch it some other time. On account of if there's one move from anybody I don't like, he's dead."

"Or she," the good-humored man added and took advantage of the other's bad grammar to say with a terse giggle, "And Harve don't like anybody much."

For several minutes before the new violence exploded upon them, the wagon and its contrastingly jubilant and despondent outriders had been moving through the fold of two humpbacked, barren hills: once again heading off the plains and into the San Mateo Mountains. The ambush that killed Nick Price, and in the manner of his dying stunned everyone into immobility for a vitally important second or so, was sprung where the hill on the right got suddenly steeper and the wagon was forced to veer close to it by the fan of massive boulders strewn at the foot of the hill on the left.

The cheerful man who had fired both loads of a double-barrel shotgun to virtually blow off Nick's head had been hidden among the boulders. Now he stood up between two of them that were almost as high as his gangling six-and-a-half-foot frame. They were a lot broader than he was. But looked to be not so hard once the final vestige of good humor had faded from his bright green eyes and the line of his thin lips had altered into a scowl. He was about thirty, and because of his tall skinniness he appeared to lack physical strength. But the granite-like quality of his facial structure would have warned that he was not a man to be trifled with even had he not announced himself so violently. As it was, nobody doubted he would relish any excuse to use the Winchester rifle he was now raking along the line of mounted men and women—while the shotgun hung at the base of his flat belly on a long strap looped around the back of his neck.

"Ditch your weapons so that Harve can come on down," the poorly dressed man between the boulders said in a homespun tone of voice that was the very antithesis of his hostile expression.

"Sure enough would like to get me a closer look at them women, Otis," Harve called down from the top of the cliff—out of Edge's sight thanks to the solid roof of the cage wagon.

But the Price brothers and the trio of women could see him. Not very well, apparently, since they had to squint their eyes to focus on his silhouette against the brightness of the sky. Plainly enough, though, to be aware of the lethal threat he posed as a backup to that presented by Otis. And just heads were moved, far enough so that dazed eyes could shift from Otis to Harve and back again—everybody forced to take seriously the sudden death of Nick and the certainty of more deadly violence if the ambushers were not obeyed. Except for one.

"Shit, he says not to move and you tell us to—" Ethan started to sneer.

Otis, without the slightest change of expression, halted the to-and-fro swing of his Winchester and squeezed the trigger. The bullet took Ethan through the bridge of his nose between his glowering blue eyes. Entered his brain and killed him before he was aware he was marked for death. Ruby screamed, Avis gasped, and Jessica fainted and toppled sideways off her horse. She crumpled, slowly in comparison with the way the impact of the lead had caused the dead man to jerk out of his saddle, his head wrenching around in a welter of blood that erupted from the exit wound in the back of his skull.

Harlan watched his brother all the way to the ground, and did not shift his enraged stare back to Otis until the corpse became inert and the inevitable flies lighted in the oozing blood. Ruby had stifled her scream by then and, like Avis, was already staring in horror at the killer, who had smoothly pumped the lever action of the repeater so that it was ready to blast the life out of another victim at the merest movement of the man's trigger finger.

"Just listen, Price," Otis instructed in the same tone as before, while his almost skeletal face emanated the familiar degree of mean intent. Speaking before the surviving brother could utter a sound, and continuing as Harve moved about on the clifftop above the wagon: "Me and my partner ain't never argued. Far as anyone else is concerned, the last order given by either of us is the one you follow. Neither Harve nor me told any of you people to speak. You remember what I told you to do? Or you want me to kill you like the others, on account of you ain't done like you was told?"

It needed a great effort of will for Harlan to contain his fury. But he realized that the alternative was sudden death. It took all of ten seconds for him to first ease his revolver out of the holster and drop it to the ground and then follow this with the Winchester from his saddle boot. Sweat stood out on his forehead, hung in his bristles, and deepened the hue of the stains at his armpits and belly before he was through. All of it erupting from the strain of maintaining his self-control.

"Kill me if you like, but why'd you have to do that to Nick?" Ruby asked dully, as tears spilled from her green eyes to cut a course through the sweat-tacky dust on her cheeks.

"Me and Harve don't kill unnecessarily, honey," Otis answered, and directed a fleeting smile at the weeping blonde. "Needed to kill the driver to stop the rig—and keep from gettin' killed ourselves, hopefully. When the rest of you got the message that me and Harve don't fool around. What we say, we mean. And then had to kill that dumbo Ethan on account of he didn't get the message plain enough. Hell, all them dead in the wagon sure do stink. How'd you talk your way into stayin' alive?"

He lowered his rifle to his side in a one-handed grip as he shifted his incurious gaze from the horseback riders to the half-breed who continued to sit in a corner of the cage wagon.

"Just borrowed some time, is all," Edge drawled with a glance toward Otis.

"I like straight answers to straight questions," Otis countered, and still his voice was a monotone while his hollow-eyed and sunken-cheeked face revealed his feelings.

"He wasn't a prisoner like the others!" the redheaded Avis put in quickly when Edge did not turn his head to look out the side bars of the cage at the tall, emaciated man who seemed on the verge of killing a third time. "He got involved by accident! Happened along when a couple of the Prices' men botched up an escape attempt! But he didn't set them free! We women got the drop on him and did that! The Prices figured Edge deserved worse than just gettin' gunned down!"

"That right, Edge?" Otis asked.

"Don't figure I could have put it better myself, feller," the half-breed replied and looked again at Otis now, having seen enough of Harve, who had appeared at the base of the cliff just before the thin man's Winchester ceased to draw a bead on Harlan Price.

Harve had a matching repeater and he kept it aimed at the broad back of Price as he ambled casually toward the line of horses and the wagon standing in the afternoon shade of the rock face. He was also about thirty. Just six feet tall, but more heavily built than his gangling partner. Dark-haired like him, but with dark eyes, too. Good-looking in a round-featured way and not provocatively tough in his present attitude. Garbed as unstylishly as Otis in his drab-colored pants and shirt and hat and boots. And, like the thin man, packing an Army Colt in a tied-down holster slung from the right side of his gunbelt. He did not carry a shotgun.

"So how come she's so hot for me not to kill you, Edge?"

"I'm just terrified of more killin's!" Avis put in shrilly, and there was a tremulous note of hysteria in her voice while her dark eyes glittered with another advance warning that the hold she had on her self-control was in danger of being torn loose. "I've seen Nick and Ethan killed. I watched the slaughter of the men you see in the wagon. And I heard about the way my brother Rod got shot down with his buddy when they tried to free the men from the prison guards up—"

"Hey, that Rod Grant you're talkin' about, lady?" Harve cut in as he moved around from the rear of the mounted trio and Jessica, who was making sounds of recovering consciousness.

"Yes, my brother Rod," Avis confirmed as she and Ruby and Price got their first close-up view of Harve: and from their reactions found him less awe-inspiring than Otis.

"And his buddy'd be Johnnie Shute that was such a wow with a rifle, huh?"

Avis nodded, puzzled now.

Harve directed a frown at Otis and muttered: "Frig it! There's two we won't get to collect on!" Then he looked back at Avis with a look of rising hope and asked: "They get it anyplace their corpses are still likely to be, lady?"

"If no other human scavengers ain't been by to pick them up, asshole, the buzzards and the coyotes and the flies and the ants will have stripped them down to the bone by now," Price rasped with heavy contempt between clenched teeth. He glowered fixedly at Otis as he made the insulting implication. But ensured that there remained on his fleshy, time-lined, thickly bristled face an expression of secret knowledge the towering thin man had better investigate before he used his rifle again.

"You want to do it, Otis, or do I get a chance to—" Harve started to say, and aimed his Winchester at Price's broad chest.

"You want to hold off for a moment or two, Harve?" Otis sounded genuinely polite.

"Sure." The shrug of the thick shoulders revealed that Harve was truly indifferent to the outcome.

"You, Edge?"

"Yeah, feller?"

"Bounty hunter?"

"No."

Otis took a plug of tobacco from a pocket of his shirt, blew off the lint, and then bit a piece. Accused indignantly: "You don't say a lot."

"He's a saddletramp figured he'd got lucky," Price said. "Rode down the trail just after Grant and Shute screwed up on breakin' us out. Me and my brothers offered him a share in our stake if he'd turn us loose. He wouldn't set us free there and then. Wanted to see the money first. I steered him to where I figured the women would be waitin'."

"Cibola Draw off of Alamosa Canyon," Harve said disdainfully as Ruby got gingerly down from her horse to whisper comfortingly to the awake but still dazed Jessica.

"Sonofabitch," Price growled, then looked as if he had not meant to utter the thought as Harve and Otis grinned their pleasure.

"You only gotta look at me and Harve to see we ain't been havin' the best of luck in the bounty-huntin' game lately," the tall, thin man allowed, and now his face was as devoid of expression as his voice. "But we turned over a new leaf. Give up ridin' around all over waitin' for somethin' to show up that's money in the saddle. Set out to go after you and them brothers of yours, Price. And the boys that was ridin' with you." He spat some dark-colored saliva at one of the boulders and it quickly evaporated to leave just a stain. "Then thought our luck was still runnin' bad when we found out you and your brothers was caught and on your way to get strung up by that Charlie McMullen creep. But next we find out from one of the boys that used to run with you, Price—"

"He ain't runnin' with nobody no more," Harve put in pointedly.

"—that you Prices never kept nothin' but a little travelin' money and some grub and like that at Cibola Draw. That the stake you was gettin' together to buy a place down in South America someplace was hid away from Cibola Draw. South of Alamosa Canyon in the San Mateo Mountains. Right around here someplace."

He gestured with the Winchester to encompass their surroundings.

"And story went, that stake was worth one whole lot more than the Price brothers and every tinhorn outlaw ever run with them. Got to seem somethin' like lookin' for a lost mine that maybe never was . . . but, me and Harve figured, what the hell! We got nothin' better to do after we spent so long bounty huntin' you and losin' out, so we might as well take a look. And then, lo and behold like they say, we hear the wagon and we see you and your brothers and the women comin' on by."

He spat some more tobacco juice and Harve put in flatly:

"Close to, Otis, the women ain't no ravin' beauties. But they're the best there are around here, that's for sure. We won't hurt them, I figure?"

"Edge?" Otis said.

The half-breed eyed him impassively.

"Harlan here put a price on this double-crossin' deal he made you?"

"Half of forty thousand, cash and trinkets, feller."

"Wow, Otis," Harve murmured through pursed lips.

179

Then brought his Winchester to bear on Price as he asked: "Shall I do it, Otis?"

For the first time in a long time, Harlan Price's anger was diminished by the weight of fear, and he had to swallow hard to force a passage through his constricted throat to give exit to his hoarse-toned voice.

"But you don't know—"

"Which one of us did he call an asshole, Harve?"

"Me, Otis. When I was askin' the redheaded lady here about her brother and that sharpshootin' Johnnie Shute."

"You need me to show you where the cache is hidden!" Price blurted, his bright blue eyes darting their fearful gaze from Harve, to Otis, to Avis who continued to sit her horse, and to Ruby and Jessica who were now standing, the blonde with the tear-run face supporting the one who looked ready to faint again—even to Edge who still sat on his haunches in the corner of the cage wagon.

But the half-breed was not looking at the abruptly wretched man who was suffering mental turmoil as he struggled to understand what had gone wrong and why he was just moments away from violent death. Instead, Edge was engaged in a struggle of his own—attempting to transmit a tacit message to the uncomprehending Avis without revealing his intention to anyone else.

The tall and slim redhead looked to be incapable of understanding anything except the fact of her own terror for stretched seconds. Until, as the desperate Price completed his beseeching survey of every face, she suddenly realized what the half-breed was seeking to convey by mere movements of his glittering eyes in their slitted sockets.

"My guess is they don't, feller," Edge said to Price, attempting to gain more time for Avis so that she might bolster her courage and do what had to be done.

"Saddletramp's right, Price," Otis said, and took the sticky wad of tobacco from his mouth, studied it, and replaced it. Then took a two-handed grip on his rifle and swung it to track the redhead as she heeled her horse forward. Demanded: "Who said you could move, honey?"

"Shoot me if you have to!" Avis challanged as the

other two women gasped. "But I'm not goin' to be sittin' right next to Harlan when one of you kill him like a—"

"No, you can't kill me!" Price pleaded. "Now that Nick and Ethan are gone, I'm the only one knows where . . ." His voice trailed off.

Otis, chewing rhythmically, transferred the new scowl and the aim of his rifle from Avis as she moved along the side of the wagon to the trembling man she had left alone at the rear. Said in his menacingly dull monotone: "Look, dumbo, if you ain't got the hang of what's happenin' yet, I'll put you in the picture."

"Kinda like the condemned man gettin' what he wants for breakfast, huh?" Harve suggested.

"You got it, Harve. Price, that place where you hid your stuff . . . it wasn't so friggin' secret. You think me and Harve would've banged off you Prices like we was swattin' flies if we needed you to tell us somethin'? No, *asshole*, it wasn't so goddamn secret. On account of somebody been there and dug it up and took most all of it. Exceptin' for some junk it wasn't worth them stealin'—or you stealin' in the first place. So me and Harve are back in the straightforward bounty-huntin' business again. Just kept you alive this long for . . ." He shrugged his narrow shoulders, "Why Harve?"

"I don't know, Otis."

"To torture us," Ruby groaned, and was ignored.

"Hopeful that all them other corpses you so kindly brought us are wanted dead or alive same as the Price brothers."

"Now, Otis?"

"Sure, Harve."

"*Nnnnnooooooooo!*" Harlan roared, and stretched long the single syllable of denial. That was extended even further as it resounded off the face of the cliff beside which the wagon had been halted.

At the same time as he vented the word-become-a-scream, he thudded his heels against the flanks of his horse and wrenched on the reins. Intent upon running down the two bounty hunters. But the men's arrogant confidence was unruffled as they displayed the strength of their partnership.

"Horse, Harve!" Otis yelled. And exploded a shot into the head of the spooked gelding: squarely between the eyes.

As, simultaneously, Harve squeezed the trigger of his Winchester: to blast a bullet into the throat and out the nape of the neck of Harlan Price.

The horse was pulled up short, dead on his feet. His forelegs crumpled and he started to fall, head going down first. But then his hindquarters came around and he spiraled to the ground. The rider lived a few seconds more, experiencing the terror of drowning in his own blood. And he clung desperately to the horn of the saddle while he dug his booted feet hard into the stirrups. Thus stayed with the collapsing animal all the way down, his grasp not released by death until both man and horse were sprawled on the ground that thirstily soaked up the blood torrenting from their gory wounds.

Loose horses galloped off while the one hitched to the rear of the wagon struggled against the restraint—pulling backwards on the rig and thereby keeping the team horses in the traces from lunging forward.

Ruby and Jessica shrieked in horror as they witnessed the death of the final Price brother and clung to each other.

Avis, having complied with Edge's silent instructions to bring her mount—which was the half-breed's own horse—to the side of the wagon, now heeled him into an instant gallop away from where the lone captive rose to his full height behind the bars. So that he had an unobstructed view of Otis and Harve—and clear shots at them with his own Winchester that he had slid from the boot on his saddle.

"Sonofabitch!" Otis yelled, his composure shattered.

"You forgot her gun!" Harve snarled, anger at his partner almost as strong as fear of Edge.

Otis swung his Winchester and the half-breed dropped the towering thin man first, placing a bullet in his narrow chest, left of center, to send him sprawling over backwards between the boulders, the wad of tobacco powering out of his gaping mouth. The second bounty hunter's smoothness in pumping the lever action of his repeater was hampered by the shock of seeing his longtime partner go down with the crimson stain blossoming on his shirt front. While the half-breed's manner of going through the same series of moves took account only of the fact that his own survival was on the line. And he threw the lever forward and snapped it back as he tracked the barrel of the rifle from the falling Otis to the momentarily stunned Harve. For a fraction of a second he thought the space between two bars was not broad enough for the angle necessary to draw a bead on Harve as the man jacked a fresh bullet into the breech of his rifle. But it was—just wide enough so that a second shot from the hip drove lead into flesh. Only into the broadly built man's upper arm where it became his shoulder. But this was sufficient to jerk him into a half turn as a shockwave of pain spasmed through his nervous system and he involuntarily triggered a futile shot into the ground. He staggered to keep himself from falling, and leaned across to unwittingly place his head in the line of fire as Edge ejected an empty shellcase and levered another round into the breech. And now Harve was sent into a full turn as he was hit fatally in the temple—gave a cry that sounded more of disappointment than of pain or fear as he dropped down on all fours, then sighed, rolled onto his side, and died.

Edge withdrew the barrel of the rifle from between the bars as he jutted out his lower lip and directed a stream of cooling air over his sweat-beaded face. Did not neglect, during the moments of easing his tension, to work the lever action of the Winchester again: in case Ruby and Jessica should prove to be not entirely involved in supporting and comforting each other, and Avis have something in mind to once more alter the balance of power.

After the series of metallic clicks and the ping of the spent shellcase hitting the corpse-littered floor of the wagon, there was just the buzzing of feeding flies for stretched seconds. Until the clop of slow-moving hooves signaled the return of the redhead to the vicinity of the wagon.

"It was what you wanted, Mr. Edge?" she asked as she rode into view, reined in the mount, and swung down from the saddle.

"Much obliged. Just need to be let out of here now?"

"Sure thing," she answered, and seemed to be suffering from a delayed reaction to all that had happened—to be in a daze as she went to the corpse of Harlan Price and needed to shift the dead weight slightly to lift the key to the padlocks from out of his shirt pocket. There were several discarded guns close by, and the half-breed was careful to watch that her attitude was not a charade designed to make him drop his guard.

Then Jessica unwittingly called attention to this danger when she said with a brand of husky-voiced scorn: "Just like men to think of whores as nothin' but pussies! Those crazy bastards must've seen the rifle on your saddle, Avis. But they just didn't figure you had what it takes to do somethin' with it."

"I didn't do so much," the redhead answered dully as she used the key on the two padlocks.

"More than me," Jessica pointed out, showing greater strength of will than the other blonde now that the killing was over.

"And me, too," Ruby put in, using the back of a hand to wipe the mixture of tears and sweat off her cheeks. "But then it never was any different. No matter where we are or what we're doin', she's always so much more . . ."

As Ruby failed to find the words she sought, Jessica said resolutely:

"But from here on in, we're gonna do our best to be as good as you at—"

The strain she had been under suddenly reached breaking point within the redhead, and as Edge came through the open door Avis let out a strangled cry, sank to the ground, and began to sob into both cupped hands. The two blondes looked in alarm from the weeping woman to the impassive half-breed, who shrugged and growled:

"Avis tries harder, but maybe the prospect of competition hurts?"

Gundown at Twin Oaks

In Montana Melodrama, *Edge had a run-in
with an outlaw named Al Falcon, but never
met him face-to-face. Falcon escaped due process of law and Edge's brand of justice in the
Montana town of Ridgeville, and when next
mentioned was a corpse in a coffin riding in
the caboose of a train at the opening of the
second Edge Meets Adam Steele book,* Matching
Pair. *The following tells how Falcon came to
be in that casket.*

THE man dressed all in black save for his white Stetson
and riding a horse that was almost as white as the hat,
reined the animal to a halt at the crest of the hill to the
west of Twin Oaks, Nebraska, and gazed wearily down on
the tiny community huddled to the south side of the curve
of the Union Pacific railroad track.

It was late afternoon and the rider and his mount cast
long shadows in the dying rays of the no longer hot sun
that would soon sink from sight behind the hill on the
ridge of which the travel-stained man rested his trail-weary
horse. He was fifty and looked several years older because

he had been in the saddle so long for so many miles: not just today. Tall and lean and burnished by the elements. He carried a Remington .45 with a wooden grip in a holster tied down to his left thigh, and a Spencer repeater rifle rode in his saddle boot.

As he gazed down out of green eyes on the one-street town with a row of frame and stone buildings on each side, he rasped a hand over the heavy stubble—gray like his hair—on his jaw and wondered whether Al Falcon was in Twin Oaks. He clucked the white gelding forward on to the down slope and vented a soft sigh as the sole sign that he earnestly wished it could end here: the trail he had followed for so long.

Evening had crept across this piece of Nebraska in the wake of afternoon when the stranger rode into town and halted his horse outside the Silver Horseshoes Saloon, which was the only two-story building in town. He hitched the reins of his mount to the rail where a chestnut gelding and black mare were already tied, the other horses as trail-dusty as his own.

As he pushed between the batwings, newly lit kerosene lamps showed him that the Silver Horseshoes was like countless other saloons in many other towns he had passed through on the trail of men like Al Falcon—but, no: nobody else was quite like the man he sought now. On the left of the narrow room was a long bar with a polished top, and chair-ringed tables were scattered to the right of a narrow aisle that ran along the front of the bar to a flight of stairs at the rear.

The bartender was a big-built, bald-headed, leather-aproned man of forty-some who smiled a welcome toward the newcomer. The only other customer was Edge, who glanced impassively at the man moving across the threshold and then continued to make the cigarette he was rolling.

"Evenin', stranger," the bartender greeted. "What's your pleasure?"

The man took off his hat and banged it against his right thigh to shed the dust from its brim as he approached the center of the bar. He leaned a hip against the front of the

187

bar, assuming a position where he could watch the stairway at the rear of the room without putting his back to the half-breed who sat at a nearby table.

"Beer to lay the dust, barkeep. And whatever you take yourself. Is that whiskey in that gentleman's shot glass?"

He replaced his dusted-off hat as the bartender started to draw the beer. Edge angled the cigarette from a side of his mouth and met the steady gaze from the green eyes of the newcomer with one of his own. Drawled:

"Obliged to you, feller. But I don't have a drink problem."

The stranger was both confused and irritated as Edge struck a match on the underside of his table and lit the cigarette. He snorted:

"I wasn't sayin' that you—"

"I can afford to buy any liquor that I take," the half-breed cut in.

"Don't pay him no never mind, Mr. . . . ?" The briefly scowling bartender set down the glass of beer and started to pour a shot of rye for himself.

"Marshal," the newcomer supplied.

"Mr. Marshal. Edge ain't the most talkative customer I ever had in my place. Here's to your good luck."

He pocketed payment for the drinks as he tossed back the liquor in one swallow. While Marshal sipped at his beer, relishing the slaking effect it had on his thirst.

"Tell me somethin'—"

"I know," the bartender cut in, and the smile he now wore contained a faint weariness. "Gonna be one of two questions, huh? I'll answer both before you ask either. First, why is the town called Twin Oaks when there ain't no trees around? Cut down the only two trees we had to build the church up at the end of the street. Second, how come the Union Pacific track curves right by the north side of town and we don't have a depot here?" His tired smile became a deeper scowl than before. "Because the folks that live in Columbus a couple of miles east of here was able to raise more of the foldin' green to grease the palms of the guys that built the rail . . . ah, hell! Guess you got the picture, Mr. Marshal? But you only gotta look around at the kinda business I'm doin' to see why I'm so bitter about Twin Oaks not gettin' a depot. Train passengers get mighty thirsty.''

While he smoked the cigarette and sipped at the whiskey, Edge kept unobtrusive watch on the stairway, the batwinged entrance, and the second customer. And was aware that Marshal was politely impatient with the bartender as the loquacious man rambled on.

''Was goin' to ask,'' Marshal said quickly when the bartender paused to reflect upon what might have been, ''what happened to your other customer? Two horses were hitched to your rail before I—''

''I got me a girl here. Name of Hannah. I figure she's part Indian, but that don't make her any less of a good looker. Adds some, I'd say. She—''

Marshal did the interrupting again, and his tone and expression emphasized his expanding impatience with the talkative man. ''Hannah's a whore, and the guy off one of the horses is with her.''

''The chestnut gelding, feller,'' Edge said.

''Excuse me?''

''The black mare's mine. In the event you have something in mind concerning the animals.''

''Hannah cleans the place, cooks, and sometimes tends the bar when I ain't feelin' so good,'' the man behind the bar rushed to put in as Marshal's resentment of Edge's implication seemed about to reach breaking point. ''But I can't afford to pay her too much, and if a man takes a fancy to her . . . well, Hannah ain't averse to showin' him a good time up in her room. When she's through with the guy off the other horse, I'll have her come down so you can take a look at—''

''It's maybe the guy off the chestnut geldin' that I'll be a whole lot more interested in seein', barkeep,'' Marshal said.

''Al Falcon?'' the bartender said, surprised. Then abruptly was concerned when he saw the way Marshal stiffened, stared at him with a deepening frown, and then swung his head slowly to peer into the darkness at the top of the stairway. His voice was a croaky whisper as he said in the manner of a plea: "There ain't gonna be no trouble, is there?"

"It should have been Al's middle name," Marshal answered, oblivious to the fact that the taciturn half-breed was surreptitiously interested in his blatantly overt interest in the man being entertained by the whore upstairs.

"He ain't caused none since he's been in this piece of country," the bartender defended.

"That ain't been long, barkeep. Al was through Julesberg less than three weeks ago."

"Right. Four or five days he's been stayin' at the Crosby boardin' house up next to the church. Restin' up. Rides his horse out for exercise every afternoon and finishes up here for a couple of beers. Sometimes takes a tumble with Hannah."

"You got a bank here in town?"

"No, sir, we don't have that."

Marshal sniffed. "Then maybe he's watchin' the train schedules. Hittin' banks is what he likes doin' best."

"Sonofabitch," the bartender gasped, and his glances toward the stairway became more frequent and more nervous. "Mr. Falcon's an outlaw?"

"Wanted in a lot of towns by a lot of lawmen, barkeep. From Denver to San Francisco and a lot of places south of there. Maybe north, too. I can't be sure."

"Any of those places put money on his head, feller?" Edge asked.

Marshal and the bartender both interrupted their grim-faced watch on the head of the stairway to direct quizzical frowns at the half-breed as he dropped his cigarette butt and placed a booted foot on it.

"Figured you might be a gunfighter or a bounty hunter or some other kind of—" Marshal growled with heavy contempt.

And yet again was prevented from completing what he had in mind by the worried bartender who blurted: "It ain't Mr. Marshal, right? It's marshal, as in lawman?"

"Right, barkeep."

"Mr. Edge there is like Mr. Falcon upstairs. He ain't caused no trouble since he come into my place a while ago."

"Lookin' for Falcon, too?" the lawman posed. And then, like the half-breed and the bartender, abruptly concentrated his gaze on the top of the stairway: as a bed was heard to creak and footsteps padded across a floor in an upper-story room.

"He headed up a bunch of hard men that robbed a bank and killed some people in Ridgeville, Montana Territory," Edge answered. "I was around there at the time, but we never did meet up. A while ago now. Was just passing through this town when the man behind the bar there made mention that the man having a ball with the whore had the name Al Falcon."

"And figured to make a few bloody bucks shootin' him down?" the marshal growled with a sneer as the man upstairs could be heard getting dressed.

The half-breed shrugged. "Like I told you, marshal. I can afford what I'm drinking. But unless something turns up soon, I'll have to sell my horse, maybe. Though I don't even know if there's money for Falcon at Ridgeville."

"The Ridgeville thing is new to me. I'm a federal marshal workin' out of Denver on this job. A thousand is what's on the wanted flyers put out over in Colorado."

"That's a state now, I hear," the bartender said huskily as a door opened and closed along the landing upstairs.

"Entered the Union August the first," the lawman answered, his voice a whisper, as he straightened up from the front of the bar, so that he had unobstructed access to the holstered revolver hung from the left side of his gunbelt. And he lowered his voice further but larded each soft-spoken word with menace as he rasped out of the side of his mouth to Edge: "Stay out of it, bounty hunter. Forget the reward. I got a sworn duty to perform. And I also got me a personal stake in this business."

The lawman stared fixedly into the deep shadows at the top of the stairs, the expression on his face wooden while his frame might have been hewn out of stone, so still did he stand.

The bartender turned his head a fraction to try to see Edge's likely reaction to what had been told him. But the half-breed gave away no sign to the tremulous, sweating, gulping man behind the bar.

He merely tipped the final heeltaps of rye whiskey down his throat, set the glass back on the tabletop, and placed his hands, fingers splayed, to either side of it. His ice-blue eyes, glittering in the light of the kerosene lamps, moved back and forth between the slitted lids, ignoring the bartender to keep an almost predatory watch on the federal marshal and the man who stepped out of the shadows to start down the stairway.

A man of thirty-five or so, powerfully built, and with a leanly handsome face. Better dressed than either Edge or the marshal. More recently washed up and shaved. His satisfaction with what had taken place in Hannah's room showing in the grin on his face and in the faintly swaggering gait with which he descended into the saloon.

But, both Edge and the marshal knew, his attitude was a charade. He had maybe first sensed the tension. Certainly when he was in a position to clearly see the other three men in the Silver Horseshoes, he knew he was going to have to go for the Frontier Colt he carried in a tied-down holster on his right side.

The lawman waited until Falcon was off the stairs, on the same level, and less than fifteen feet away before greeting him:

"Hi, Al."

Falcon's green eyes set in an element-darkened face under a shot of blonde curly hair did not move along their sockets anymore. And it was obvious he had discounted the bartender and relegated Edge to a slot below the lawman in the order of trouble to be dealt with.

"Hi, Nat. Still the good guy?"

The lawman slowly raised his right hand, delved into his shirt pocket, and briefly displayed the federal marshal's badge that was inside. Said as he did this: "Give yourself up,

Al. You've robbed a lot of places and killed a lot of people doin' it. Only right you should stand trial for some of that. Be punished if found guilty.''

Fal~on shook his head very slowly, and a look of melancholy spread over his face. It was as if he were already mourning the death of this man before him whom he had yet to kill.

"It's taken me a long time to track you down, Al,'' Nat went on. "Now I've caught up with you, I'm goin' to take you back. Dead or alive. Your choice.''

"You're choice, hero,'' Al Falcon countered, and the sadness was gone, displaced by a killer grin. "A choice sucker.''

He drew so fast the move was a blur of speed. Only his right arm was in motion—he was so confident of making the kill he did not even turn to make himself less of a target, nor drop into the gunfighter's crouch. In one part of a second the Colt was in the holster, and the next instant it was leveled at the marshal and the hammer was cocked.

While the marshal could only start a groan of despair as a look of the dread of dying began to form on his face. For although he had a hold on the wooden butt of his Remington, he had not fisted his hand into a grip to begin sliding the revolver from its holster.

But then a shot rang out, shattering the tense silence and causing the lawman's groan to expand into a cry. But of the expectation of pain rather than pain itself. This as the bartender vented a gasp of amazement. For it was not the gun in Al Falcon's hand that had exploded the shot. That stayed silent and unmoving and not wisping smoke from the muzzle. While, the killer grin sliding off his good-looking features, the outlaw looked down at the bloodstain blossoming on his chest, left of center. And toppled forward with the rigidity of a felled tree, dead before he had the chance to raise his head and look at the man who had shot him.

The half-breed sat almost in the same relaxed attitude as before. But now just his left hand was splayed on the table to one side of the empty glass. His right had streaked off the table, drawn his own Frontier Colt, cocked the hammer, and squeezed the trigger the moment the muzzle was clear of the holster. And now, as both the bartender and the marshal shifted their shocked gazes from the inert form of Al Falcon to look at him, Edge clicked back the hammer again, and rested the smoke-trickling barrel of the revolver on the tabletop, aimed at nobody.

"Shit, mister, you must've had that gun outta the leather before Al Falcon started his move!" the bartender croaked.

"You want to kill him for accusin' you of doin' that, mister, I'll forget I'm a lawman," the federal marshal snarled, and shot a contemptuous glance at the bartender as he dug into his shirt pocket for the star.

"But that Falcon, he drew so fast I could hardly see his friggin' arm move!" the bartender protested, still so in awe of what he had witnessed he hardly had any room left in his mind to fear the ramifications of the lawman's ire. He shook his head slowly from side to side as a dull-faced woman with an overripe body started uneasily down the stairs. "I can't see how anyone can get a gun outta the holster faster than that."

"Al's slowed down, barkeep," the marshal countered as he turned to face the bar and leaned both hands on it. This as Edge rose from his chair and slid his killing gun back in the holster. "He used to be a whole lot faster."

"Sonofabitch," the bartender gasped.

"And I was faster than that," the tall man in the white hat went on as the just as tall one in the black hat stooped to pick up the dead body. "But we were both a lot younger then." He pinned the badge on his shirt front.

"Damnit, he was a good customer and a fast payer," the sullen, plain-faced whore complained.

"He used to be almost as fast on the draw and a straighter shooter than me," the lawman put in dully.

"Tell me something," Edge said as he straightened up, the corpse draped over his left shoulder.

"Me?" the lawman asked, placing both hands on the bartop again as if he needed its support to keep from shaking.

"Just how personal was your personal stake in this law business?"

"Name's Nathanial Falcon, Mr. Edge. Don't roll off the tongue so easy nowadays, but that carcass you got was my kid brother."

"Sonofabitch," the bartender murmured.

"Taught him all he knew, I figured," the marshal added. "But he learned some more after we went our separate ways. It appears."

"Or maybe you just got older and slower, feller?" Edge posed pensively. "Am I doing you a favor if I take him—"

"You saved my life," the elder Falcon brother interrupted. "Maybe on account of I'm gettin' older and slower. Or maybe because him and me were brothers of a different kind—he could kill me, but I couldn't bring myself to kill him. I ain't sure I can thank you for savin' my life and mean it. Am sure I'll thank you to haul that no-account outlaw killer outta my sight. City of Denver'll pay you for your trouble. Pour me a whiskey and leave the bottle, barkeep."

"Hey, mister!" Hannah the whore called after Edge as he carried his burden toward the batwings beyond which a crowd could be heard gathering to investigate the firing of a shot in this quiet town. The unattractive woman still disheveled from her last sexual encounter gestured toward the marshal. "Some men, they drink to forget a bad thing. It costs a little money to do that. For maybe less money when it is added up, another man, he could easy forget what has happened here, in the arms of Hannah?"

She arranged her fleshy body in what she assumed to be an alluring pose and spread a provocative smile across her overblown face. Edge had halted with one hand hooked across a batwing to look impassively back at the whore over his unburdened shoulder.

"Why should I want to forget anything?" he asked, and made to push between the doors.

"So you proved you could draw faster than him!" Hannah snarled in a challenging tone. "That Falcon, he was the best there was at somethin' else, mister! He was like a machine, that one! He could go on and on, time and time again like he was a . . .''

But Edge had stepped out of the Silver Horseshoes Saloon and now he went to the chestnut gelding and transferred the corpse from his shoulder to the saddle as the whore abandoned her attempt to goad him into an angry response.

''Harlot!'' a woman in the crowd of shocked local citizens rasped. ''That kind makes me ashamed to be female.''

''Yeah, lady,'' the half-breed growled sourly as he began to secure the body over the saddle. ''And there are all kinds of females make a man glad to know his machine can be hand-cranked.''

Chapter Seven

AVIS GRANT, Ruby Rivers, and Jessica Boone were what they looked to be. As whores they had worked bordellos in El Paso, Tucson, Yuma, and a whole string of tent cities where there were more rumors than pay dirt. They had been in a house in Tucson when the Price brothers, Johnnie Shute, and Avis's brother came by to raise some hell.

"They were all drunk and the lights are never bright in them kinda houses," Ruby said, taking up the story as Avis fell morosely silent after a great deal of animated talk. "And her and Rod hadn't seen each other for a whole bunch of years. And—"

"And he almost got to put it into her is what happened," Jessica broke in quickly, as the other fleshy blonde paused to eye the redhead quizzically—seeking permission to reveal the close call with incest.

Now Ruby glowered furiously at Jessica, but when they both looked at Avis it was to find that she was emerging from the moments of introspection with a grim smile on her dark-eyed face.

"It didn't happen is what's important, I figure," she said evenly, her head cocked to one side to pose the statement as a query to Edge.

The four of them had moved away from the fold in the hills under the sheer wall of rock where the Price brothers and the two bounty hunters were sprawled in the utter stillness of death, their corpses by now, doubtless emanating the stench of putrefaction. Maybe the more recent dead stinking as bad as the corpses of Chester Rankinn, Austin Gatlin, Billy-Joe Delany, and the Comanche, which had been dragged out of the cage and dumped in a less than dignified heap before the wagon was set rolling again.

Or, it could be, there was not so much left of the bodies to decay and smell so high now: after there had been time for the buzzards and the coyotes and a whole host of lesser-fry scavengers to take opportunist advantage of the gory leftovers of this latest example of evil with man's desire for riches at its root.

Sitting now on his saddle between the cage wagon and the night-warming fire something less than a mile away from the slaughter scene, Edge slowly ate a plate of chile beans and jerked beef, and reflected that it was better to be alive and feel stupid than to be dead and unable to feel anything at all. Which was not a profound thought, he acknowledged, but even under ideal conditions he had never considered himself a deep thinker. And circumstances were far from perfect this seemingly quiet evening at the end of a harrowing afternoon. For he did not trust the apparent innocence of the terrain surrounding the night camp and he maintained a conscious surveillance over the moon-shadowed ruggedness of the rocky hills on all sides. This while he also remained on his guard against the three women who superficially appeared to be entirely concerned with the sensations of deliverance: but this state of their minds would not last forever, and it could just as easily be sooner rather than later when a sense of security allowed them to entertain avaricious thoughts.

After the redhead had gotten over her weeping jag in the wake of the killings, it was she who suggested they should look for the place where the Price brothers' cache had been hidden: ". . . because those guys said there was still some stuff left. Not worth so much, but when people are as broke as we are, every damn thing is worth somethin'." Ruby and Jessica had to agree with this, but had looked to

Edge for advice. He had appeared to be on the point of moving off to again pick up the trail he'd been riding before he allowed himself to get sucked into this new experience with evil: but it had seemed to take just the prospect of a heaped plate of hot food to persuade him to go along with the women. He astride his horse while the whores rode up on the wagon seat, all the other animals hitched to the bars at the rear.

The women regaled him by turns with tales of their sordid pasts in the whorehouses of Texas and the southwestern territories: sometimes exuberant and at others almost morbid as their moods changed in relation to the unbidden intrusion of memories from or responses to much more recent events. At first cheerful while the wagon rolled through the failing light and cooling air of the ending day, following the half-breed who was tracking the sign that not too long ago had been left by more than just Otis and Harve; then, when they reached the place where the Prices' ill-gotten gains had once been secreted, the whores were plunged into deep dismay as they surveyed the twilighted scene of broken-open crates, ripped sacks, discarded valises, and sundry items of abandoned clothing. With, here and there among the litter scattered over a confined area before a shallow hole in the ground at the base of a ten-foot-high, needle-like outcrop of rock, an occasional glint of metal or other shiny substance. Something about the way the fast-diminishing light bounced off these objects made it clear just why they had been left amid the debris of emptied containers and unwanted clothing. They were made of base metal and the stones were of paste.

Edge began to build a cooking fire with what was combustible from amongst the junk while the women looked without hope for something of value that might have been negligently left behind. But whoever'd gotten there first had been thorough. And the whores began to recover from the effects of their disappointment that was not, after all, unexpected: and they took over the chores of attending to human requirements while the half-breed saw to the needs of the horses. Since there were eight saddle mounts and two from the traces of the wagon, it took him some time to bed them all down in the mouth of the ravine that cut into the hill immediately behind the needle of rock that had marked the Prices' hiding place.

While he tended to the horses, Edge remained disinterested in anything save the task at hand and the potential danger from within or beyond the night camp. Then, as he took his ease on his saddle, and food smells and heavy eyelids began to numb his awareness of everything but hunger and weariness, Avis picked up the threads of the women's earlier conversation.

The supper was served, and with each of them on a different side of the fire, the talk and the listening continued. Talk that was fundamentally about greed for money and the lengths the women were prepared to go to satisfy their avarice. At least that's how their audience of one heard it as he remained alert to the first sign of danger and pondered upon the way his own aspirations for wealth had yet again brought him to the brink of a violent death. But he did not, as he used to in the past, experience disconcerting self-anger as he acknowledged his rainbow-chasing stupidity. While Avis, Ruby, and Jessica told him how they had come to be tied in with the Price brothers, Shute, and Rod Grant, he simply called himself a fool for making yet another grab for the crock of gold: at the same time as he relished the mere fact of being alive when so many others were dead.

"That would have been hard to live with, I guess," he replied to Avis's implied query about her close call with incest.

"Even for a whore," Ruby said reflectively, peering into the fire.

"It goes on a lot, I hear," Jessica murmured, withdrawing into the same state of detachment as the other thick-bodied blonde. "On homesteaders' places and other places, too, where families live God knows how far away from neighbors. Fathers and daughters, mothers and sons, brothers and sisters."

Avis nodded. "Yeah. Real strange when you think about

it. Us being whores and yet it makes us sick to our stomachs thinkin' about gettin' screwed by . . ." She shrugged her shoulders. "But then, even whores gotta have somethin' to believe in, I figure. So maybe it ain't so strange?"

Again she eyed Edge in search of agreement. And he finished his supper and set down the empty tin plate, only now noticing how little the women had eaten. He answered:

"What a person believes in is nobody else's business."

"What do you believe happened here, Edge?" Avis asked.

Now he shrugged as he began to roll a cigarette, and replied: "The bounty hunters found somebody who used to run with the Prices and knew where they stashed their stake. If one man knew, so could a lot of others. Or just one who had some friends."

"Friends?" Ruby asked.

Edge struck a match on the butt of his holstered revolver and lit the cigarette. "The sign shows that four or five riders were in this neck of the woods in the past day or so. That's two or three not counting our unfriendly neighborhood bounty hunters. If it was worth the trouble, I could take a closer look and come up with the exact number."

"Too scared to make a try for the loot until after Harlan and Ethan and Nick were bound sure as night follows day for the rope?" Avis said.

"Or died some other way," the half-breed replied, rising wearily to his feet.

"You gonna bed down already?" Jessica asked.

"He's had a heavy day," Ruby pointed out.

"We all have, one way or another," Avis added.

Edge stooped to pick up his saddle and glanced at each woman in turn through the heat-shimmering, smoke-veiled air above the fire. As if to check that the distorting effect of the energy-charged air really did improve their looks by acting to soften the gauntness of the redhead and to thin down the fleshiness of the blondes' faces.

"Leaving, ladies," he told them as he straightened up again, saddle draped over his left shoulder.

"But why?" Avis demanded a bit angrily while Ruby and Jessica cast nervous glances out into the moon-shadowed terrain beyond the firelight's limit.

"Obliged for the supper. There's nothing else I want from you."

"You weren't gonna be offered nothin' like that, mister!" The redhead's anger had expanded at the implied slight.

"Not if you don't want it," Jessica hurried to add. "But you can share the fire, and we'll fix breakfast for you in the mornin', and—"

Edge touched the brim of his hat with his free hand and said: "Obliged, but I ain't a herd animal and—"

"You sayin' me and my friends are cows, mister?" Avis snarled.

Edge sighed. "No, lady. Was about to explain that I prefer my own company unless there's something I need tied in with running with other people."

"But—" Ruby began.

"Aw, let him go if he wants," Avis growled.

Jessica shivered and added fuel to the fire, more for the light than the warmth. She muttered bitterly: "There's frig all we can do to stop him, seems to me."

Edge had moved into the ravine as the trio of whores resigned themselves to being left alone. While he saddled his horse, he could hear the redhead trying to persuade the blondes that everything was going to be fine—reminding them of how many nights they had spent at Cibola Draw without a man to protect them.

"I guess we have to be grateful you ain't takin' the wagon and spare horses?" Avis sneered as the half-breed led the chestnut gelding out of the ravine and swung up into the saddle. "We're hopin' to raise a few bucks on them for all the trouble—"

"I don't understand a man like you, Edge," Ruby put in with a pensive shake of her head. "You don't look the type that can be so contented to go through all you did and come out of it with nothin'."

202

"It takes all types to make a world," he replied, tipping his hat again, before he wheeled the horse and started to ride slowly back the way they had all come.

"Be a hell of a lot better world if some types weren't around in it!" Avis yelled after him.

Edge murmured softly so that only he heard: "I try to make a contribution, lady." This as he struck a match on the Colt butt to relight his cigarette which had gone out. There were no more words shouted after him, and no exchanges among the women loud enough to reach his ears. But he could sense their gazes upon him. Did not look back over his shoulder until he was certain that intervening solid ground rather than insubstantial moon shadow hid him from the night camp. Cast the backward glance to ensure that none of the women had moved along his tracks to keep him in sight after he rounded the shoulder of the hill.

Then, certain that he was unseen, Edge slid the Winchester from the saddle boot and brought his feet clear of the stirrups before he thudded in his heels and commanded the gelding to gallop: came sideways off the animal as he lunged into sudden high speed. The dismount had to be hurried but could have been smoother. He landed awkwardly on one foot and was unbalanced so he went sprawling to the hard ground amid the swirl of dust kicked up by the pumping hooves of the racing horse. The clatter of hooves masked the sound of his impact, his rasped curse, and the coughing jag triggered by the dust motes in his throat.

He rose to his feet feeling bruised and parched, but the day just ended had held worse discomforts for him. And, after a few cautious strides on rising round, he found that by favoring his left leg with a limp he was not forced to wince every time he set down his foot. His progress toward the crest of the hill became even more cautious as the sound of galloping hooves faded into the distance, and he drew nearer to the night camp of the three whores. He saw the fringe glow of the fire at its highest point first. Then heard the mumble of voices, which got clearer and clearer until he was able to discern what was being said although he was not yet in a position to see the speakers.

". . . well, I say we're well rid of him and when you see—"

"All I said," Jessica cut in on Avis, "was that he's the kind of man that maybe I've always been lookin' for."

"Ugly as sin?" Avis challenged.

"I thought he was a real good-lookin' guy," Ruby said defensively. "Kinda broodin', maybe. But I like them kinda—"

"Shit, you ready to forget about that Mex creep and listen to what I got to tell you? Or ain't you interested in bein' rich?"

"Rich?" Jessica gasped. "But—"

"Don't kid around, Avis," Ruby protested, close to the point of anger, as the half-breed reached the vantage point he was aiming for at the top of the ravine's western side—where he was able to squat down with his back to a hump of rock that prevented his silhouette from being skylined.

From here he was able to see that the women had remained seated on the ground on three sides of the fire. None of them seemed to have eaten any more supper. Now Avis rose to her feet, brushed the dust off her dress, and began to pace back and forth in a manner that came close to suggesting arrogant triumph.

"That hard-nosed Mex greaser got it right, sweethearts. Two more men other than those bounty-huntin' creeps were around here just the other day. Johnnie Shute and Rod, that's who."

"But—" Ruby began.

"Just listen, why don't you. And find out how your old friend from seems like every crib in the country is gonna make your fortune for you!"

"Ruby, let's do as she says," Jessica urged. And both the blondes sat there attentively, like fascinated children listening to a story told by a much-admired adult.

Avis reveled in their deepening attention as she continued to pace and to explain: "I've known about the place where the Prices hid their stake for a long time. Harlan could be real stupid when he was liquored up, and one of them times when he was drunk, he brought me here to boast about how much they had stashed away. Promised me I could go to South America with them if I kept on being good to him."

She shivered briefly, as if at a fleeting memory of being good to Harlan Price. But this hardly interrupted her flow. "Then the stupid bastards got themselves caught by the law. And it took me all the time they was in jail waitin' to get tried to persuade my chicken-hearted brother we oughta take the money and run." Now she interrupted herself more pointedly to emphasize: "Not just Rod and me. You and you and Johnnie Shute as well."

The two blondes nodded enthsiastically, accepting her veracity and urging her on to the climax of her story.

"Well, after that judge sentenced the Prices to hang, Rod told Johnnie what I had in mind and together they worked up enough friggin' courage to go through with it. But, like I told that Edge creep, more or less . . ." She smiled at the memory of her mockery of the half-breed: "They was too scared to make the move until they were certain Harlan and his brothers were good and dead. And when they reckoned there was no way to be sure of any hangin's takin' place inside of a prison, I came up with the plan for Rod and Johnnie to bushwhack the friggin' cage wagon and kill every man aboard it!"

She sounded proud of herself.

Ruby undermined her good feeling when she accused: "You could've let me and Jessica in on it while we was all waitin' at the draw in Alamosa Canyon, Avis."

"Yeah, I could've! But, shit, a whole lot of things could've gone wrong and I didn't want no comebacks on me. You know how mean the friggin' Prices were."

"Somethin' surely went wrong, Avis," Jessica said angrily.

"And how! When I saw the stranger drivin' the wagon with all those guys over and above the Prices in the back, I knew I just couldn't do nothin' about it except what Harlan told me. I couldn't kill all that many people."

"If you'd started, I sure wouldn't have helped you," Ruby growled,

"Me, neither," Jessica added.

"So I just played along." She shrugged. "Figured, what the hell! Rod and Johnnie were dead and couldn't get me in trouble. And I was the only other person knew what the plan had been." She smiled and recommenced her near strutting again. "But then it all worked out for the best when that couple of coldhearted bounty hunters done what Rod and Johnnie didn't do. Figured the Mex might be a problem, but he took himself off and so took care of himself. If the worse had come to the worse, we could always have given him a share."

"But a share in what, Avis?" Ruby demanded and stood up. Jessica imitated her move and then both raked their gazes over the fire kept alight by empty containers and the discarded receptacles scattered across the ground between the fire and the hole at the base of the pinnacle of rock. "You said your brother and Shute were here—"

"Layin' the smokescreen, Ruby," Avis answered in a gloating tone. "See, I figured that if Harlan had shown me where the stake was stashed, he might have told others. Or Nick or Ethan might have told. Whoever it was, somebody slipped up, because them bounty-huntin' sonsofbitches was here." She waved a hand to encompass the campsite lit by the flickering fire. "It was my idea for Rod and Johnnie to spread all this crap around and make it look like the stuff was gone. And it sure as hell fooled that Otis creep and his sidekick, didn't it?"

"So where—"

"Follow me, sweethearts," the gleeful Avis interrupted Jessica. And augmented the invitation with a beckoning hand as she swung around and headed across the campsite, went by the needle of rock, and passed thirty feet below Edge's lookout point to enter the ravine: where the horses snorted their disapproval at being disturbed by one, two, and then three women forcing a way through them. "And forget about that peanuts of twenty grand or so the Prices told the Mex about!'' Avis crowed, her voice disembodied in the inky blackness of the ravine's bottom. ''There's a hell of a lot more than that and we'll all have to sweat some to get it loaded aboard that cage on wheels.''

Perhaps the three whores did not sweat in the chill of the night air as they came and went from the depths of the ravine. But they underwent considerable exertion in hauling out crates and cartons, sacks and bags, and a broad range of items that were not packaged—handguns and rifles, tables and chairs, lamps and framed pictures, ornaments and even some books.

Often, as the loot of countless holdups was packed into the rear of the prison wagon, Ruby or Jessica would question the sense of bothering with anything except the sacks of money or crates of gold and jewels. But always Avis urged: ''Everythin'. I want everythin'.''

Once when the chore was almost finished, Jessica asked how much Avis thought they had, and the redhead waved a hand in a dismissive gesture and claimed: ''Oh, millions maybe.''

A lot less than even one million, Edge guessed as he waited for the right time to make his move. But a lot more than the figure the Prices had put on their hoard—Harlan had probably figured the half-breed wouldn't believe the truth about its actual value.

''That's it then?'' Jessica announced gratefully as she and Ruby struggled to the rear door of the prison wagon, which was now low on its springs, and set down on the ground the heavily laden topless crate they had carried from the ravine.

The jumbled contents of the box reflected the dull redness of the dying fire, and Edge recognized them as gold and silver religious artifacts just as Ruby did.

The blonde whore trembled as she straightened up, rubbing the small of her back, and said, ''I've done a lot of lousy things in my life, Jessica, but I ain't never stole nothin' from a church. I don't want no part of any money these sell for.''

"Neither of you got anythin' to worry about," Avis announced evenly, but with something in back of her voice that caused the two blondes to gasp in fear as they swung around to look at the redhead. This as Edge stared down at Avis where she stood beside the needle of rock—and did not trust himself to make his intended move for fear of startling her into unpremeditated action. And then it was too late.

With totally cold-blooded forethought, the woman squeezed the triggers of the matching pearl-handled revolvers she held in each hand. Ruby and Jessica shrieked in terror. Avis moved away from the rock, thumbed back the hammers, and fired two more shots. And only then did the half-breed jerk himself out of the uncharacteristic shock he'd experienced when the opening shots exploded: looked from the woman with the blazing guns to the two who had dropped to the ground as the bullets tore into their flesh.

Ruby was on her knees, hands splayed at the end of fully extended arms. Jessica was sprawled out on her back and jerked from side to side. Both were screaming and both had bloodstains on their gowns at the belly.

Edge would never know if the first or second shots or all of them had hit the whores. But now he made a coldly calculated decision to check his finger on the trigger of the Winchester as Avis emptied both her guns into the women, sending Ruby out on her back in the same manner as Jessica. Then reducing both women to unfeeling, unmoving utterly silent corpses. With liquid crimson now staining their faces as well as their gowns.

She had to thumb back the hammers and squeeze the triggers just once to become aware that the revolvers were empty of live bullets. She was standing between the dead whores by then, and when she opened her hands the guns dropped onto the corpses, their muzzles still wisping acrid smoke.

Avis dropped hard to her knees and began to sob. She clasped her hands in front of her breasts, tightly interlocking the fingers. Edge thought it was unlikely she saw the box of religious artifacts just a few feet from where she knelt.

He left her weeping and praying and went to retrieve his horse. While he was doing so, justified his decision not to intervene once the shooting had started—on the grounds that out here in these barren mountains it was better to be dead than to be dying from a bullet rotting the intestines. This he could accept. He found it less easy to admit to himself that the shock of seeing the woman kill her two longtime friends had stunned him into a stretched second of inaction.

He located the chestnut gelding some half mile away from where he had commanded the gallop to commence. More than enough time had passed for the horse to recover; but he had more than enough time to accomplish what he still had to do, so he led the animal by the reins at an easy pace back to the scene of the latest slaughter. He did not set out to make a great deal of noise, but neither did he take any great pains to muffle the sounds of his approach.

He saw Avis before she heard him.

She was in an attitude of prayer again, but not in the same place and now she was standing up. Not weeping anymore, although the moonlight—the only source of light now the fire was out—gleamed on the tracks of her old tears when she turned to look at him. She had been standing, head bowed and hands clasped at her breasts, a few feet away from the needle of rock. The hole at its base had been filled in and two silver crosses from the box of stolen ornaments had been placed on the recently disturbed dirt.

The corpses of the blonde whores were obviously interred beneath the crosses. When Avis recognized the man who advanced on her, leading his horse and giving no sign of aggression, she vented a choked cry, whirled, and lunged toward the area where bloodstains showed the bodies had been.

"You insulted my father, lady," Edge said coldly, his ice-blue eyes in their slitted sockets gleaming more brightly than the silver crosses on the makeshift double grave.

"And now you're going to aim guns at me . . . which you know I object to."

He was perhaps twenty feet from her as he finished speaking, and he released his hold on the reins of the gelding at the same moment she came up from her stoop: to turn toward him from the waist and level both revolvers at his chest. Revolvers he knew she would not have thought to reload. But which she did not realize were empty of live shells until she thumbed back the hammers and squeezed the triggers.

He powered toward her in long strides as she stared desperately down at the useless guns. Then jerked up her head to stare at him with hatred blazing from her dark eyes as she made to hurl both revolvers at him. But he was close enough then to thrust out his arms and fist his brown-skinned hands around her frail wrists. He tightened his grip and her scowl of repugnance became a grimace of pain.

"Drop the guns, lady," he rasped through clenched teeth.

"You bastard!" she hissed, and pursed her lips to signal an intent to spit in his face.

"My folks were married, but I'll overlook that," he told her, then pushed her hands up level with her shoulders and jerked them down to her waist. He made no alteration in the way he clasped her wrists—so that the bones inside the sparse flesh in the trap of his fists snapped with a dry sound.

The scream she vented did not sound dry at all. And when the searing intensity of the pain hit her nervous system, actual wetness was spurted from her throat as she brought up what little supper she had eaten. Before her brain refused to condone further punishment of the conscious being and plunged her out of awareness.

Only when her slender frame became limp did the half-breed let go of the broken wrists above the empty, useless hands. But he did not leave her crumpled on the dirt. He hefted up her easy-to-carry, uncontrolled body and placed it in the rear of the wagon, draped unceremoniously across some untidily stowed freight. The key was still in one of the padlocks and he transferred it to his shirt pocket after closing the door and turning it in both locks. Then he adapted lariat ropes to form traces and harnessed six animals to the heavily laden prison wagon and unsaddled his own gelding before hitching him with the other spare horses to the rear bars.

He knew the whore was awake and watching him as he completed his preparations. She had done some groaning and spilled more tears as she gained consciousness, but after she recalled the circumstances of her predicament she quickly quieted down. She could think of no way to alleviate her discomfort, though: except to appeal to her captor.

"You broke both my wrists."

"One for insulting my Pa's nationality and the other for trying to kill me."

"But the guns weren't loaded," she protested, fighting back an impulse to wail.

"I knew it. But for a while, you didn't."

He made a final circuit of the wagon and its team and the animals hitched to the rear. She had worked herself into a half-seated posture, her back against the barred side, when he next saw her.

"I went a little crazy," she offered, as he dug the makings from a shirt pocket and started to roll a cigarette. "All this stuff in here. I just couldn't bear to think of sharing it. They were my friends, but they didn't take any of the risks. You've risked a lot. Right from the start . . ."

"And I plan on getting paid for my trouble. Just like I did from the start."

"But the folks who used to own all this stuff . . ." She sobbed and it sounded of frustration. "They'll pay just a couple of cents on the dollar of what it's worth."

He struck a match on a horizontal bar and lit the cigarette. She vented a despairing sigh and asked:

"How did you know to come back and . . . and that me and Rod planned—"

"Heard you tell the other two about the scheme to steal

from the stealers, lady," he told her. "Came back because of how easy it was for me to leave."

"I'd have cut you in, you know. If you'd been . . . well, I let you outta this cage after the lousy bounty hunters were killed, didn't I?"

"Owe you for that."

"So I'm collectin' the debt."

"You already did. I just broke your two wrists. Not your neck. Take it easy now. We got a long trip ahead of us."

"I went crazy there, so I know what it's like!" she shouted after him as he moved forward and climbed up on the driver's seat beyond the solid partition. "And you're actin' worse crazy! You can't deny you're bein' stupid not takin' all the money and stuff that's aboard this friggin' wagon! Or maybe you are, damnit to hell! I bet you're gonna get rid of me so you can have it all and no one'll be left alive to know about it!"

"That's the way you figured to play the game, lady," he told her evenly as he knocked off the brake and worked the leather and rope reins to move the six-horse team into a tight turn.

"Shit, everyone's greedy and everyone's willin' to cheat when the stakes are high enough, big man!" she snarled vehemently.

"Way things are, you have no monopoly on greed and cheating, sure enough," he answered.

"I friggin' know it."

"We all took chances. And it's you who's going to go directly to jail, lady. And I plan to collect a whole lot more than two hundred dollars."